D1078928

GREETINGS, HERO
AIDEN O'REILLY

Greetings, Hero
By Aiden O'Reilly
Honest Publishing

ISBN 978-09571427-5-6

Manufactured in the United Kingdom
by Lightning Source UK Limited

Cover: Slava Nesterov

CONTENTS

Human Behaviour   3

Roman Empires   15

A Fine Noble Corpse   29

A Drop to Warm my Blood   48

Three Friends   71

Concrete Triumphant   88

The Re-education Camp   98

Self-Assembly   104

Greetings, Hero   118

Contempt   199

Lost and Found   237

The Laundry Key Complex   247

Unfinished Business   259

Stripped Bare   276

Words Spoken   298

HUMAN BEHAVIOUR

In the paved *Hinterhof* they cut yucca into thin slices of starch. Plopped it onto the hot oil. The good food aroma filled his head. Warm evening air rose from the concrete all around. He felt alert, palms dry, nostrils clear. There were eyes behind his eyes, gulping down what they saw.

In this city he fell in love with the side walls of houses; high planes of bare brickwork, nothing for the eye to fix on. He loved the deleted buildings on Berlin's streets, those missing teeth, the flash of sky like a lifted skirt. And in the back courtyards ragged weeds straggled up through the cracks.

This is not decay. This is the beginning.

'Here is Wilma, she studies sociosomething,' said Klaudia. She was keen to find him someone interesting to talk to.

Wilma goes to mambo dancing classes.

Wilma plays the double bass.

Wilma arranges pebbles at the bottom of thick glass containers.

'Hello Wilma,' he said, taking her damp chubby hand. Was her name Italian? Her hard black pupils and gelled black hair confused him. She looked like she'd been licked into shape. The clean, new-born appearance disturbed his eyes. He felt he could not see her properly. A strand of hair or crease in her finger took all his attention. Her voice was quick, a little lilt constantly seeking assent.

'What are you doing in Berlin?'

'Looking around. Learning German.'

She smiled and waited like she'd caught him speechless and knew it.

'But if you want to learn German could you not do it at a university?' Making fun of him, perhaps. Or maybe the idea of hanging around to learn German sounds bizarre to people here.

'It's better to do it in the country itself. On the streets like. It's the only way to learn a language.'

'You are right,' she said after a pause. The yucca! She bounced over to the grill and took the pan off the flames. The grill was home-made, a small stack of reclaimed brick with a scrubbed iron grid on top. Hand-shaped patties that couldn't have been meat sizzled gently. It will be a vegetarian grill party, Klaudia had warned him, half proud, half apologetic. Red and green peppers roasted along the edges of the grid. Wilma picked one up, slid the burnt skin off with one finger and ate the flesh. He tried it out, standing alongside her.

Took a pepper off the grid and tossed it from one hand to the other to cool off. The carbonized skin came away in one pinch. It was sweet and clean and fruity underneath.

The charcoal smoke curled lazily upwards in this chasm formed by the backs of houses. A smoke that drew neighbours to lean over their balconies, and drove flies into an ecstasy of drowsiness.

Then he went to the bathroom and saw the contraceptive device. Took it in his hand. She had left it there, and could foresee someone touching it, if only to get at the antiseptic behind. Anyone could get a burn or a graze on a night like this. No one would mind a slight cut, a release of blood when it flows so warm and the skin heals over so quickly. She could surely foresee someone touching her device to get the antiseptic, or the plasters, or the toothpaste.

Could she foresee this? He zipped open his fly. Touched the little round ring to himself and watched a fold unstick in response.

He walked back out to the yard where the smell of cooking thickened the air. The girls were rearranging the chairs to be upwind of the smoke.

'Ah, Kevin, if you need to wash your hands go in the kitchen,' Wilma called.

He remembered now, there had been no washbasin, only a bath and the toilet. Dutifully he went back inside and ran cold water over his hands at the sink. The window sill held a motley collection of little objects. A wire nest, a corkscrew, a smooth bun of stone with a dip in it. He placed his finger there, stupidly, there was only grimy cigarette ash. Again he turned on the tap. The jet slapped his hand to one side, curled on the enamel sink, and threw a splash over his T-shirt. What might have been the towel had an embroidered image of a sun-god on it, so he let it be. It was warm outside, he would soon dry off.

'How is the socio-bio studies?' he asked her. She was caught by the abruptness of the question. Straightened up from the brick grill, surprisingly tall.

'I study history of art and art therapy,' she said.

'Not sociobiology?'

'No, that's Wilma.' She indicated with a nod. Wilma had put on a bright floral headscarf. Her black fringe jutted out below it. The scarf made her laugh. She put her hands to her cheeks, flicked four fingers with a dismissive gesture.

'Oh, I didn't actually meet you yet,' he laughed to cover himself. She found a place to put down the tongs and gave him her hand. It was slimmer than Wilma's, and her face was more acute, eyes a shade more grey than brown, nothing at all like Wilma in fact, but for an instant, distracted by the similar gelled black hair, anyone could be mistaken.

'Sylvia,' she said with that initial eagerness with which people introduce themselves.

'Kevin,' he said.

'Yes, Klaudia told me. It's interesting to meet you. You are the first Celt I have met.'

He considered the implications of this.

'You are a Celt, aren't you?'

'As far as I know all my parents and grandparents going way back are all Irish, yes.'

'So you have original Celtic genes?'

'My grandparents and so on are all Irish as far as I know, so I suppose yes.'

'What happened to your T-shirt?'

He rubbed the damp cotton, a bit pointlessly. 'It's only water. From when I was washing my hands.'

'I can get you a dry one from my sports bag. I only wore it for a couple of hours.'

She left him there with the tongs. He leaned over the grill to flip a few of the soya burgers. The heat passed through his damp T-shirt. He moved back, afraid that the wet spot would have evaporated entirely by the time she got back.

Meat contains toxins that accumulate. The liver has to work harder to purify the blood, the sweat smells and irritates the skin. Klaudia had explained this patiently to him, perhaps viewing him as a potential convert to vegetarianism. He still could not fathom this tall athletic German woman who had befriended him on his first day. She had invited him to her apartment for dinner. He had arrived with a bottle of red wine and she sent him back out to the shops to pick up the ginger root she needed for her recipe. Then she seated him at a candle-lit table and proceeded to grill him about his parents, his brothers and sisters, his ex-girlfriends, his religious views. He opened up freely, told her of the all-boys school he had gone to, his older brother's time in jail for possession of cocaine, his sister's flirtation with depression, how he didn't go to mass but was good friends with a guy who had studied for the priesthood. She listened keenly, directing his account with a few probing questions. Tell me if you argue with your brothers, she said. Tell me if you visit your grandparents. Tell me how it is.

When she got up to make coffee he realized he had no urge to ask her the corresponding questions. Not even an elementary sense of fair play induced him to ask her. Ethiopian, Colombian, arabica or mild blend, she asked from the cabinet. Arabica, he said at random. Good, she said. Ach, Kevin, you have such interesting things to say about yourself.

He watched her now, this untypically freckled woman who knew him like a book, as she rearranged bark mulch around the miniature pine.

'Here,' said Sylvia, handing him a brushed-cotton T-shirt. He unfolded it, brought it to his nose to better catch the scent.

'You have nice perfume.'

'I'm not wearing any,' she laughed, 'that's my skin.' She sniffed at the T-shirt. 'No, no perfume except a tiny tiny bit.'

He stepped back, turned to one side. Whipped off the damp T-shirt, aware of his pale freckled Celtic skin, soft round arms that belied their strength, spidery chest hairs, each one curling away independently. His soft skin took on imprints easily; the band of a pair of trousers, strap of a shoulder bag, little twigs and grit if he lay down on the grass.

The fresh marine-blue T-shirt hugged him. He pulled down the hem on all sides. This taut material that pressed against him had hours before pressed against her breasts and stomach, sprung a crease where her back dipped between the shoulder-blades.

'Thanks,' he smiled.

'It looks better on you.'

'I'll give it back at the end of the night, though it might get stained by then.' By way of answer she tugged the hem of her own top. A couple of charcoal marks criss-crossed it, a few tiny specks of oil from the spitting grill. She dusted off some carbon black.

'Do you want me to keep an eye on them for a while?' he asked, taking the tongs from her hands. She took away a couple of the roast peppers on a plate and sat down on the grass patch. This yard was a communal space surrounded on all sides by four storeys of eroded brickwork and rusting balconies. An elevated rectangle of well-kept grass, a few miniature pines in barrels, a loose stack of old brick, an old horse trough with a sheet of glass over it – the herb garden. Klaudia came over with more neatly patted cutlets sprinkled with chopped basil.

'How do you know Sylvia?' he asked.

'We did music lessons together. She was in the same school as me before that but I didn't know her back then,' she answered.

'She's a good friend of yours?'

'Yeah, I can say so. We were all on a trip to Turkey last year.'

'Just girls on the trip or did boyfriends go?'

'Just girls. The boyfriends stayed at home.'

'So she has a boyfriend?'

Klaudia opened her mouth to answer, hesitated, thought better of it.

'Oh Kevin.'

'What?' he said indignantly, wanting to provoke a

reaction, to see what that tone of voice meant.

'Why don't you ask her if she has a boyfriend if you want to know?'

He looked into the inscrutable eyes of this woman who had set about making him her friend in such a rigorous manner. It seemed to him her bare arms and legs were too firm to be attractive. They were beautiful in form like the limbs of a gazelle. He could picture him and her grappling in stylized moves, her hand under his elbow, his hand on her thigh, without the least trace of arousal. She was too clean, odourless. If he licked her she would be tasteless. When she had bent over to show a judo movement it was with neither coyness nor a girlish innocence. It was the action of someone who would find it faintly ridiculous – yet perhaps human in an old-fashioned sense – to be told this was erotic.

Yet when he looked now at her high arched eyebrows and narrow nose it was obvious she was good-looking. A natural straw blonde, with fine wintry hair, a shapely ear that was unaccountably flushed pink.

'Your ear is red – do you have the 'flu?'

'What?' She touched her earlobe and her face looked pained. 'Yes, it happens sometimes when I am a little run down.'

He looked at her and tried wilfully to see her in a different light. To feel the heat of that earlobe on his lips. Press with his hand her breast, naked behind her coarse cloth blouse only inches in front of him. He imagined touching the space between her legs in an action devoid of intimacy. Her eyes narrowing to bring out the oriental tinge of her features. He felt the stirrings of interest, a tentative rising in his loins. And if she saw it? Oh Kevin, she might say, in a reproachful tone.

The kitchen/living room is long and cluttered with wickerwork, books, little *objets d'art*, CDs and plants. There behind the table he sees her sports bag. Badminton, she said she played. Through the window he sees the steady curl of the grill-smoke, hears the thin voices of summer. The bag is half open. He takes her shorts and sports bra, feels the limp texture of things that someone has worn. The clean feminine scent makes him sleepy. He could lie down on the sports bag and close his eyes, drowsy with a fast-beating heart. But this is a time for action. The firstlings of thought must be the firstlings of his hands. He zips open his fly, presses the damp delicates against his crotch. He feels purified, filled with confidence. Now he is ready, now he has abandoned himself to hunter's magic.

He walks straight up to Sylvia where she's flipping burgers on the grill, puts his hand over hers and steers the movements of the spatula, like someone teaching a child.

'Hey, cut it out,' she laughs. He takes a burger and walks off.

Wilma, where is rubber ball Wilma? He scans the courtyard, the window into the living room, the doorless sheds where the bicycles are kept. Wilma with the damp hands and cherry dot scarf. The only thing that could slow her down was her bulging bosom. He felt an obscure sympathy for a girl who has to carry the burden of heavy breasts, deep folds trapped under a tight bra, perspiration enclosed in the sweltering weather. He pictured again the way she had chased a roast potato before it rolled off the concrete.

'Where has Wilma gone?'

'She went to a neighbour upstairs so she could phone her school. She has no phone here,' says Klaudia.

They drag the table out from the kitchen and eat off plates. The sun has dipped below the tall apartment houses. They talk about people they know, what work they are doing and what countries they have visited recently. They chat about old friends from the schooldays.

It is time to go. They shake hands, give a small hug.

'I am glad you have met my friends,' laughs Klaudia as they walk back towards Prenzlauerberg. 'Now you know more about me.'

Out in the wide streets the night air has turned chilly at last.

'I left my T-shirt behind,' he says. 'I'll have to go back.'

'It's not so important,' says Klaudia.

'I know, but I'm wearing Sylvia's T-shirt. I don't know when I can give it back.'

And so he runs back: runs first, then walks slowly the last stretch. Loses heart, walks by the door, resolving to leave it for another day as Klaudia suggested. But the same Klaudia waved him off with the T-shirt. He had to return it.

Wilma answers the door. She says no, it is not late at all, come in, did you come back the whole way? The last inch of wine is in the bottle, the cups and plates piled on the sink. He goes to the dark end of the kitchen, excuses himself, and changes T-shirt. Half-heartedly offers to wash it, smiles at Sylvia, holding her eye, and she smiles slowly back. Something is understood between them. He feels physically weak with anticipation. The breath trembles in his lungs. He feels a need to cling to her to regain balance, a need so strong he laughs at it, strokes her arm with his fingertips.

She moves away, picks up her sports bag, swings it deftly over her shoulder.

'I have to go now. I'll leave you kids alone. See you tomorrow or whenever.' She smiles the same knowing smile, gives a wave to both of them.

'Wilma,' he says when the door closes, 'I missed you when you disappeared today,' presses against her in the hallway, their mouths meet, her full breasts warm as kittens against his chest. She throws off a scent like spiced tea.

'Really?' she says, surprised, 'Really?'

They struggle onto the sofa, push the table away with their legs, striving against each other for release from their physical natures. See! he says, I can touch you all over. See, she says, I can touch you wherever I want.

Afterwards she pads over naked to the fridge, adjusting the brassiere she hasn't taken off, and returns with a carton of juice.

'What are your long-term plans in coming to Berlin?' she asks. 'What is your relationship with Klaudia? What activities do you do?' And then: 'Are you a moral person? Would you cheat at work?'

He yields to the barrage of questions with a resigned feeling of deja vu.

'You're so strange,' she says and flicks him. 'I don't know what you're thinking.'

'Strange?' he says puzzled, intrigued even, 'In what way strange?'

Roman Empires

Read this!

Are you aware of the **truth** about the Romans?

Do you ever stop to wonder about the **pernisious** influence of a corrupt version of history?

Are you aware of the true **extent** and **power** of the Roman Empire?

Here are some quotes which I have garnered from *current* second-level school history books. These books have been

examined and approved *at the highest level* as being suitable
for the education of the *nation's children*.

"The Romans brought the concepts of law and justice to
Europe"..**LIES**

"... concrete ... one of the main advances in technology
which came from the practial genius of the Romans ....**LIES**

". . . under the Antoinines never have so many people lived
their lives in a state of uninterrupted harmony - the fruit of
wise rule..**LIES**

"civilisation as we know it came from Rome".................................
...............................**LIES & PROPAGANDA**

I have been to **Abyssinia** (Ethiopia) and seen concrete
footpaths and steps constructed by the workmen of
Nicodemius III, dated reliably to 228BC using Carbon.
The Ethiopians were racing chariots **on concrete** while the
Romans were plodding through **mud**. Who would dare
to claim that our own roads will be free from cracks 2226
years from now? Examples and accounts of the true nature
of Roman rule are plain to all who examine the facts, and
refuse to be misled by 1800 years of lies & propaganda.
Anyone who believes that the power of the
Romans was crushed out of existence in 448AD
is living in a fairy world, a world of beautiful
fragrant pink flowers, with pots of gold at the
end of rainbows, a world where larks fly down
onto your hand and sing to you and where the
animals never eat each other.

The real world is not like this

In the real world the corrupt and malicious influence of the Romans continues unabated, as strong as ever it was. This is attested by the prevalence of varnished versions of history as well as by attitudes and politics that can only be described as Roman.

On the ides of March 278AD, one hour after dawn, Junvius Matrius, a Dacian who had incurred the displeasure of the Princeps for some minor misdemeanour, was taken from his home in Apulia and forced to fight in the circus. He was killed by his well-armed professional opponent. This was no isolated case - there are many like him.

------ **THIS IS ROMAN JUSTICE**

As far back as 600BC the Alexandrian Pharaoh's priest Akkian Xeros wrote a tract pointing out the adverse effects of lead piping on health. Almost 1000 years later water in the Roman home was still being supplied through lead, leading to learning difficulties in young children.

------ **THIS IS ROMAN TECHNOLOGY**

After a hard day's work, the typical Celt returned to his wife and children. Some neighbours might pay a visit and together they would listen to the bard (or fildh) recite long poems from memory. Afterwards they composed songs on a 36-stringed harp, while the elders drank modest amounts of beer. The typical

Roman on the other hand got his entertainment from watching two gladiators gouging each other's eyes out at the circus, or watching the naked wives of other men at the baths.

------ **THIS IS ROMAN CULTURE**

Some people say that this happened a long time ago. They say they have other things to worry about. Yet what could be more important than refuting **1800 years of lies and propaganda?**

For more information contact:
New Idea Publications
James Dwyer
42 Russell Ave
Dublin 2

McNally & Co. Printers   8 Fosset Lane, Dublin 2

Justin rapped the brass knocker and took a step back. The door swung open and a lean man in his seventies smiled in high delight and invited him inside with much ado. Justin followed down the sparse hallway, a well-hoovered hallway with a coat-stand, umbrella bucket and nothing else.

'Is it gifts you are bringing me Justin? Or is that something for your young lady that you're carrying with such delicacy?' He spoke in a theatrical way which never failed to bring a smile to the student's lips.

'How are you keeping, Mr Dwyer? It's a book actually. Very old edition.'

The older man ushered him into the sitting room.

'It's from the reserve catalogue,' Justin continued, 'so I have to give it back tomorrow. I thought you might find it useful in your 'research'.'

'Wonderful, wonderful.' The amateur historian twined his fingers together. 'You're a mole for information Justin, a bloodhound on the track of knowledge. If I might express it so.' The student grinned like a small boy being praised by jolly uncles.

'But let's get our priorities right. Take off your coat and I'll make a pot of tea. You must be exhausted after walking here, in this weather too. Wretched.' He spat out the last word.

Justin flopped down into the sofa. A coffee table got in the way of his legs and he pushed it forward. Calm sounds of cups and saucers clipping against each other came from the kitchen. He flicked though the antique book and set it back on the table.

An excess of energy spurred him to his feet. He scanned

through the book cases and examined the undersides of ornaments. The tiled mantlepiece held an elaborate clock, flanked either side by a set of grotesque Lords and Ladies. Justin wondered briefly if the man had ever been married. He could simply ask – it was hardly an embarrassing question.

The walls of the room held a series of framed black-and-white photographs of Roman ruins. He unhooked one and examined it. Four men in shorts and wide-brimmed black hats grinned back at the camera. Perhaps they were laughing at the sight of themselves wearing Spanish sombreros. They had the hard-jawed looks men used to have before the sixties.

'I see you are struck dumb with admiration for the perfection of Thamugadi, Justin.' Dwyer set down the serving tray on the coffee table. 'You could build a cathedral on top of that arch and it wouldn't budge. "Simplicity of conception united with beauty of form." The mighty arch. The concrete they started using during the Empire years has all crumbled away but those stone blocks are still in perfect condition. A farcical concoction of concrete that crumbled to dust. Sit down for this tea. Crumbled into dust, but the simple arch survives.'

Dwyer let the mahogany-hued tea pour into the cups and scratched at the tab on a pack of gingernuts. The wrapper gave way and biscuits spilled out. Justin set down the photograph and helped pick the biscuits up off the carpet. He followed Dwyer's example and put them back on the plate. It was an old but well-hoovered carpet.

'Do you know the secret of how to make an arch? You put in the keystone first! Did you ever hear that one?'

'I did not.'

'How such magnificent buildings could be made using such simple instruments is a marvel, Justin, an enigma to this day. Your mind is sharp, you know about physics and computers, don't you? Maybe you could put the Thamugadi arch into the computer and see what comes out. Did you see what happened when they let the computer loose on the shroud of Turin? The face of Jesus rose up from the cloth surface in three dimensions.'

'It might be possible all right to put in the dimensions and analyze the stresses. It's all vectors,' mused Justin.

'No problem to a mind like yours! Maybe you would find it was actually the launching pad for a missile – they had a form of gunpowder you know. They had the principal idea. They knew about ballistics from old Archimedes. Maybe they were planning an air-raid on the rebel province Mauretania.'

Justin could not tell if this was another irony.

Dwyer picked up the antique volume. He gauged the heft of it and ran a finger over the embossed leather. 'Is it all eulogy and the obsequious praise of Roman lackeys? Not another book that sings the praises of that dismal bastard – excusing your presence – Marcus Aurelius?'

Justin had been in the library feeling diminished by the nine foot high walls of books that surrounded him. His four year degree basically involved absorbing knowledge from these books and reconstituting it. He got the notion of seeking out the book with the oldest publication date. This would be something that nobody had done before, he reckoned. He found himself working his way faster and faster along the shelves. Slip out a volume, flick to the title page, calculate the Roman numerals, slip back in. He had got as far back as 1816 when he became aware of eyes upon him. He took the book that he had in his hands to the reading tables and studied it closely. To his surprise he found a spirited discussion of the moral dissolution rampant in the Gordianus family. It was in much the same vein as some of Dwyer's rants.

'You've unearthed a fine morsel Justin. This is a nugget of truth you've mined. I've heard tell of this author, the name is familiar.' Dwyer leafed through the pages reverently.

'So you think it will help you in your research?' asked Justin.

'My project, Justin, "my project" I call it. My days of scrabbling in the dust are over. I don't have the health for it.' He shook his head and his voice coarsened. 'You wouldn't believe it Justin. Digging out trenches with a dental pick. Sitting in the mud for hours. Now it hits me in the hip joints and the knees. The shoulder I wouldn't mind; I won't be lifting crates any more. But I still have to walk. If you can't walk to the shops you're a cripple, plain and simple.'

Justin had nothing to say to this.

'Tell me Justin, do you have to rush off now? Do you have a minute to spare for me?'

'Absolutely. If there's anything you need me to get from the shops, it's no problem.'

'The shops? No, no. I want your opinion on a matter. Your scholarly opinion. I've designed a poster to increase the people's awareness. The next phase of the project. To shake them from their complacency.' He reached between the sofa and the bookcase and drew out a cardboard tube.

He unrolled a scroll across the table, then together they held it up against the wall.

He allowed Justin time to read it from top to bottom. 'What do you think of it?'

Justin nodded slowly. 'It attracts the attention.'

'That's the aim Justin. To attract attention. To illuminate! Are there any mistakes that I missed?'

'No. Well, why do you write "varnished" there? Did you mean "tarnished"?'

'Varnished, tarnished. It's a tricky one. Yet varnish itself is a sort of tarnish in the way it covers over what's already there. In fact it doesn't cover completely, otherwise it would be paint. It colours pale timber in an effort to make it look like a better quality. Varnish is almost clear, hmm. It's like we're all looking at history through rose-tinted varnish.'

'Maybe best leave it as it is,' conceded Justin.

'Or would "garnish" be the word that hits home? You can garnish a pig's ear but it will never be a sirloin steak.'

Dwyer let go of the bottom and the thick paper curled up into a roll. He indicated a few dozen such rolls wedged at the side of the sofa.

'I've been to McNally printers and he gave me a good deal. A very nice, pleasant man he is, very knowledgeable, you can see an innate intelligence in his features. Well-read too, we had a chat about the symbolism in Moby Dick. He has his own ideas there, I wouldn't argue with him. He ran off forty-eight copies on his machine. Churned them out quicker than your eye could follow.'

He gripped Justin firmly by the hand and his keen eyes gleamed. 'Will you help me, and help this project of mine, and maybe do a little to push back the curtains of ignorance?'

Justin gave a quick nod.

'All I'm asking you to do is put up a few of these posters where the public will see them, and I'll be very grateful. Very grateful indeed.'

'I could put some on the Greek & Roman boards at college.'

'Marvellous. I appreciate it. But not just the notice board. I'm not trying to appeal only to academia. I'm not a nutcracker. This is important for everybody, not just your doddery professors ... I was thinking you might put one in the window of Brendan Byrne's place.'

Justin had a vision of himself standing before the sharp-nosed shopkeeper, the latter holding the poster before him at arm's length and reading aloud in a drainpipe voice. 'Byrne's minimarket? It might be out of place there. It's generally only ads.'

'Maybe you could try the church door? The old convent wall, that's public property, no-one can say a word to you there.'

'I'll see what I can do. Thanks for the tea and everything. I have to get back for a tutorial.'

Dwyer pressed a roll of posters onto Justin's palm and curled the fingers of the other hand around it.

'You're a warrior,' he said. 'A scholar and a warrior.'

'Sure I'll see what I can do.'

'And remember Justin,' he said.

'What?' Justin turned at the doorway.

'Never forgive them. Never forget.'

Late, late that evening, after the library had closed and only a few heads remained bent over books in the study room, a lone figure skulked through the corridors. He looked furtively about him and held what appeared to be a cudgel in his right hand. The figure slipped into the toilets at the sound of jangling keys. When the jangle and footsteps had receded, the shadow slipped out again and rapidly taped up four posters in succession.

His duty fulfilled, Justin felt a weight lift from him. He strode freely across the cobblestones. It would have been easy to dump the posters in the nearest bin, but that would commit him to telling a direct lie. Maintain a steady course between lies and the brutal truth, that was his policy. He resolved to steer clear of Dwyer for a week or so, allow time for this project to die a natural death.

'Every morning, when I stand in front of the mirror for a shave, and our dismal northern skies are raining down outside, I think about Romulus Augustus and the swarming hordes of huns and I rejoice that the Roman Empire has fallen. This was the end of servitude to worldly power, and the opening up of minds. This is something to be thankful for.'

Justin was back in the plain sitting room, once again sipping tea from a cup with a saucer. He struggled to follow Mr Dwyer's extended discourse. A sunbeam penetrated through the trees in the back garden and made the mahogany veneer on the coffee table glow a fantastic orange. The conversation, the teacups, and the scent of warm books elevated him to a realm of pure appreciation. It did not occur to him that, except for a few small details, he could be in the sitting room of his own parents' red-brick semi three streets away.

The threat of heavy fines on the short-loan had prompted his return sooner than he'd wished. Mr. Dwyer had been delighted to see him and was in a celebratory mood. The campaign had gone very well so far. Several neighbours had seen the posters he'd pinned up in the local shops, and were keen to know what it was all about. He had high hopes for the next phase of the project, which he assured Justin he would shortly reveal.

Dwyer was now well underway into a detailed account of the intrigues of the Severus family and the extent of their influence through five generations. The man could randomly access an immense wealth of names and detail. He threw around names of senators and consuls like they were friends he had fallen out with.

'The people are not thankful enough for the world that they have today. Look at all the countries on the map Justin: Switzerland, Belgium, Croatia, France. They should all be celebrating their freedom from the rule of Empire. It could have gone on forever you know.'

'Interesting point,' murmured Justin. 'Yes, I guess it could.'

'All the peoples of the world, forever looking to the one central source of validation. No sense of anything more important than entertaining yourself and eating well. And now there are those who dream of the resurrection of Empire and the rule of one law, one society, from the Baltic to the Sahara, and from Galway to Constantinople.

Bring back Caesar, we want a real emperor instead of some shopkeeper's daughter: that's what they say. We had better be careful Justin, or some fine morning there'll be a knock at the door and a man from the Praetorian Prefect demanding tax from us.'

'Do you really think there are actual people who want a resurrection of the Roman Empire?' asked Justin. The older man stared at him as though he were a half-wit.

'That's exactly what they're trying to do! They haven't stopped trying since 476. Do you not have eyes in your head? Caesar, Kaiser or Tsar, it's all the same to me. The same way of thinking and the same blood-line. Civilisation my arse! They very nearly made the whole world into a race of slaves, slaves of the sword themselves as they were. Your professors won't tell you that. Your professors will wallow in ignorance.'

'I think they know their history quite well,' ventured Justin.

'Not a bit of it. They know only the facts.'

'Well I have my own opinions about your theories. In fact, I think a lot of your ideas are a bit far-fetched. A bit too far-fetched altogether.'

'What's far-fetched? That millions are ignorant of the history of those bastards from the Tiber and their modern-day lackeys?'

'There's been a lot of history since. The French revolution, Marxism, no less than two world wars. The Romans are a long time ago.' Justin reached for his coat. He had no stomach for an awkward scene.

'A long time?' said Mr. Dwyer, 'You have no sense of

History at all. *His ego nec metas rerum nec tempora pono. Imperium sine fine dedi.* You don't have a word of Latin in your head? Some scholar you are. Some fucking scholar.'

'Well if it's cursing we're at now.'

'You think history is not worth cursing for?'

A knock at the front door interrupted them. A perplexed look crossed Dwyer's face.

'The bell must be broken.'

Justin slipped in front up the hallway, saying his goodbyes with forced politeness. Then he remembered why he'd come at all. He muttered and squeezed past Dwyer and back down to the sitting room for the library book.

A damp-haired teenager in a padded jacket came in and looked about uncertainly. Behind him was a teacher from Justin's old school. Justin said a brief hello as he passed them, on up the hallway, squeezing his way and nodding to each person he knew: Mrs Begley and her crony Mrs McGuin, Phil Brady the software coder, Ms Doyle the history teacher, Jim Flynn's dad, Austin Burke the organiser of the community games, Rory McCarthy the metal-detector fanatic who had donated finds to the National Museum, all coming to hear that the Empire has fallen and now we are finally free.

A Fine Noble Corpse

Children swung from the bars of the frame. Their voices were small and hard like pebbles. Even the smallest ones clambered up the metal ladder and were fearless of sliding down. Their legs and arms were nut brown from the sun. Summer had started early; there had been a full month of such weather.

In the city he came from, such a ramshackle climbing frame would have been cordoned off. The sandpit too would be closed as a health and safety hazard. It might conceal glass and dog shit, and children could pick up diseases.

Mothers sat on the bench and smoked. They ignored the tireless squabbles of the children. A mess of cigarette butts had accumulated at their feet. The sandy loam stretched in front of them to where the children played. The pit where the children played was a zone of deeper, cleaner sand.

'Aunt,' said Anna, 'can we leave these upstairs?'

'Is it yourself?' squealed the woman in delight. 'Who is the young man you have?' Anna flapped her hands impatiently.

'Stefan. You'll meet him tomorrow.'

'Did you get the Holy Communion presents?'

'They're all ready. Is there anyone upstairs to let us in?'

The aunt leaned back her head. 'Just himself.'

'How is he?'

'Quiet enough. Sitting up above, recording away.'

Stefan pushed open the sheet-metal door and let Anna in first. The steps were bare and gritty. The walls had a smooth finish with the appearance of salami in greytone. They bounded up the stairs, glad of the cool air. He sneaked a kiss on the back of her neck as she knocked on the door.

A leathery face peered out. Eyes sunken in, gums exposed at the base of the teeth. His thin lips worked soundlessly for a couple of seconds. 'Anna,' he blurted. 'You're back.'

'I'm back every month, Uncle Bartek.' She pushed ahead to the kitchen and unpacked bouquets and presents. Bartek followed her, his mouth hanging slack. He walked with carefully-placed steps, not exactly feebly, but the walk of someone who does not trust the ground. Then he noticed Stefan.

'Take a seat. You'll have a coffee? Sit down.' They entered a black cavern of a room. Heavy curtains hung over the windows. The air caught at Stefan's throat, his tongue felt sticky. He tasted cigarette tar. 'Don't mind the things there.' A pair of long scissors and what appeared to be a box of medical equipment lay on the table.

'You develop your own photographs?'

'Which? No. That's audio tape.' The thin man seemed pleased at the mistake. 'See? Six point four mil,' he said and unwound a strip from a reel.

Stefan's eyes adjusted to the dark. He made out a row of glass-fronted cabinets. Shelf upon shelf of thin boxes. Audio reels, each labelled and dated. He flopped down onto the low sofa. The long open box held several instruments of dull-grey surgical steel. Aged but flawless.

'Do you see how this thing can splice the tape? Do you see the way it cuts at an angle?' Bartek sat beside him and leaned over. Stefan caught the whiff of a deviant body chemistry. An inorganic smell that shrivelled his stomach to a knot.

Anna poked her head in. 'Uncle,' she said, 'where is little Monika?'

Bartek stared hard at her. His lips struggled, perhaps forcing back a curse. When he spoke however, it was in a subdued tone. 'She'd be down in the playground, as far as I know.'

'Oh Jesus – she was one of the girls on the swings and I didn't even notice.' Anna put her hand to her mouth. 'I think I was looking straight at her.'

'This is the tweezer – German production – and this the guillotine, and this is masking glue.'

'You have the old style audio reels.'

'That's it. That's it. High fidelity.'

'Uncle. This is Stefan. Will I make some coffee?'

'Stefan, pleased to meet you. Oh yes. I believe you lived abroad for a while?'

'I was in London for six years.'

'Dead right to get the hell out of this hole. Me? I'm too far gone now. Nobody wants to employ a living skeleton.' He rose up, gaunt and unsteady. Sucked in a breath through his nostrils. 'It would be proper order to offer you a beer, but I can't. I don't keep any in the house. One whiff of alcohol and an inner battle wages.' He held his ribs. 'Sometimes I can't even walk past a shop where beer is sold. I take a walk the odd time to get air. At night though, when the shops are closed.' He gave a nod towards the kitchen and lowered his voice. 'It's a shame that I can't drink a beer with you. If I was a decent uncle, me and you, we'd get blasted drunk together so I could see what kind of person you really are.'

He sat again, resumed his demonstration of tape splicing. His mouth smacked dryly in concentration.

Jestadaj, the labels said. Yesterday. Stefan walked along the cabinets reading dates in the dim light. 1971 – 1976, not a month missing. The cursive script was meticulously executed. Strokes of ink leached a penumbra of red and orange. With every step along the row of cabinets a sick feeling in his stomach intensified.

'Jestadaj,' Stefan read aloud.

Bartek took up the song in a tuneless chant. '*All my troubles seemed so faw away. Now a need a place to hide my way.* That was the name of the radio show. Jestadaj.' He sprang up and opened a cabinet. 'Bay City Rollers, do you know these?'

'Yes. *I only wanna be with you.*'

'Yes, yes. Now you have it. Gilbert O'Sullivan?'

Stefan shook his head.

'You don't know Gilbert O'Sullivan?'

'No.'

'*I told you once before and I won't tell you no more get down get down get down.*' He stamped the floor viciously on the last three beats.

'Where did you get all this music?'

'I recorded it from the longwave radio. The authorities didn't like that. The evil influence from the west. Creeping into our innocent little country like the Colorado beetle.' He took down a squat jar, set it flat on the table. He eased the lid around and it came loose in the palm of his hand. A thick black liquid lay within.

A wild notion ran through Stefan: this was the drug that kept the man alive, kept those jaws moving, muscles twitching, long after the body should have turned soft and decayed.

'You'll have one too?' Bartek took out a pouch and rolling papers. The life-breath whistled in his nose as he tapped and rolled. He concentrated hard to keep his fingers from trembling. His tongue searched for enough moisture to seal the gummed edge. They both sat back on the couch. Stefan rolled the smoke around in his mouth and inhaled lightly. Bartek sucked and hissed at it, his dry lips unable to form a seal. The tip at last glowed and kindled.

'I dunk them in there when they're finished. Deadens the smell.' He indicated the jar of tarry liquid.

Stefan had given up smoking years before for the good of his health. But such concerns were remote here. He looked at the dark wall. A framed photograph of three long-haired young men. They lounged against the display window of a shop, big sneering grins on their faces. He did not recognise Bartek directly, only by eliminating the other two. He did not know what they were doing now, but knew enough not to ask.

'Do you go out much?'

'It's as much as I can do to go to the local shops. I get dizzy in the heat of the sun. The doctor said …' – and here he jumped up again, as he did frequently during the visit – '… he said he cannot understand the nature of my physical organism. He says he measured my blood pressure and sugar levels and I should be dead twice over. He said my metabolism is doing a tightrope walk. One drop more, he said, will kill me. And I believe this. I truly believe this.' His eyes challenged Stefan to refute him. 'When I got out I drank sixteen cups of coffee a day. I needed to have something going into my blood to keep me steady. They gave me tablets at the clinic. But I pushed them away. *I didn't battle alcohol to get addicted to these. Keep the little white tablets.* They're only a sedative, she said. *No, keep the damn things*, I said.'

'When was this?'

The man counted in his head. 'Fifteen years ago, sixteen.'

A noise came from the kitchen.

'You and Anna, hey? You like her, yeah?' Stefan snorted in reply. 'You'll be happy with her. Not a beauty queen, but she's got a nice body, short and stocky. That's the best kind. And she's been well brought up.' Bartek crossed himself, from forehead to stomach level, left to right shoulder. 'Nominen bominen bubblegum bubblegum,' he said. 'You can get on well in the world when you do what you're told and believe the priest at mass. Stick to the home and the church and you can be happy in a place like this.'

'It's been a long while since I was in a church,' said Stefan.

'You've lived abroad.' The way he said it, the word held some of the meaning it used to have – the West, Freedom, the real world outside. 'Tell me, you've seen the candles. Do other places on earth have this fucked-up religious psychosis?'

He had seen the candles. Stretched out along Ulica Marcinska for five kilometres. Normal street lighting had been switched off. No light came from any business or shop; just the glow from thousands of lanterns. The smell of wax rendered the air itself sacrosanct. It had been like that in every town and city for three days after John Paul II died.

'You'll be happy, she's a nice girl,' he assured Stefan again. Anna shouted from the kitchen to say they should be on their way. 'You're not the type to cause trouble. I bet you're a good boy with her, holding back the urges. Know what I mean? Yeah I can see that, you're not one to make life difficult.'

Sun shone on the concrete slabs. Green weeds pushed up through the joints. In another month they would be baked away. A drift of sand lined the new tarmac road. The slabs, the blocks, the road too all looked as though they had been set haphazardly on a shallow bed of sand.

He approached her slowly, not knowing if this was the goodbye scene. But she was jumping with impatience and he reconsidered that maybe last night was not as significant as it seemed at the time. It made him happy to see her in good humour and he broke into a jog.

'Quick,' she said, grabbing his arm.

'Why were you waiting outside? I would have gone up to collect you.' He took off his jacket and loosened his tie. It was not hot, but soon would be.

'I don't want my family fussing over you.'

'Oh, the *family*,' he mocked. He wound his free arm around her, pressing her backwards.

'We have to go.' She wriggled. Then fell limp; let him have his way. 'That's my mother over there,' she said in a pause between kisses.

A small round woman stood on the pavement opposite, hands on hips, dressed like a peasant, long skirt and headscarf. 'Oh my God,' she squealed, and ran inside.

'Will you get into trouble?' he asked.

'Don't mind her, she's mad,' said Anna. Bells rang out. It was a thin, dislocated sound. 'Come on, we have to hurry. Jesus, I don't even know where it is.'

She clutched her things and ran straight-legged across the tarmac. In this part of town the apartment blocks stood at angles to each other. Wide spaces stretched between them.

'Are you sure it's that way?' The ringing seemed to him to come from a different direction.

'How should I know? It's a brand new church.'

'I say we go this way.' They walked and ran in spurts, out past the allotments, to the outside of town. A low circular building lay off the road ahead of them, surrounded by tilled land. Cars had pulled up outside. Some drivers, with no sense of decorum, had driven right up to the doors.

'So I'll tell you about Asha, ' Anna said. 'We didn't know each other at all as children. I remember meeting her at confirmation or something, but that was all. She didn't go to the same school. Somebody asked me once, that Asha, she's your cousin, isn't she? And I said, Nooo, I don't think sooo. I was embarrassed that I didn't know her, because you'd be supposed to know your own cousin. And just imagine that person went straight back and told Asha and then her mother knew and she said never speak to those people again. So I used to see someone like her in the street and think hmmm, maybe that's her, but she doesn't look like someone who's just had a baby. She probably doesn't recognise me any more. I grew up quickly, for a while, people said they didn't know me from one day to the next.'

Anna spoke rapidly. He found it hard to follow her sometimes.

'But you finally got to know her?'

'Oh yes. I jumped out at her and said, *you're my cousin*. Straight away we got on well. She's just like me. Same fashion, same way we laugh at mad things. But a different physical shape.' She closed one eye and traced a curved outline with her finger. The woman standing before them now tilted her head, made a pretend frown.

'This is my most favourite cousin, Asha. Asha, this is Stefan.'

'Pleased to meet you Stefan. Her only cousin.' Asha wore a brown bodice with criss-crossed strings drawn in a bow. She looked wholesome. 'Monika is inside rehearsing with her schoolmates. The whole thing is half an hour late.'

They filed along the pews. Each clasped something in the hand: Stefan his jacket, Anna her handbag, Asha her *décolletage*. They sat bolt upright and prepared their minds for an hour of blankness.

Children stood patiently in the aisle, swaying perceptibly. 'Child psychologists agree,' the priest said, 'that the age of criminal responsibility begins around the age of eight years. Though you may teach these children, they are not a product of that teaching. What is the nothing out of which a child creates a conscience?'

These were strange words for a priest. Stefan looked up to check for the white collar. He tried to follow the sermon, if indeed it was a sermon. At last the words fell into a more familiar priestly cadence. The woodcut stations of the cross, stained glass windows and smoke from incense imposed their own discipline. He woke from this to realise it was still the homily and there were at least forty minutes left to go.

One child turned her head, grinning and inviting others to grin with her at this outlandish garb. Never been in a church before, Stefan could see. She looked delighted at the whole dungeons and demons atmosphere.

One of them was hers. Maybe even this one.

The thought made him queasy, the profane secret at the heart of the world. He eyed her sideways, this Asha, the tied cleavage she wasn't thinking about, the country garb she wore. She looked like any girl who might catch his eye in a bar. Nothing to suggest another person had come out of her, eight years ago when he was just starting senior level at school. Back then he would have been the type to snigger if a girl like her walked past in the yard. Could she tell that when she shook his hand?

Anna on his left tugged at his elbow. Time to kneel. She joined her hands and bent her head forward. This genuine fervour bothered him. During the six weeks he'd known her there had been nothing to suggest this. Perplexed, he fell to his knees alongside. As he did so, his abraded penis caught in his underwear and he winced.

The previous evening they had gone to the sports bar. This was a flat-roofed building originally built to be a changing room for summer bathers at the lake. A gully ran down the centre of the bar room. He sipped at his beer. It didn't feel right to get drunk in a place with hard tiles and steel chairs.

'Here is where me and the girls used to sit,' said Anna. 'We spent all the last year of school here, every night. Then I passed the exams and never came back. The barman asked one time, *where's the spiky-haired girl with the* – and he trailed his fringe over his eye, the way I always used to have it.'

She was happy for him to visit these places which were now relics of her past. They stumbled down the pathway to the lake shore and veered off on a track among the trees. This was another secret place. He tripped her up and let her fall on top of him. Twigs and briar ground into his back. She didn't get off him and he moved his hands over her. Lights from the street spangled through the branches. He knew that from the well-lit road absolutely nothing could be seen in the woods. But it is hard to believe in one's own invisibility. He backed her up against a tree, trying to find a foothold on the bulbous roots.

They waited until no-one was on the road before

emerging. The undergrowth caught at their feet, scratching and stabbing their ankles.

'So this is where the town girls bring their boyfriends,' he said.

It was the wrong thing to say.

'Do you think I take boys in the woods to fuck?'

'No,' he said.

'Do you think it's my habit to take boys in among the trees to make them spew?' Her face was pinched together in hatred. She walked on ahead of him. He jogged up alongside. She swerved so as not to see his face, walked with straight steps, seeing nothing but the path at her feet.

'I didn't know what I was saying,' he tried.

'You bastard. You could have said something to make me happy. And instead you come up with the most horrible thing.'

She cried all the way home. He felt exposed; people would see them. A stranger in town, a sobbing local girl. This was the inevitable end of things. He had not thought that words could have such an effect. He had not meant anything. It felt trite to just say sorry. Like putting a penny in the right slot.

He caught up with her again at her doorstep. She faced him, letting him see her tears, the wrong he had done her.

'Say something,' she said. 'Say something that would make me happy.'

And so he did.

The children craned their necks to see the action: two priests blessing a basket of loaves. A loaf was handed to each child, who kissed it and held it in front with elbows bent at right angles. It was a pose as iconic as those depicted in the paintings in the alcoves. The new church could not yet afford statues. A teacher passed along the procession, keeping order in the lines.

It was over. Anna bent over to exchange whispers with one of the communion girls. The girl jiggled with excitement, her braided rope flailed out. Her fingers dug into the thin crust of the loaf. She tripped along inside her satin robe, two and a half steps to every one of Anna's.

'This is the most cleverest and sexiest girl you'll ever meet,' said Anna.

The girl squirmed in giggles.

'And she had to memorise pages of stuff for today.'

The girl took a rolled sheet from her sleeve and handed it to him. She looked nothing like Asha.

'And her name is Monika.'

'Hi, Monika.'

'Say something funny to Monika.'

Guests milled about from table to table in the garden. A few weathered men stood under the eaves and closely observed the activity. They had the look of people waiting for their chance to come. From time to time one might offer to help the women carry out the trays of food. Wide boards of shaped melon with skewered strawberries and kiwis, plates of cold meats, boiled white sausage, gherkins, chicken drumsticks. Temporary timber decking had been set up for the most important tables. Asha's mother had spared no expense.

A screech of excitement: the communion girl, dragged

out by the hand to meet the grandmother. Moments later Stefan too felt his hand firmly gripped. He felt hemmed in by the tables, the handclasp, the cluttered trays of food.

'This is my grandmother. She has all her wits about her, and isn't doddery at all yet,' said Anna.

The old woman placed her hands on his shoulders so he had to stoop. Hunker down, Stefan, like a good boy. She asked him where he was from. She told him she had lived there for two years, the people there were honest people and could be trusted. Stefan gritted his teeth, smiled. His thoughts were on the man in the curtained room.

There was no beer or vodka on the tables; it was not that type of occasion. Some of the men sneaked away from the party and came back to stand by the shed with bottles of beer behind them on the windowsill. A bottle was offered to him, but didn't accept. It was all right for them, but perhaps not for him.

He selected some cold cuts on a plate for himself. 'Whow,' he breathed out. It was meant to indicate how hot it was. Asha smiled at him and tightened the strings on her décolleté. He rolled his eyes to show how ridiculous an idea it was that he would be looking at her cleavage.

Time for photographs: Asha and Anna under the cherry blossom, little Monika between them. 'Just a second,' said Asha, running to pick up an axe that was lying outside the woodshed. Monika squealed and struggled to escape. Asha held her by the shoulder and poised with the axe aloft. Cameras snapped, people chuckled uneasily, a voice called out for an end to the nonsense.

'What was that about with the axe?' he asked Asha. Music

played loudly from speakers placed out on the windowsills.

'What?' she said and leaned forward. With a slow movement he reached down and tightened her front strings. 'My goodness,' she laughed, flinching at last, 'you'll have to watch yourself.'

He picked up a slice of melon, panicking at the thought that the daughter was her daughter, and how quickly he had forgotten this. Her brown eyes mocked him.

He sought a random exit from the situation. 'Have you ever been abroad?'

'How would I go abroad?' she said.

Anna came back, and the two women were soon laughing about the old days, growing up apart as kids, and the time when Asha and her mother moved down to the cellar.

'Her father Bartek was so crazy. He used to pour methylated spirits through a loaf of bread and squeeze out the alcohol. So one morning he went to the local shop and said, *A loaf of bread please.* The shopkeeper narrowed her eyes at him. *Your good wife bought bread at eight this morning, why do you want bread at this hour?* And she ran him out like a stray dog.

'So he goes to the cosmetics kiosk and says, *Good morning madam. A bottle of Przemyslaw aftershave, please.* And the lady stoops to look through the hatch at him. *I know your type*, she says. *A half-litre of aftershave, eh? And you with a wife and child.* Bartek throws up his hands. *Jesus fuck. No bread, no aftershave? I'm going for a beer.*'

The chair legs squeaked across the boards. 'Steady on,' he said, and pushed the mass of female limbs back into position.

'No bread, no aftershave,' Anna squealed again. 'God, he was a laugh.'

'And what was that about the cellar?'

'When Asha was little, Bartek went really mad for a while, psychotic mad, and chased them round the kitchen with an axe. *Parasites*, he roared. *You're sucking the life from me!* Asha and her mother locked themselves into the cellar. Later, when he was asleep, they crept up and took mattresses and blankets down with them, set up house in the basement. They cleaned it up and set down mats. Set up an electric stove for themselves.'

'It was embarrassing to go to the shops,' Asha said. 'They used to give me extra food for free. I wanted to stay in and hide.'

'And meanwhile the lord of the realm roamed freely in the two rooms upstairs, playing music at maximum volume night and day.'

'Bartek,' Asha explained, 'had this dream of being a famous DJ. He ran a rock 'n' roll radio station for two weeks, until the *Militia* drove up and took away the equipment. The two weeks of being a radio star went to his head. He used to write letters to foreign DJ's, even to the bands themselves in Manchester. There was never any reply. *The red bastards have me on their files*, he used to say.'

'More likely the British radio stations had him on their files. Warning: Don't answer this Polish nutter.'

'Still.' said Stefan. 'He must have been a real rebel against the system. Running a pirate radio station back in those days.'

'Bringing crappy seventies music to the nation,' laughed Anna.

'Will he be along later?'

Asha looked at him, puzzled. Was this a joke that has gone over her head?

'Invite Bartek?' said Anna. 'You mean, the Bartek we were just talking about?'

'Nobody here would speak to him,' said Asha. 'They would turn their backs on him. He hasn't left the room in years.'

'But he is well remembered,' laughed Anna.

Stefan laughed too. He had tried to think things back into the domain of the normal. That all things were, at the back of it all, ordinary. But they weren't. In a room on the fourth floor the dead man sits at a table splicing tapes. Blood like creosote. Preserved beyond his time. He'd make a good corpse, laid out straight in a coffin of the same hue. A fine noble corpse.

He looked with mixed admiration at Asha. She smiled back, a mocking smile to one who could never understand the intensity of her life.

'Monikoo, show Uncle Stefan your presents.'

The chubby communion girl trotted over. He followed her into the house, down a corridor to a freshly-painted room. She showed him her set of beads made from milky purple amethyst.

'How much money did you make today?' he asked. She searched his face, looking for a signal to laugh.

'I'm only keeping a hundred and giving the rest to mama.'

'You're a good girl. A hundred is enough for anyone.'

'It's loads of money,' she agreed. 'Have you got one of these?' She showed him a pocket games machine.

'No. I couldn't afford one.'

Monika looked pleased at this. *An ordinary plausible kid*, he thought. *Funny how kids can be more conventional than their parents.*

Seven years in London had changed him. He felt himself above village taboos. He had seen what he wanted and was worthy of it now. She thought herself beyond touch because of the child. She had learned to despise the small-town admirers who only ever made their approaches when drunk.

He went to the kitchen to pour a jug of water. The old brass taps creaked and had to be turned through several rotations. It was as warm and humid as May can get. The promised rain had not arrived. 'Asha,' he said to the cupboard as he waited for the jug to fill.

She came in with several plates.

'Asha. It's good to see you.'

'Anna was wondering where you were.'

'Anna is a nice girl.'

'I'm sure she is,' she laughed. 'You already got fresh water? Better take out glasses too.' Her bare arm stretched past him. He passed a hand around her, lightly, so she turned to him, a puzzled look on her face. Their bodies shifted off balance, pressed against each other.

Then a dizzying crack to his jaw. Tears clouded his vision and he stumbled back thinking, *that noise, that was me being hit.* And then he thought, *that was no slap, that was a punch,* and to his amazement he's on the floor and she's not there. He feels shame: under an evil influence he had attempted to take sexual advantage of a young mother. No, he is shocked: the violence bred in her bones has reared its head. There were no borders to what she was capable of. Or no: she had only intended to slap him, but the glass was in her hand. Perhaps she hadn't noticed the glass in her hand.

All possibilities are equal; there is no starting point to think about what has happened, no reason, no proportion. She was nice to hold.

A sharp pain shot vertically up his cheekbone. He realised now why it is named the eyetooth. Realised too that those who have been chased to the cellar by a man with an axe do not know the bounds of normality.

He got up, staggered for the bathroom. In the corridor he saw the front door open and thought briefly about leaving. He splashed water into his mouth and spat. Gargled and spat several times but the water still ran red. His heart was pumping too fast. He held a wet cloth to his forehead and thought his way back to calmness. Nothing too serious had happened. One tooth was wiggle-loose. No sirens were wailing, no women screaming.

He waited as long as he safely could before he would be missed, freshened his face one last time in the cool water.

'Tooth infection. Flared up on me again,' he mumbled his way past a couple of the remaining guests. At the end table three pairs of female eyes watched him, awaiting his next move. He had no idea what they were thinking.

A Drop to Warm my Blood

Oleg had finished his shift at the gas plant and was having a quiet one at Pascal's place. A teenage girl came running in to the barroom, a young slip of a thing with a fluffed hood framing her eyes. All sorts of people came into the bar these days, and it was not unusual for a woman to have a drink on her own. Oleg knew better than to leer without first being certain of her provenance. And indeed, after casting a glance around the room, the girl approached him with a wary look.

'Uncle,' she said, 'I'm to tell you that Grandma is ill and in the hospital.' She pulled down her hood.

'Good Lord,' he said.

'She collapsed yesterday morning and was brought in.'

'Is that the way it is?' The Grandma was surely ninety

and not for long in this world. Oleg felt big of soul at being the recipient of tragic news.

'Aunt Anna says you're to go to her house and move the bed up into the spare room.'

'For what?'

'Dunno. Visitors I suppose.'

'Oh yes indeed. Bad news travels fast.' He nodded his head, thinking of the extensive web of the Grandma's cousins, nephews and nieces from abroad who might come to pay their regards. There would be news of those who got out long ago, plates of smoked ham and salami, bottles of duty-free, a certain atmosphere of respect.

The girl was casting sidelong looks about her. Plain wooden benches, a grimy tiled floor. And the men, mostly swaddled in their coats, although the place steamed with warmth.

It felt like a critical regard to Oleg. He felt she was memorising details, compiling a mental report. To be held against them, the men, at some unknown later point in time.

'Indeed I'll do that. I'll be sure to do that,' he said.

'Fine. I'll go on then.' She looked at him from under her hard-edged fringe. She was his sister Wanda's child. One of his nieces. He always confused the names – there were some three or four girls of a similar age – several years between them perhaps, but time passes so quickly.

He recalled her as a child however; this one precisely, he was sure of it. He had nicknamed her the Queen of Absurd one long-ago family Sunday. The family – the extended family that is – had all been out in the garden grilling cuts of meat and drinking cherry liqueur. That was the days when he was still invited to such occasions. Twelve years ago now, to judge by the length of her legs.

As the girl twisted her way between the tables to reach the exit, Oleg wonder what way things generally worked these days. Whether a girl like that would still be a virgin, or expected to be a virgin, or whether people gave a thought to things like that. The world was changing.

'Pascal,' he said, 'draw us another large one. I just got terrible news. The mother-in-law took a turn and was taken to the hospital.'

'The Grandma? Christ Oleg.'

'She'll hardly get out alive.'

'Is that the way it is?'

'Has to happen some time.'

'There's truth in that.'

Oleg sank a draught of beer and it warmed him. He decided he would go straight home after visiting the hospital. It would show respect.

A hardened shell of ice coated the footpaths. Snow had fallen at the beginning of winter, and the surface was well beaten down by now. On windless days such as this, coal smoke formed a thick stratum over the town. They said it was bad for your lungs. It had been good enough for them all as children. But now the trend was for health and environment, and all manner of things were regulated and banned. Industrial buildings in the town centre were not permitted to burn coal and those further out needed taller chimneys.

This didn't bother Oleg personally: it meant more buildings had to switch to gas, which meant his job was all the more secure.

He reached the high street. Here the cobbles were well-scraped and he could walk with a longer stride. They had been discussing the matter in the pub, not an hour earlier. Several cases of acquaintances who had slipped and fractured bones on nights such as this. The cold weather, they agreed, made the bones more brittle. Oleg was no longer young, and he feared the treacherous hard-packed snow.

The hospital was a four-storey building indistinguishable from any other in the town, except every window was lit up. The light illuminated clouds of vapour. Steam issued from vents and ducts that ran along the outside. That was the way it was in that town: the buildings looked like they had been turned inside out, their inner circulation exposed to the world.

It took a lot of energy to heat that hospital. A lot of gas piped along a dedicated line from the plant.

Oleg stamped his feet on the entrance mat and shook his coat. Bouquets of flowers stood in metal cylinders in the hallway. This confused him. He thought for a moment they were set out so visitors could take a bunch in to the patients. But that didn't make sense: you get nothing for nothing. He touched the petals to check if they were real and went on down the white-tiled corridor. He looked back at the wet footprints he'd left, but there was nothing he could do about it.

He followed the signs to the critical ward, and indeed there was the Grandma on a bed under the window. She looked pale, her hands clasped on her lap. Anna came at him fluttering, making much of the situation.

'Will you give the woman some peace, she's in a frail

state.' Oleg backed off. The Grandma's eyes were closed, she hadn't yet seen him. He made a shush gesture with his finger as he backed out. The space between the trolley beds was narrow. Loose metal swung and clanged.

'Get out to the corridor,' she said. She was doing what she did well: making him look like a boor. 'What has you coming over here?'

'Isn't it the right and proper thing to visit the Grandma?'

'Did you move the bed up to the spare room?'

'I came straight here. Like any decent man.'

'Decent,' she repeated. He had no reply. Not here, in this place, where she might raise her voice (a privilege he would not be permitted). And this from a woman who had said, *I will have nothing more to do with you.*

It was pointless to stay and take abuse. He would move up the bed, of course he would; out of civility, out of family duty.

'The bed,' she called after him, 'take the bed up to the spare room.' He waved off her annoying voice, wished her away, wished her eyes away that she might not be watching as he moved his bulk down the corridor. The passageway was cluttered with buckets and wheelchairs. He murmured a respectful greeting to a nurse as she palmed her trolley to one side. Not far enough. The tails of his coat caught in some protruding wires and he had to apologise again, standing there while she knotted the cables together and squeezed them out of the way.

Anna, however, did not stop to watch him. She returned to the ward where Grandma sat up asking where everyone had disappeared to.

'The nurses,' she complained, 'they spend more time putting on make-up than they do out on the wards. I haven't seen a nurse all day.'

'Now that's not true Grandma. You were asleep a lot of the time.'

'Asleep? I close my eyes for one second and they run off and leave me for hours. You couldn't be awake long enough to catch those nurses.'

'Did the doctor see you again?'

'The doctors keep well away. I hear them laughing with the nurses. There's funny business there all right.'

'They're all sinfully lazy.'

'They're not lazy when it comes to certain things,' the Grandma grumbled.

Anna tugged the corners of the bottom sheet around the mattress to make it sit neatly. The fabric felt damp in her fingers. Food stains trailed down the mattress cover and onto the floor. It was true the nurses were not very attentive. She sighed and crossed to a recess, left of the entrance. A stainless steel sink with an antiseptic dispenser. Buckets and mops. And, in a cupboard under the sink, bottles of cleaning fluids, steel wool, and various disinfectants. She made up a warm chloroxylenol solution. She had done a year of nursing training herself, years and years ago.

'Lift up,' she said, and folded the blankets to one side. She wiped down her mother's body with a moistened cloth.

'Look at me,' said Grandma. 'A sack of old bones.'

'Be quiet now.'

'Only a bother to people.'

'Ah now.'

'I pray to Jesus to take me up to him.'

'Ah now.'

'It's not worth the trouble. Leave me in peace.'

Anna rubbed her with a towel. The terry fabric was harsh, like a scrubbing pad. She rolled up cotton tissue instead and swabbed the skin dry.

The old woman continued to talk about how she would be up with the saints soon. With her own mother too, who would have her place amongst them.

There were five other patients in the ward. But they were half-comatose and no longer a presence in the room. Their exhalations brought an organic bluntness to the dominant odour of isopropyl alcohol. Every so often one might gasp in spasms, bite at the air alarmingly.

Grandma was different. Her face was framed by a mane of white hair, her expression as peaceful as a cherub's. She joined her hands across her lap, and even when her eyes closed in sleep she did not slump to one side. She was not like the others, who had fuzz sprouting from their scalps, features neither male or female.

A nurse appeared at the door momentarily, pursed her glossed lips.

White steam outside curled against the window panes. Vapour bloomed and dipped in the wanton draughts of air. The view out of the window was a frosty, steamy confusion, cut through by glimpses of steel ducting and seamed sheet metal. Not a view that anyone would want to gaze out on. And so nurses and patients alike turned their gazes inward.

Wanda bustled through the double doors with her coat over her arm. 'How long have you been here? Did she eat anything since?'

She turned to the Grandma. 'Now why won't you eat? Why are you refusing food?'

'I'm not refusing food nor anything like it,' the Grandma averred.

'The nurse said you didn't eat a mouthful of dinner.'

'What nurse?'

'The nurse on station. She said you ate nothing at dinner time.'

'Oh the stink of it, the slop they serve here.' Grandma twisted her mouth in distaste. It was not like her to complain about food. She had brought up her daughters to believe that hardship was a virtue. She always chose the two-day old vegetables at the market. Crusts with schmaltz was wholesome food. She had been strict and loving with her daughters. Now, as is the nature of things, the wheel had turned.

'What stink?' scolded Wanda. 'It's your imagination. They get the best of meat and vegetables in here. I'd be over the moon if I had some of it instead of the jars we're still eating from. Sit up. Go on, sit up.'

The old woman wedged out her elbows and made an effort. Anna slipped in an extra pillow behind her back.

'Now. You have to eat.'

'I'll eat, I'll eat.'

'But you didn't. You haven't eaten all day.'

'Stop your fussing. I don't want to stuff my face.'

Wanda turned to a nurse who was changing the drip at another bedside.

'You. How long has she gone without food?'

The nurse looked up, startled. 'She picked at it, but it's hard to say if she ate any.'

'Do you see?' Wanda said indignantly to her sister.

'She's not well, don't you see she's not well?' said Anna. 'She doesn't feel any hunger in her state. There's no use forcing food on her if she can't hold it down.'

When the sisters conferred like this they talked at normal volume. The Grandma, when not being directly addressed, sank back on the pillow. Her eyes narrowed to water-logged slits.

'I'll make up an egg custard. She has to get some vitamins into her.'

The nurse working at the bed nearby interposed. 'There are sufficient nutrients in the intravenous.'

The two women followed her eyes to the transparent pouch hanging from a steel hook. It sagged like a bodily organ. A thin tube dangled, ran underneath bands of gauze and into a catheter on the back of the patient's right hand. This interface of flesh and the needle repelled the eye.

'Man does not live from bread alone.' The Grandma's eyes opened. 'I have eaten all that God in his mercy gave me grace to eat.'

'Ah now,' the sisters murmured.

'Whether I eat or not, I'll not be long among you.' There was a silence. 'I'll be praying for you on the other side. I pray Oleg will see sense and that God may forgive him. I pray you'll all have happiness and peace of heart.'

'We will Grandma.'

This God-directedness had begun some decades earlier. There must surely have been a time when Grandma was just another hard-working mother in the town. As the years passed, she had accumulated dignity as others accumulate money. She had tended the war graves before any formal committee had existed. There were other more obscure graves that also she tended. But if she swept the sand around them and placed fresh flowers, that was too trivial a matter for the town magistrate to investigate, and not in any case explicitly against the law. It would be noted however, and years later brought into consideration when deciding what students should be given scholarships to university.

The Grandma had warned her children against the dangers of alcohol and petitioned the local bars not to sell to minors. Yet when the time came for her own sons to stagger home drunk she didn't preach to them or nag them. She prayed that the drink would leave their souls intact.

There were stories about her that went further back. The kind of stories few bothered to relate, because it was not healthy to have too much interest in the past. She had witnessed the horrors of the war and seen an unremembered number of her older siblings die in those times. She had been taken to work in a factory, or rather cleaning the dormitories of the factory workers. For three years she did not step outside the premises. She made light of this episode. Although she spoke often of the suffering in her life, it was always in the most general sense, implying a suffering common to all.

Grandma brought seven children into the world. Her eldest grandchildren, through the eldest son Jacek (and Daria, who had married well), were now living in Canada and the USA. She kept photographs showing little children standing beside a Christmas tree with hundreds of lights.

There had been a couple of letters in the last ten or fifteen years, but no more photographs. Those children would be grown up now, speaking English, perhaps with children of their own. And Anton's daughters too, wherever they had fled. The mother had taken them abroad and married again, and nobody could blame her.

There was a joke that went around about the supposed extent of Grandma's influence. It was said she had played a role in the banning of the plink-fizz hangover tablets. Along with other women of the town, she had held a placard in protest outside the chemist shop which sold them. For weeks they maintained a sporadic blockade.

Her objection to the tablets was supposedly because a headache was God's punishment for getting drunk, and it was sinful to artificially elude this punishment. It made for a good story, and so it spread.

The truth was more complex. The television advert for the tablets depicted a wild party with the voiceover: *we all get drunk on occasion, sometimes you just have to let it all out.* It was a voice that insinuated itself into people's lives. Nothing like it had been heard before. Adverts up to that time had shown attractive young couples having breakfast in a sunny kitchen, laughing schoolchildren, roses in a vase. This one was different. It simultaneously scorned and seduced people with its knowing voice. It may be true that Grandma identified it as the voice of Satan made manifest. Some weeks later the advert was withdrawn, the product taken from the shelves.

Oleg packed his toolbox and made his way across the frozen cobbles to his wife Anna's house. They had never gone through the formalities of a divorce. He had signed some document that ceded his rights to the house. Probably it had no legal status, but he let matters rest. He was the man, and so he was the one who had to move out, that was all there was to it.

Anna had left the front door unlocked for him. It had been several years since he'd set foot in the house. He descended the stone steps to a blast of warm air and the heady scent of must and pickles. A cast-iron boiler was burning, circulating hot water through the house. He stopped to admire the boiler and examine the pipes for leaks. It still worked as well as the day he and Anton had installed it, over thirty years before.

Oleg pulled away a heap of rags and papers to uncover the old iron guest bed. It was a weighty mass of iron struts and springs. He would need his ratchet wrench to take it apart, maybe even his angle grinder. He checked to see where the socket was and dragged the bed to the middle of the floor.

His body felt cumbersome as he worked. He panted with effort. He felt fine working the eight to four shift at the gas plant, even though there was plenty of lifting and twisting. But the least physical effort after hours left him exhausted. For this reason he hated doing repairs around the house and would hardly bother to tighten a leaking tap.

As he straightened his back the musty smell became more definite. It was the unmistakable whiff of fermentation. It could perhaps be a crate of neglected peaches. He set out on a hunt, guided by his nostrils. Past the five-litre jars of compot, way back behind the teak dresser, the heavy antique kilim – and there it was. A demijohn with the valve sticking up. A froth had leaked beneath the airlock and left a sticky residue down to the wicker. He uncorked the fragile tubing and tested the aroma. Apple cider, with yes, more than a hint of peach. It had been left there a long time and was well mature. The demijohn was too weighty to lift, so he lay on his side and tilted the neck towards his mouth. The fluid was fruity and mellow, full of nourishment. But lying on the hard flagstones hurt his elbow. Oleg pulled out the kilim and laid it over the floor. This worked fine; he could prop an elbow on the folded end of the rug, tip the jar to his mouth, and sip at leisure like a Turkish sultan.

He saw poor Anton's things on the shelves. His fitter's toolkit, a pressure gauge, several old pumps – stored away down here out of mind. This demijohn and glass airlock were Anton's too, but at least someone was getting use from them. It pained him to see these tools corroding away. He knew it would not look well to ask for them. He could simply take them, but that was too big a risk. Left down here as a ludicrous memorial, unseen.

Poor Anton, he recalled. In those last months, as he moved beyond anyone's trust or concern, Anton was not allowed into Pascal's pub. The regulars did not want to know him anymore. He was a disgrace, an embarrassment to anyone who ever drank himself into a stupor arm in arm with him.

But for so long he had been a font of good humour. The turns of phrase he used could still be heard in the plant canteen. *You Zulu warrior. Strap me up vertical and let me blast away.*

The bread that daddy Anton brought home had a strange

industrial smell. The children were overheard complaining. He used to pour the meths through a half-loaf and collect the neutralised liquid drop by drop. Then he would toast the loaf to drive off the methyl. He knew his chemistry, engineer Anton, with a diploma and all to his name. He could talk the talk of phase transitions and relief valves, and continued to do so in obscure metaphors long after the plant had let him go.

His wit and bluster had seemed invincible. He would slap a bottle of violet methylated spirits on the counter in front of the check-out girls at Netto minimart. 'French polishing the old dresser,' he would wink and smile broadly, 'have to get things shining.' And the girls would smile back. They would laugh and joke with him. So brimming with good humour, exuberant, it seemed he could carry the day. He created a new reality where drinking methylated spirits was no longer an unspeakable act of the doomed, but a counterstroke of wit, a cunning coup against the Machine. And we all know what the Machine is.

When Anton fell there was no rock-bottom to hit. He neglected the basic things like washing and shaving. In the summer months he took to sleeping wherever he collapsed in a drunken stupor. He fell out with his old friends one by one, even as he became best friends with the next stranger on the street who would stop to listen. And still he could brighten their day.

It was ugly, the way things went in the end. Something only old women would chatter on about. The past is gone and done with, let it rest.

But wasn't he inspiring in his day, arms thrown apart to

dispel the gloom, singing for all the world to join in with him. Exultant.

Oleg hammered and twisted to loosen sections off the bedframe. Each rust-locked bolt needed a spasm of effort. He took an armful of irons up to the loft room. Heat rose from the whole house and settled there. It was the driest part of the house, and yet left empty most of the time. He pushed aside the boxes of Christmas decorations that were stored there and set to work, laying out pieces the way they would fit back together.

He tensed as the front door latch snapped open. Footsteps on the bare boards. Anna was back. She would resume her attacks, smell the drink on his breath, notice the scrapes on the walls and bannisters. He shook his head, anger seething up his veins. *I want nothing more to do with you*, she had said. Jesus Christ, he muttered, and swore to drop his tools and walk out if she started her nagging. Because once that woman started, it was like a drill that clicked to a higher speed no matter what you did.

'I'm not going up near you, work away,' she shouted up. A few moments later he heard her voice on the telephone. She was speaking distinctly, an earnest solicitous tone. It was the relatives abroad. Oleg paused and listened carefully. First flight out, seven hour difference, changeover in London.

They were coming. Good food would be set on the table. There would be an atmosphere of abundance and respect. He, Oleg, would be allowed take his place at the table. For the sake of the visitors all rancour would be set aside. Amongst company he was at his best. He could tell stories to hold all their attention. Stories of the antics at the gas plant, local scandals, family histories, all brought out to shine again. Anna and Wanda too, their eyes would sparkle.

Oleg heaved at the spring base and it slipped into position. It wasn't quite right, but it would do. Any engineer could tell you: when you took a thing apart, it never went together as perfectly as before. He put a hand to the bed and it swayed. The headboards would steady it. Time to pay another visit to the cellar, and maybe take a break for a few minutes and sample the liquid preserves.

Anna was in a quandary. The visitors had asked her to book rooms for them in a local hotel. She had dismissed this idea, insisting she would accommodate them with relatives and family friends. No member of their family would be sent to the communist-era high-rise hotel on the outskirts of town.

But now that she set down the phone, she was troubled by second thoughts. These visitors from Canada would be accustomed to high standards. Born in the village, but no longer of the village. And of course the younger generation with them had never even seen the home country. In the heat of the moment, she had felt compelled to treat them like family. But there was no certainty that they would act like family.

Footsteps approached from the back door of the house. It was Wanda's daughter, breathless after running, yet as pale as ever.

'Aunt Anna, they were trying to ring you on the phone. Didn't you hear? Didn't it ring?' She looked at her aunt with panicked eyes. She was the bearer of bad news, and was afraid to utter it.

Anna spoke calmly. 'It's Grandma, is it? What happened?'

'Her heart stopped for over a minute.'

Anna put on her coat. 'And is she conscious now?'

'I don't know.'

'Come on then. Don't run. Running won't help anyone.'

They walked quickly nevertheless. A doctor was at the bedside when they arrived. The Grandma was sitting up straight. There was a bloom to her cheeks. She did not look like someone whose heart had stopped just minutes before. But that would be the adrenaline injections. It was a false vitality, the precarious surge of a flame consuming itself. An electrocardiograph beeped intrusively.

The sisters conferred with the doctor. The patient was in a weakened state and not yet stable. There's only so much, he said in a low voice, that we doctors can do. Anna told him of her own training as a nurse, way back decades ago, and he nodded respectfully. She's comfortable now, they agreed. She's not in pain.

Anna plumped up the quilt and tucked in the edges.

'Daughters,' Grandma spoke up. 'Daughters dear.'

'We're listening.'

'We'll share a glass of red wine. Go on, get out the bottle.'

'Grandma,' laughed Anna, 'there's no red wine here.'

'There's a bottle hidden about somewhere. The nurses come in when they think I'm asleep and take a swig for themselves.'

'Now don't be ridiculous, there's no wine here.'

'I think there's a bottle hidden under the windowsill.'

The sisters smiled at this fancy, for of course the old woman was a life-long teetotaller. There was never a drop around the house when they were growing up. And there were no windowsills in this room.

Grandma lifted her head to stare at the beeping machine. 'What time is it?' she asked sharply.

'It's ten in the evening.'

The Grandma looked from one face to the other. 'And what has you still up at this hour? Go on to your room the pair of you.' She reached out her left hand for something familiar that should be there by the bedside. Her hand grasped at the air and a perplexed look crossed her face.

Anna took her arm and tucked it in back under the quilt. 'Shhh now. We'll stay up a while with you.'

'Oh Lord, but the times back then.' The Grandma spoke low and quickly. It was an account of matters that they had heard before. Those who had gone abroad, those who had made poor decisions in life. Names wandered in and out of her narrative, and it was hard to know what generation of Marias or Annas she might be talking about.

Oleg came in at a certain time. He had brought a flask of coffee to disarm any bad feeling. The sisters were grateful. He told them he had set up the bed solid and steady as a rock.

'Anton,' the Grandma said, 'turned to the bad when he was only as tall as your knee. He had badness in him through and through.' They had never heard her speak like this of her dead son. But from her subsequent mumbled words it appeared her mind was back in the time before Anton died, and so she was scolding the living, not the dead. 'Poor drunken Anton,' she said, he's like a cat after cream.'

Oleg snorted merrily and looked at the two sisters to see

if they would join him in a grin.

The Grandma spoke then of times further back; of her sisters, a girl whose surname had to be kept secret, a borrowed bicycle, a malicious haircut from a supposed friend. Some of the people involved in these events were on their way from thousands of miles away, with their credit cards and suitcases with wheels.

'I've had my fair share of hardship,' said the old woman. 'I always made dresses of the cheapest cloth. Always made do with the poorest cuts of meat. And you, all of you, have a secret drop to cheer yourselves.'

'No mother, we don't.'

'I can see you all smiles. I know you have your secret pleasure. But you leave me out.'

'No mother,' said Anna. She forced an indulgent smile.

'Go on. Let me have my share. A glass of wine to put a smile on my face. A vodka to warm my heart. A drop to liven my blood.'

Anna looked behind her and peered out in the corridor, but Oleg was not there. He had gone off for one of his breaks.

'Shut up,' she said, 'shut your raving.'

'I know you have your special bottle stashed somewhere. You have your secret sips to keep you going. And me, bearing all sorrows with nothing to help me.'

'I swear, I don't touch a drop,' said Anna in tears.

'What are you crying for? Can't you see her mind is addled?' said Wanda.

And indeed it was a ridiculous accusation. There were only three places in the town to buy alcohol, and people gossiped. The women who drank were well known for it.

'A swig to gladden my soul, after all my sorrows. Would you deny me that? To warm me and bring a drop of sunshine. I know you have your secret help. A naggin of vodka, a glass of cherry liqueur.'

'I can't stand it, give it to her. Give her something.' Anna looked wildly about the room as if there might indeed be a bottle by some other patient's bedside.

Wanda grabbed her sister by the shoulders and held her. Anna shook for a few seconds with tears, then wriggled free and fled the room.

'Hush now mother,' said Wanda. The Grandma continued to talk about a bottle under the windowsill, a secret bottle for the three of them, a bottle that would be forgiven.

'Hush now,' said Wanda. 'Hush, you'll wear yourself out.'

Anna was gone some time. When she returned, she and Wanda took it in relays to watch and to smoke. The Grandma sank back on the pillows. But later she livened up yet again and talked about the cherry preserves she'd made last autumn, and how her glasses were broken but it was not worth repairing them now. She continued talking even when her voice had faded, so the sisters could not distinguish what she was saying. On and on she talked, apparently making sense.

People came and went through the night. Oleg brought more coffee and bread rolls and went off again. At some point the nurse came in and asked if she should turn off the machine. 'It's entirely up to you,' she said.

The colour had faded from the Grandma's cheeks. Her skin turned thick and waxy. She sunk into sleep. Her features lost their familiar set. It was unsettling to look at her and not recognise the person who had been talking only hours before. It was the talk that kept her going, and now she had finished speaking. She breathed in a couple of times, like someone trying to catch the start of a sneeze, and was dead.

The sisters continued with their prayers. Some time later Wanda went out to fetch the duty nurse from her station. The nurse pulled out the catheter and lowered the head rest. She left a clean covering sheet, but the sisters did not use it. Anna disconnected the drip bag and emptied it carefully in the sink. She washed it under the tap and threw it in the bin.

Oleg appeared shortly before noon. He sunk down on one knee onto the tiled floor and stayed in that position until his joints ached. He gripped the rails on the bed and pulled himself up. It was over now, and so sudden. Perhaps it was just as well that he had not been there for the last moments, to see the women all in tears and he unable to do anything about it. She brought him a chair, Anna did, but he did not want to sit. After a long time he asked if there was anything he could do. She shook her head; there was nothing, they didn't need any help with the arrangements. He could call by the house in the morning if he wanted.

Oleg stamped his way through the grey snow. He was touched by death. One fall on the snow in these temperatures and he too would not live to see dawn. Life is long, he reflected. He had another forty-five years to go if he lived as long as Grandma. And the turmoil of his younger years was already long burnt out of him. The fire that burned in him, the things he could have done, the person he could have been.

He had tried to be content with the ordinary events of work and family, to cover up the bitterness at the heart of things. Not to be taunted by what could have been, by the thoughts of another life he could be living somewhere far away, if he had had the courage. For there are places in the world that are cursed, places that tell you who you are and what you cannot be.

So he had stayed and tried to do the everyday things in an everyday way, and to keep from her what was real. But he let out a glimpse of the hard horror at the back of things and she had run to her mother.

Thus he learned the lesson. No matter if your own life is thwarted, you keep a lid on it, you don't pass it on to others.

'Pascal,' he said, 'A double of plum brandy. The Grandma passed away.'

Pascal crossed himself and sighed. 'I'm sorry to hear it Oleg. That's rough.'

Oleg sat alone at the counter. One day you are here, the next you are gone and other people are there. He felt the force of these paltry truths, these things too trite to mention. This is what all the deliberations of philosophers came down to.

The door opened and some familiar-looking young people stood there uncertainly. They understood from Pascal's frown that they should close the door against the cold. But they whispered together for a moment, giggled, and left without so much as an excuse-me or kiss-my-ass.

The likes of them would have good office jobs, holidays abroad, central heating. A new world was coming, that belonged to those who knew nothing of suffering and crushed hopes. They would have no need of religion or drink. And good luck to them, thought Oleg. Why not live like that, if you had the chance? Though it was otherwise with him, forty years left and already too late. And all he had learned, of how to endure, was useless now.

The barman Pascal dried the counter and wondered when Oleg would ever go home. It was disgusting that on the day of his mother-in-law's death he would be in the bar, boozing. And everyone knew the despicable things he had done or attempted to do. Such a man was a stain. Darkness and pain followed him. But what could you do? What could you do except pass the normal polite comments and wish that he soon leaves.

The door opened. It was the young people back again in their jeans and bright thermal jackets. This time however an older man wearing a suit was with them.

'Excuse me, we're looking for the hospital. The Saint Martin hospital?' The man's accent was oddly old-fashioned and formal.

Oleg jumped to his feet. His eyes streamed with tears. 'I think I might know who you are,' he said.

THREE FRIENDS

When viewed from the row of boutiques at the pier, the cathedral seemed to have been hewn straight from the rocky peak. A series of terraced gardens sloped down from its triptych of doors.

Inside it was light and dry and cool. In place of statues, wall paintings in pastel colours reached up to the vaulted ceiling. Three backpackers wandered from chapel to chapel in silence.

'This kind of place is far more interesting to me than Florence or Chartres. These Gothic arches are legendary. If I had my charcoals with me I could just sit and sketch them all day,' said Christoff, a tall Belgian with a pagan-shaved head. When their route brought them southwards of Vienna he had attracted mistrustful stares in every town. Not that he noticed; he greeted the trembling old shopkeepers with the same geniality as ever, leaning across the counter in all his innocence.

The past week had contained a month of experiences, each day a rollercoaster ride through time. This was the first place where they'd stayed more than one night. After half a dozen cities in eight days, a feeling of pace and motion coasted them along.

The three friends rested on a low stone bench set into one of the exterior alcoves of the cathedral. There they found, crudely scribed into the stone, the board pattern for the same game they'd played on the overnight train journeys. Three concentric squares – the ancient game of Merrills. Christoff insisted on playing right there and then, with coins for pieces. He said he could feel the influence of the workmen who had played there centuries before, he could feel their spirits join with his.

A security guard stood watching them, as though to memorise each move and countermove.

'Someone doesn't want us here,' said Colin.

'Ignore him, we're not doing any harm,' said Christoff.

'We need to sort out somewhere for the tent.'

'You'd sleep on a rock. You'd sleep on a moving, shaking rock.'

'Time to go.'

On the long intercity trips Colin had slept soundly stretched out on the steel floor, waking up with a cross-hatched pattern pressed into his right cheek. Bullet-headed, black-haired Colin, the others wove a mythology of warrior-clans about him.

'That's the kind of spot we're looking for. There.' The third friend, Hans the Dutchman, pointed down to a bare expanse of grey close to the rocky shore. The regular ridges and right angles indicated it was man-made. Perhaps a holiday apartment development abandoned when the currency crashed.

The guard ignored their cheeky goodbyes. As they trooped down the corkscrew bend road it became hard to track where the vacant space had been and they argued about where to cut off through the shrubs.

The hotels had charged inflated prices, calculated on the basis of their passports no doubt, and there was no camping site on the island. It was Christoff's idea to trust nature and sleep sous les belles étoiles.

They rolled the tent out in the wind shadow of a ridge of blockwork. Nothing to do on such a balmy day but take a siesta. Who knew what way the weather would turn at night? It was best to get some sleep stored up.

Elderly strollers looked down disapprovingly at the sleepers. A man with a dog stopped and gazed at them, as though to drive them off by force of will. He called his dog to heel in a loud voice.

Hans and Christoff discussed the ethics of the issue and came to the conclusion that, though it was a minor disrespect to the environment to camp out in the open, in this case they were morally justified as the hostel prices were extortionate.

'I never thought there'd be a place like this here. It's like an oasis in a desert.' Christoff looked around the dance floor.

A girl in a taut lycra top glanced over at them, leaned back against a pillar. She had black hair and blitzy, glinting eyes that latched on things and held them in their grasp. Her glances locked onto Christoff, the drinks bar, the door, Colin, the bar again.

'There are many interesting girls here.'

'So I've noticed,' said Colin.

'Why didn't we find it before? It's a hell of a lot better than those plastic-coated cocktail bars,' said Hans.

For the previous two evenings they'd wandered from the harbour to the marketplace and back again, sitting in kiosk-sized bars and learning the bar attendants' names. After the bars had shut they'd prowled energetically up and down the sea-front. From several luxury apartments they heard pounding party music and saw the pulse of disco lights. They made jokes about yacht club posers and playboy tycoons.

Then on the third evening, along the waterfront where they'd tramped on every cobblestone, they found a night club. Not just any night club, but an industrial-music night club with the names of top Dutch DJs stencilled around the doorframe. Hans had spotted the cut-out coffin from the street. They followed a black arrow down a lane between high warehouse walls. An old woman at the door took their money and would not let them carry their raincoats inside. She looked the same as the old woman in the state museum, or the one at the gallery. Wherever there was an admission price there was a grandma with her hand out.

'I don't know if people here appreciate what they're getting,' said Hans. 'That DJ knows his shit. This is from a Rotterdam band called 'Loave'.'

Colin nudged the other two. 'Look at the way those chicks are dancing.' A girl wearing a pilot's cap stared at the ground as she hopped twice on one foot and twice on the other.

Christoff shrugged. 'She's just doing her own thing.'

'I wasn't laughing at her,' said Colin, 'it just makes me laugh to watch her.'

The girl had been standing in front of him, almost leaning back against him, for ten minutes. The dance floor was crowded; lots of people stood with their backs to the wall to take a rest from the pulsating throng. She didn't move away from him, but remained just standing there, the nape of her neck close enough to breathe on. She had dark hair, too burnished a colour to be natural, straight hair that curled in to an abrupt end high on the back of her neck, and she stood there very still. He was straight-backed against the wall, his chin almost resting on her shoulder, and felt that now, now surely she must feel his presence, must sense it, pressing so close, and it seemed to him she must, she did, and she accepted it and he accepted hers and their auras – which had at first resisted each other – were now mingling, creating tiny links of attachment. A few moments more and he no longer felt uncomfortable standing so close to her, and knew that he could speak to her whenever he chose. In any case it wouldn't be possible to squeeze past without saying 'excuse me'. He waited, feeling ever more calm.

He touched her shoulder lightly and she turned to look up at him.

'Sorry, do you know who the DJ is by any chance?' Her face was an attentive blank. 'Sorry, do you speak English?' he added.

'Yes I do. What did you say about by chance?' Her accent was foreign, her syllables tumbled and breathless.

'Sorry, what was that?' he asked.

She smiled and spoke in a firmer voice. 'You asked me something first.'

'I was wondering who the DJ is tonight.'

'Who is?'

'The DJ – the guy up there who plays the records. He's got pretty good taste.' He suddenly felt that the question might seem pretentious. 'Because the stuff here is so weird; it's all the latest stuff.'

She smiled brightly. 'It is weird music. It's very modern, isn't it?' She had turned fully towards him now, standing almost under his chin.

'It's so new, some of it I've never heard before,' he said.

'It's interesting music,' she said, perhaps reluctant to reveal her lack of knowledge. He could see her face more clearly now. She had strong features and dark slashes of eyebrows. Her hair was straight and shone red in the light. Her features were too forceful for her to count as a stunning beauty.

The music stepped up a pace. Most of the crowd were out dancing. Someone heading for the toilets squeezed between the two of them, and she took one step back to let him through, then one step forward again. Colin smiled at her and felt suffused by her presence, and neither of them spoke for a while.

'Are you here on holidays?' he asked.

'Yes. I am here two weeks now.'

'Where do you come from?'

'I come from Croatia.'

'Really? I've never met anybody from Croatia before. What's it like there?'

'It's always boring. My town is not very big.'

'Why did you come here?'

'My parents have a summer cottage here. We come here every year since I was small.'

'Yeah, it's a beautiful place,' said Colin.

'It's so boring. It's a place for babies to go on holidays.'

He laughed at this.

'It's true,' she said. 'It's just for mothers and their little babies. This club here is the only interesting place and they never say what day it will open.'

'It's a strange place,' agreed Colin. 'No music pubs, no other night life, everywhere shuts at the dot of midnight – and then we stumble across this place after being bored stiff every night.'

'Who are you with?'

'Two friends of mine from college. Christoff from Belgium and Hans from Denmark.'

'And you?' she asked.

'Scotland. Inverness.'

'In the what?'

'Inverness. It's a town. In Scotland.'

She looked at him with unconcealed admiration. 'Don't you wear a skirt or something?'

Colin laughed. 'I have worn one yeah, a couple of times.'

'I'd like to see you in a skirt.'

He looked down at her light yellow and orange skirt. She pushed one brown shapely knee forward.

'I wouldn't wear your skirt though.' She laughed giddily.

'It's called a kilt anyway; the skirt that Scotsmen wear.'

The music changed rhythm and melded into Lou Reed's 'Walk on the Wild Side'. She rocked to this with her shoulders.

'Can you dance to this?' he asked.

'Ssshh.' And then, a moment later, 'What does 'Do de do de do' mean?'

He hesitated, examined her puzzled expression. She broke into a laugh.

'Fooled you!' She pushed him lightly on the chest. They went out on the dance floor for the next couple of tracks. They were fast energetic mixes with no lyrics. She kept her eyes mostly to the floor and danced with a minimum of leg movement.

The music changed again to a dense percussive tangle. They stood a moment trying to find a rhythm.

'Let's stop,' she shouted in his ear.

'That's my friend Christoff!' Colin pointed. Christoff was the centre of attention, performing a squatting dance to the impossible music. People pulled back to form a circle around him. He was a strong dancer, able to copy the acrobatic movements seen on music channels.

'He's like a rock star,' she said. 'Is he in a band or something?'

'No, he's an ordinary guy. That shaved hair and chains make him look strange, but he's a straight-forward kind of guy. In Belgium no-one looks at him twice. He's always concerned about being fair, and world justice and all that stuff. You'd have to see him helping old women with their bags.'

'No, I don't believe it,' she said.

Colin looked around for Hans, so he would have something to say about him too. But Hans was nowhere to be seen.

They both stood against the wall again and talked about the people dancing on the floor, where they might be from, what kind of people they might be. Each sentence they exchanged was tagged with a skittish laugh.

She sat on the parapet and looked up at him. He had to say something. She didn't look as if she was going to say anything. He had to find something to say.

'I really needed to get out for some air,' she said. 'Too many people tonight.' She closed her eyes and leaned back, swinging her legs to the muffled beat. The more she looked relaxed, the more Colin felt uneasy. He wanted to sit beside her, to take her in his arms, to get back that feeling of being soothed by her presence. He was outside of it now, distant again.

'Will we go down to see the harbour?' he asked.

'Why?'

He shrugged. 'Just to see it at night. It might be nice. Or we could go back in to the music.'

'It's nice here for a while,' she said. He sat down beside her. Colin was wondering if she was really beautiful, the incontrovertible beauty only seen on television or in a magazine. He was trying not to look too long at her. The girls at his college were all ordinary, some better-looking than others. They all had faces he could look at. But with this girl he felt unsure of himself, as though such beauty demanded something special, and he must find out what was needed to attain it.

'Actually I have to ring my parents before eleven.'

'Oh?' he grinned. She was younger than him, a year, possibly two. It was a significant difference. 'You have to ask your parents if you can stay out late?'

'My parents went up to Rijeka for the week. I promised I'd ring them.'

She stood up and brushed the back of her skirt with her hands.

'Will you wait for me here?' she asked.

'Yes,' he said, and looked around. 'Right here?'

'No,' she laughed. 'Inside of course. You're not a bus-stop.'

'So where did you go?' Hans asked with a big grin, 'making contact with the natives?'

Colin grinned back. 'Not exactly a native, but close enough.'

Hans hooted. 'So you hooked up with a girl! I was only testing you out.'

'Where did you two go to?'

'The queue for beers was enormous, we went out for a quick one at the umbrella bar. So where is this girl?'

'She had to go out make a phone call.'

They could see Christoff coming with the beers. He calmly held the beer bottles aloft and edged his way through the dancing masses.

'This is the guy,' said Hans, 'who chats up three girls at once – and in French. He gets a grade A for that – Hey,

Christo,' he said loudly, 'those girls of yours are slipping off the hook. Did you tell them you're a barbarian?'

Christoff grinned. 'I don't know if they are just playing or if there'll be something more.' They clinked bottles and drank down the Blonde Beer as the label proclaimed.

'Guys, see the time. One of us has to go down and bring the bags up,' said Christoff.

Each morning they went to the ferry terminal to stash their bags in a locker. The building closed at ten to midnight.

'Maybe we'll all go down, this place is not going to stay open much longer,' said Hans.

'No,' said Christoff, 'we have to drink the night to the dregs. Never abandon the night.'

They decided to choose the old-fashioned way. Hans had a box of wooden matches they used to light the gas stove. He took out a few and rattled the box. The game was to guess the number of matches left, and whoever was most wrong would go for the bags. They retreated to a table close by the toilets to count the matches. After taking an inordinate amount of time to make a few simple subtractions, they discovered that Colin was the loser. They quickly agreed he was to pitch the tent on a sandy area close to the abandoned foundations.

He waited outside. The bass boomed down the narrow lane and out to the quiet harbour. He walked to the entrance door and back again to the parapet and the flowering shrubs. The air was so still that each stopping point had accumulated its own scent. Then he saw her, half running, half walking, her skirt flapping against her legs. She waved and slowed to a walk.

'It's just my hard luck,' he said, 'and when the music was really getting good.'

'But it's nearly over anyway,' she said.

'Will you be here tomorrow?'

'I can't. I have to go to the next island on the ferry. I promised to visit an old friend of my mother.'

'Oh!' he said, at a loss for words. 'Well maybe we'll be staying a few more nights here – I don't know, we've other places to see. Will you be back by then?'

'Yes, maybe,' she said.

'Then maybe I'll see you here again the day after tomorrow?'

'Maybe,' she said, 'but you know you'll probably meet me walking around if you're still here. The town is so small.'

'Yes, it's so small. If you're out at the beach, the place we're camping is on the other side of where the steps go up to the cathedral. You know it? The place where the concrete walkway ends and there are some building foundations?'

She nodded and said nothing. He needed to find courage and found it and took her hands.

'You can come and visit me in Scotland.'

'That would be nice,' she said, 'but that would be too expensive to me.'

'Then I could visit you in Croatia,' he said.

'You would come from your country to Croatia just to visit me?'

'Yes. You're ... I've never met anyone like you before. You're a special person to me,' he said awkwardly.

'Oh really?' she said, and took her hands away from his. 'You see too much in me. You see too much in people.'

Colin didn't know what to say to that. He waited for her to say something more.

'Well, do you want to give me your address so I can write a letter?' he asked. She went back to the cloakroom to borrow a pen. She sat on the low wall and wrote the address with such deliberation that for one dark moment Colin had the thought that she must be writing a false address. Why should she give her real address to a stranger she'd just met? Perhaps it had been too forward of him to ask. He could, after all, be any kind of freak. But then after handing him the slip of paper she smiled and leaned forward and kissed him, swiftly, probingly.

'It was really nice to meet you,' she said. 'Maybe you will really still be here when I get back on Thursday?'

His watch said he had four minutes. He jogged to the ferry station feeling light-hearted and alert, his mind racing. Off-season flights were cheap. He could fly direct to Vienna and then get a train. The whole thing could be done for less than a hundred. Tomorrow he would check the ferry landing times and on Thursday he would wait in one of the harbour cafes, drinking coffee and reading all afternoon

Christoff strode out from the seething breakers. The sun was dazzling, but did not yet have heat in it. He reached the band of bare rock studded with limpets and picked his way more cautiously. The water ran in rills off his naked body. He leaned forward with hands on his thighs to recover his breath, then turned and looked back out to sea.

Hans was the more expert swimmer. He was aiming towards the shore further down where there were no rocks.

The sky over the hills of fields behind them was flecked with clouds which would soon dissipate. Christoff reached the sand and jogged the last few steps to where his clothes were bundled. He picked up a towel and patted his shaven head, then peered down at his shrivelled genitals.

Hans climbed out of the water, and made his way on a converging path to the patch of coarse grass where Colin lay sleeping. He had simply lain down on his isolation mat with a sleeping bag pulled over himself. His two friends pulled dry towels from a disordered heap and scrubbed themselves vigorously in the cool morning air.

'I really needed that,' said Christoff.

'Especially after last night,' said Hans.

'I really needed that too,' said Christoff with a laugh, 'I haven't had sex for six months. I've been living like a monk. I needed to clear out all the tubes.' He inhaled deeply through his nostrils. 'Now I feel my yin and yang energies are back in balance.'

Hans laughed. 'You know, I'm not sure how I feel about that – sleeping with the same girl as you. It kind of feels strange. I'm not sure if it was a good idea.'

Christoff acted offended. 'Do you want my doctor's certificate? Anyway, maybe I should be worried about what you might have?'

'No,' laughed Hans, 'I'm sure it's all right. I was more thinking about her. You don't think she was a bit weird or anything?'

Christoff grinned. 'She just wanted to have sex, and more sex. What's so weird about that? I doubt if she can sleep with whoever she wants in smalltown land where she comes from. Over here she can have her fun. She was all revved up though, I've never met a girl like her. If I think about her I'll have to go cool down in the water again. Don't make me think about her.'

'She was a real dark-eye beauty,' said Hans.

'Don't make me go back in the water, I said. Just the thought of her gets me going again. Hey, how many times did you do it?'

Hans snorted, reluctant to give an answer. Colin had woken up and lay still with his eyes shut. He was wondering if this was an elaborate ruse to make him regret being the one who had to leave early. At the same time, it would be typical for Christoff that events would take a turn to the bizarre.

'So how many times was it?' asked Christoff.

'It depends on what you mean by 'sex',' said Hans.

Christoff hooted and slapped his thigh. 'How many different kinds are there? Oral? Axial?'

'Aw come on,' said Hans.

'OK. Put it this way, how many times did you come?' asked Christoff.

'Give it up,' said Hans.

'OK. OK.'

'Did you two meet some girls?' asked Colin, sitting up.

'Yes,' said Hans, 'some wild thing from Croatia. It was a crazy night.'

Colin felt a fungus taking root in his stomach, swelling and seeping pores into his bloodstream. He forced his voice to speak.

'And will you meet her again?'

'No. I'd love to,' said Hans, glancing up at Christoff,

'but she's gone to visit relatives on the next island. We'll be gone by the time she gets back. Actually I don't know if it's a good idea to meet her again. It was a once-off kind of thing.'

The fungus swelled and bloomed and burst, flooding his system with its poison. Hans noticed.

'What's wrong with you? Oh shit ... was she the girl you met?'

Colin shoved his feet into his shoes. He could barely see out through the water in his eyes. He snatched several times at his laces before he could tie them. Perhaps it was not the same girl. He seized on erratic memories of the previous night. Her narrow fingernails, the home-stitched hem on her skirt.

'It's not possible. Stop, Colin. What was her name then?' asked Hans. 'Jolita or something?'

Colin had never thought of her by name before – the name didn't sound like her. She had thought it hilarious that he'd only asked her her name after they'd been chatting for more than twenty minutes.

'Yes,' he said. He unbuckled his rucksack and crammed his sleeping bag into it.

'Oh shit, oh shit. We didn't know,' said Hans.

'It's not our fault,' said Christoff. 'Hey, where are you going?'

'Leave him alone,' said Hans, 'he'll be pretty mad, he's a Scotsman remember.'

'Is he going to leave us? Just like that? He's a strange kind of guy. Remember on the Vienna train –'

'Let him cool off.'

Colin sat on his rucksack and peeled an orange. The woman at the market stall hadn't understood him and had pressed a bag of a dozen into his hands. He sat in the shade of the ticket office. The next ferry to the mainland was in two hours.

Christoff slowed to a halt and stood over him.

'Honest, I swear we didn't even guess. We never saw you with her last night.'

'I know. I know that,' said Colin.

'You must have liked her. She was a nice girl,' said Christoff.

Colin was silent.

'You know, I admire you,' said Christoff.

'You do?' said Colin, confused.

'I don't know. You're so – passionate about things. You believe in things. I'm not like that. I kind of envy you. A girl might shoot herself in the head for you, but not for me.'

'That's no use to me,' Colin said grimly.

'Were you ... in love with her – a bit?' asked Christoff shyly.

'Just go back to Hans.' Colin began to walk away again.

'Look, I'm sorry,' said Christoff following him. 'I said I didn't know. Be fair! Tell me straight out: are you going to bear a grudge about this?' Colin stopped in his tracks, turned and looked him in the eye.

'No,' he said and reached out a hand.

Concrete Triumphant

'Would you lift up, don't be stooping.'

The craftsman leaned down and gripped the hawk over the white knuckles, holding it up from below. He slapped and smeared the mortar, scooped a glob deftly onto the trowel. Hurled it at the eroded joints in the chimney breast, sealed it in with the trowel edge.

The loaded mortar board sagged again, inch by inch, until it rested on the stringy black hair of the boy underneath. His face was streaked with grey stains from the cement, his nose red-raw from the cold and the brisk friction of his sleeve. Grains of sand ground into his fingers, working their way under an old plaster. It didn't hurt now, but he knew it would later. He peered up from under the board and willed strength into his drooping arms. The master scooped the mortar onto the trowel in one fluid motion and turned to the work again. Again the hawk sank slowly, and again the white knuckles on one side released their grip as the boy scrubbed his nose. He shook the blood back into first one arm, then the other.

They were on a scaffolding erected at the gable end of a house. It was a Victorian redbrick in the old residential part of the city. The father was up on a trestle pointing the chimney base. He slapped the mortar into the empty joints, pressed it in with the trowel and smoothed it over. Each time he slapped on a trowel-full, a good portion of it skited back, streaking the lower brickwork on the way down.

The mortar board became lighter. The boy could spare the attention to look across at the upstairs windows. He could see white lacy curtains, empty window boxes, wet leaves on window sills. He could see through the lace to the room inside. An assortment of bottles and spray cans stood on the inside ledge. A bright orange wardrobe with a mirror set in front. It had to be a woman's room. Little pictures, or postcards, were stuck all over the door. His eyes searched the crumpled bed clothes, trying to follow the shapes of the discarded items on the bed.

'Is it heavy? I said, is it too heavy for you?' The voice broke through like a fistful of gravel hurled at him. He strained his arms and raised the hawk again. If he hung his head to one side it didn't ache as much. He counted slowly.

From this position he could see the rows of slanted black roofs, the bushy crowns of trees, and all the little chimneys pushing out their smokes. It was a different country up here. You could giant-step from roof to roof, clamber across the mound of a treetop, and reach the flat expanse of the factory roof. From there you could make your way along the top of a high wall to reach more distant archipelagoes. More of the city is roof than road, he suddenly thought. The roads are not roads, but canyons cutting through the world of roof-level. Back gardens are hollows and pits into nothingness.

The houseman's wife appeared and stood cautiously to one side of the scaffolding. 'Are ye ready for a bite to eat?' she called up.

It won't be long now. The thought idled through him, holding him steady, warming him, waiting for the lights to change. Any moment now. But the craftsman disdained to be seen rushing in for lunch as soon as it was called. The woman stood below, looking on at the work in progress, as was her prerogative.

The boy rested the hawk on a spud of the scaffold, relaxing in the security of her gaze. He resumed his strategy of stepping from roof to roof, and now built the network of telephone wires into his landscape. Over these precarious bridges you could reach the church. The tiny three-runged ladders at the top of each telegraph pole provided temporary resting-places.

'Ah givvus a bit,' the voice intruded (but, under the gaze of the housewife, not as harshly as usual). The boy lowered his head to take the strain and offered up the hawk. Looking down he saw the round red face of the woman smiling at him. She called again, 'Don't be letting it go cold on the plate.'

There was no reply but the bristle sound of a stiff brush on bricks. The wet grit skited down into the boy's face. He screwed his eyes half-closed against it. At last his father climbed down from the trestle and threw the trowel and brush into a bucket of water. He thrust the bucket into the boy's hands. 'Take this, would you?' Spoken through the nose and mouth together.

'By God there's a bit of a chill out too, you young lad must be frozen,' the woman said kindly.

'It's all right,' the boy said. It was awkward to be treated with such consideration.

'Go in and eat the food while it's still warm.' The boy looked up at his father still scouring the wall and hesitated, unsure of which authority applied. 'Go on,' she said. The boy went ahead inside.

The sink was in a scullery next to the kitchen. He went through and washed the cement from his hands under a strong gush of warm water. There was a bar of soap and a bottle of detergent but he didn't want to interfere with her things. Outside he heard the woman scolding, urging his father to use the good warm water inside. The boy shook his hands vigorously. Life now fully seeped back into them. Too fully. They were two fleshy lumps of red stained with paler blotches, and now the pain seeped back too. He wished he was back at school, though there was nothing he had hated more than school. Maybe next year he could go to London, earn good money by painting people's railings, get his own flat.

The woman had prepared a stew, served not with potatoes but with stacks of bread. Through the window they could see the lawn, now with tracks of mud where they had dragged the scaffold pieces.

'That's a powerful stew,' the craftsman said.

'Only a bit of meat and carrots, you need something

warm on a day like this, and the pair of you way up in the elements.'

'That's all you need in a stew, barley and a slip of onion. You know an onion keeps off all kinds of colds and flus. There's a power in an onion.'

The father reached out for another cut of bread. His thin hands were appallingly abused. The remains of a bandage clung to the middle finger. The skin on the sides of the knuckles was cracked radially. One of the cracks seeped blood. Veins and tendons interplayed on the back of his hand. The fingernails looked like worn saw teeth. They were alive, but had the appearance of things, of abandoned tools. The thumb nail was split in two from the quick, and a hard growth filled the space between.

'What kind of meat is that in the soup?' his father asked.

'Just a bit of an old lamb is all.'

'Lamb is a great meat. People long ago used eat a lot more lamb. I don't like pork. The Jews never eat pork, that's a fact. When I was young we'd have to kill the lambs ourselves. We'd run after a wild one in the fields with a knife and cut its throat. We'd do all the butchering ourselves, and me only twelve years old. And then there'd be lamb for dinner that same day. A very healthy meat, so they say.'

The woman stopped eating and stared at him intently. 'That's right, that's right,' she said. Nothing more was said for some time.

'That's a great gossoon you have there.'

The boy shifted on the hard chair. The teapot pleasantly gurgled tea into the cups, and for a long while the spoons clinked round and round.

The woman squinted and caught his father's hand in hers. 'Look at the state of your hands. I'll go get a plaster for you.' The man looked at his hands as though puzzled by them and drew them out of sight under the table.

'Don't be bothering. It's as well to let the air at them.' He picked at the tattered threads and let them fall to the floor.

'Will we have to set up another level for the chimney?' asked the boy. The man paid him not the least attention.

'Put this on you – give me your hand,' said the woman on her welcome return. She held his hand steady on the back of the chair.

'Now you're fixed. It'll hold together until five o'clock.' She winked at the son.

'Thanks for the bite to eat,' said the man, and pushed the chair back into place under the table, a concession to the female domain of the house.

Outside the grey clouds had sealed together.

'Clean that filth off the lawn, and that, and scrub that mortar off the wall. We can't leave it in that state. These kind of people are used to having their homes tidy, not like a pig sty.'

The boy picked up the yard brush and started scrubbing.

'HOW WOULD YOU USE A YARDBRUSH ON A WALL?' his father bawled. 'Take that scrubbing brush there, and are you listening? Don't finish it until it's finished. Get all that filth away and give it a good scrubbing. Get those things out of your way first – DON'T PUT THEM ON THE LAWN, for Jaysus' sake! Can you move a little faster? Did you not get enough to eat? Take a grip on the brush and move yourself.'

Perhaps there was some good reason why the handbrush had to be used instead of the long-handled yardbrush, but the boy only passively perceived that the easier option was forbidden. He dipped the brush in the water and scrubbed the wall, dipped and scrubbed and found a rhythm, and then he was away, thinking of nothing, and was lost inside the pattern of the brickwork and the angles of the scaffold framework. Time passed, any amount of it, cloud-lengths of time, rolling on to five o'clock.

A shout called on him to pass up more planks. So they were going to raise another level. This was a welcome change from the scrubbing. When enough planks and poles were up on the platform, he climbed above his father and stood on the bare poles. His father in turn passed the materials up to him. The boy noticed the clenched-jaw effort his father had to make every time he pushed up a plank, and the way he squinted his eyes against the hail of grit. Finally they both stood on the new boards and began to attach the lengths of pole.

Up at this height the scaffold didn't have the same solidity as on the lower levels. It would be nice if the woman came out, the boy thought, and saw the way he was able to clamber about at such a height, with the whole construction swaying at every step, and she might shout at him to be careful and mind himself. It was getting late, he could see from the way the clouds were tinged with colour close to the horizon. They secured the poles provisionally, tightening the bolts home with finger and thumb.

'Get me a number sixteen spanner, would you?' his father said.

'Is it in the car or in the toolbox?'

'Sure you'll find it anyway.'

The boy descended the ladder, watching the world become normal again. He searched quickly through the toolboxes, found nothing, and went out to the car. The sun at the end of the day broke through the clouds and lit up everything horizontally. All the little glowing houses, hundreds of gable ends, all in need of pointing. The car had stored up heat inside. He rummaged through the back, suddenly aware of the passage of time again, and at last found the hammer.

His father was busy fixing in the new poles. He seemed not to notice neither the boy's absence or arrival.

'Here,' said the boy, holding out the hammer. The father looked at it and hesitated, and then in little more than a whisper: 'Is that a number sixteen spanner?'

The boy looked at it and his lips wavered, but he answered in a firm voice, 'Yes,' and held it out. His father reached out slowly and grasped it, looking into his son's eyes for signs of defiance, or stupidity. There was only calm certainty.

Touched on some raw nerve of superstition, the man said no more. Old intimations came back to him. There was a wedge driven into reality and it was threatening to crack apart. Slowly he fitted in a section and hammered it home, and then shook his head and muttered, For Jaysus' sake, a hammer! But there was nobody to hear this appeal, and he found that, after all, he didn't need the spanner.

The next time he spoke to the boy it was in a more subdued tone.

'Can you hold up the cross bar?' They worked together

wordlessly, the boy following the movements of his father.

A trickle of sand from above formed a tiny dune on the boards. The boy thought of holidays on the beach in the time before his mother went away, the hill at the end that was all theirs for two weeks. It was a sand hill with a circle of marram grass. Whenever strangers crossed onto their territory they would be challenged and forced to acknowledge the true owners. Between themselves they'd had battles to see who would be king of the hill. It had been a laugh when dad had made a campfire at the back of the caravan. They'd boiled up tea and roasted potatoes like a real cowboy camp.

His father climbed with surprising agility up onto the slates and clambered around to the other side of the chimney. He demanded the slate rip and a bucket, and told the boy to lay out the planks and fasten them in the meantime, handing him down the hammer.

This surprised the boy. His father had never asked him to do such an important job before. Usually he was given the most simple repetitive tasks, just washing and cleaning up. He looked up and down the platform, figuring out what length would fit where. The planks were stacked vertically on the platform below, within easy reach. He began working steadily, pulling up a plank from below, fitting it into place, hammering through the long metal pins. They stuck out the other side and he hammered them to curl back and grip the timber, like he'd seen his father do. From here he could see the ragged scraps of clouds lit up in red along the horizon. He licked his abraded fingers and spat. Down at ground level things were darker, though up at that height it was still bright. With a feeling of contentment he realised that time was limited. The day was drawing to a close; soon there would be stars. In the room across the street a light was on already.

'IS IT ALL FINISHED, IS IT?' the gravel voice assaulted him. He jumped up with a shock and tapped at the nearest metal pin to hammer it home.

'Is that steady? Is that something you could stand on and work?' His father tested an edge plank with his foot. The boy quickly grabbed a clamp and slapped it on, pulled it closed. One turn of his fingers tightened the nut. His father stepped fully on the plank. The clamp slipped a little.

'Is that fast, is it?' his father repeated, 'And this one, and this one, is that well-fastened?' His father bickered hoarsely, pointing at another plank. He made his way towards it. The boy grabbed another clamp and ran to fasten it. Too late. His father jumped onto the plank with his full weight.

'DO YOU SEE!' he roared in triumph as it slipped from under him, 'YOU CAN'T DO ANYTHING RIGHT!'

He'll land on the lower platform, the boy thought quickly, as the figure keeled over and down. But there were no planks left below. The figure fell and fell, and the head slapped with a resonant clang against the bar at the bottom level. The boy stepped cautiously up to the edge of the platform and looked down at the small crumpled corpse lying across the dark scrapings of mortar. The grey greasy strands of hair were clotted together, and an ooze of blood thickened over the concrete.

The Re-education Camp

They have taken my parents to the re-education camp. 'Go easy on them,' I say, 'they are old and come from a village.'

'We mean them no harm,' they answer, 'but their ideas offend us all.'

When I visit them – twice a year at least – they are delighted to see me. Yes, they are keeping well, they have satellite television now, they have vitamins and skin creams, duvets instead of blankets. It is a pleasure too for me; we get along fine as adults. I like to listen to them talk about the old days; they have a precise memory of names and extended family connections. I have amazed my colleagues on occasion by telling them that, for example, a second cousin is related to a famous politician.

'How do you know these things?' they ask. I tell them

straight out. It's no shame to have parents in the camp. It could happen to anyone.

'It gets cold here,' my mother says, putting on a shiver. 'Water collects on the walls and runs down.'

'Condensation,' my father nods his white head. 'Poor air circulation. It never used to do that in the old house with lime plaster.'

'No,' I tell them, 'you just haven't learned how to adjust the settings.' That's always the way. They forget too quickly the discomforts of lighting a coal fire, just like they forget how much time they wasted washing things by hand, scrubbing floors, standing in line at a telephone box.

My mother's voice drops. She leans toward me in the dark living-room. Out of habit they never switch on the lights until the last daylight is gone. 'You wouldn't believe the things they are telling us now.' Stay longer than an hour and they begin to speak freely. They think I am one of their party. I lower my eyes and say nothing.

'They say the Vatican is abolishing limbo. The baby souls go straight to heaven.'

I scrape my foot along the skirting. Examine my fingernails. Things are worse than I expected.

'And all the prayers I said through the years, what will become of them?'

'I'm sure they'll be ... reassigned,' I say.

'Aaagh,' she makes a noise of dismissal. Father shouts from the kitchen, 'The potatoes need teeming.' He swaps pots on the rings and fiddles with controls. My mother joins him in the kitchen and they make a drama. Steam rises and they forget to switch on the ventilator.

Dinner is proceeding nicely when my mother starts again.

'They are telling us that now one man will be able to marry another.' I say nothing to encourage her. My father mashes the potato with the back of his fork. He was never a thinker, but he had his progressive views as a young man, and greeted the early stages of the change. I have seen photographs of him at a demonstration in the fifties. I think his views have got more reactionary since entering the camp, but he says less and less at every visit.

'And you're not allowed wear a cross at work,' continues my mother. 'Do you wear a cross at work? I can get you one as a present. And young Gilligan, who set fire to the plant, was sentenced to get counselling. Counselling, so he can find himself. I know the kind of counselling he deserves.'

'The economy is going downhill because people are not spending enough. It's wrong now to save money, so they tell us.' It's my father this time, he doesn't like my mother to monopolise the conversation.

I bear through it as best I can. Before I leave I fix whatever needs fixing. The motion-sensor light that wards off thieves needs adjustment. The silicone sealing in the windows leaks in spots and I ring the number listed on the guarantee. I set up instant dial on the telephone yet again. No matter what goes wrong they will obscurely hold the new regime to blame and fail to see how comfortable they really are.

When my mother was fifteen she swore devotion to the Mediatrix of all Graces and chose St. Joseph to intercede on her behalf for the souls of the faithful departed. In the five years she worked in the post office, she earned enough to pay half the down payment on a house (nobody knows this outside the family.) Electricity came to the area, and when she prayed her eyes were fixed on the flickering red bulb and not on the sacred heart above. When it burnt out one night she knew what it was to fear for one's mortal soul. The night vigil invested her with the courage to address the priest as he left the sacristy. Child, he told her, if the flame strengthens your faith then yes, God is in the flame. But if you want to switch it off that is also right and fitting.

In the village my father came from, a local man hammered holes in a disc of galvanise and ran a pipe to the outhouse. He was the first in the province to build himself a shower. The people sniggered into their hands. Only the youngest children dared to point and say, 'There's the man who stands up naked to have a wash.' And when his wife passed, 'Do you think … ?'

So you see there is good reason to forgive them. And when I meet my colleagues at the re-education admin offices – I freely admit that is where I work, my parents will never read this anyway – they are full of understanding. Understanding, yes, but judgement still has to be made. Am I to treat them more leniently just because they never had the power to impose their ideas? But we are not grim about our work. We crack the whip of irony, look on benevolently, and wait for them to come over. One irreverent joke would be enough to have us laughing good-naturedly with them. Lighten

up, that's all we're saying. Lighten up, don't take things so
seriously, and you're already half-way out of the camp.
Inside the re-education camp they cluster with their own
kind at sheltered corners. I see them from a distance, necks
stretched toward each other, nodding. Their eyes gleam,
the wind carries the rustle of whispers. A few steps closer
and they stop the conversation to shout over to me with
genuinely hearty greetings. They are shameless in their
dissimulation. This bothers me; it shows the depths of their
deviancy. I am made to feel like a child who has blundered
into a conversation that doesn't concern him. 'What was
that you were talking about?' I ask, but the question gets
lost in the greetings. I don't pursue the matter: it's not a
constructive way to proceed.

They are hungry for ears to listen to their kind of talk.
It's ugly to see their bony fingers tremble with zeal and the
spittle rise to their lips. They have only a few more years;
why can they not just relax and enjoy life?

Sometimes though, I can see they want to make me
proud of them. They have been scrupulously friendly to
every girlfriend I introduced, no matter what her race or
habits. They tell me, as though it could possibly interest me,
that the noodles from the local Chinese take-away are a very
healthy food.

'That Mr Larkhill is a very friendly chap. He was
looking at the way I was chucking at the window catch. Oh
no Madame,' – my mother was clearly impressed by this
word – 'let me show you how to do it. And he brought
out a hand drill and bored another hole just a fraction of
an inch further along. You'd want to see the way it works

now. As smooth as I don't know what. My name is Mister Larkhill, he told me.' She gave a nod I had last seen when I announced I had graduated with honours.

'And he sat there where you are now and drank tea without milk, and instead of biscuits he asked if I happened to have a square of chocolate.'

Mr Larkhill is from Mali and is as black as coal dust. He sweats something terrible, and the whites of his eyes are splintered with red.

I know what raced through my parents' heads. I know the ugliness that stains them through and through. Yet when I relate the story of Mr Larkhill it will go to my parents' credit. The colleagues will laugh and say the old pair are at last getting in tune with the times. No, I want to tell them, you should hear what they really think. I keep my silence, half because there is little sense in being meticulous with such hopeless cases, and half out of sentimentality.

SELF-ASSEMBLY

When he came home that day Eugene found a long box in the hallway. He dragged it into the living room. It was of a size that might contain a guitar, or some longer instrument. A white label on the lid stated: *Contents: Self-assembly woman.*

He got out a steak knife and slit the brown tape at the edges. Inside were a number of pieces, separately wrapped. He lifted one up and picked at the wrapping. No bubble plastic, just layers and layers of pulpy paper. The object inside looked like nothing he had ever seen before. He unwrapped a few pieces and laid them out on the floor alongside the box. A few stubby tubes and bulbous shapes with snap-connectors embedded. The colour was a neutral skin tone except for the roughened grey ends.

Eugene took the largest section and felt the heft of it.

It was a lower leg without doubt. It felt complete in itself, something you might like to keep beside you on the couch and stroke every so often. By now he was beginning to believe the box contained exactly what it stated on the lid: a self-assembly woman. His curiosity aroused at last, he rummaged through the box for an instruction leaflet. 'Lucky for me it's not a kitchen cabinet,' he thought. The results of his DIY project some months previously had been laughable.

The wrapping paper soon littered the floor of the room. He ate his evening meal sitting on the couch, and watched television for some time. At last his attention was drawn again to the box on the floor. The sight of the two limbs he had assembled bothered him. It was not right to leave it incomplete.

He searched for the torso. It was not as easy to identify as he expected – just one oblong lump among the others, not even as heavy as the thighs. When he had attached the arms and legs he had something resembling a human body. But it was unsatisfactory. The skin was too even in tone. It felt unpleasantly putty-like. All in all, it was no more realistic than a plain shop dummy. He wondered how he could have expected otherwise.

He tried to get the body, or what pieces he had already assembled, to sit up on the couch. It was surprisingly heavy. The box had not seemed so heavy when he had dragged it into the living room. The limbs put up a leaden resistance. He took an arm and made it wave, bending the elbow repeatedly. Now he tried to get one hand to rest casually on the arm of the couch. It was useless; he felt like he'd never seen a human before, didn't know what angle the elbow should be, the way the legs should cross. He stretched out his own arm and studied the way his fingers moved to grasp the handle of a teacup. But he was tired after working all day. He concentrated too hard, and in the end his arm was moving woodenly, gracelessly.

It was after midnight when he left it there, limbs jutting at odd angles. To get even one finger to rest in a lifelike position seemed impossible. He scrunched up the wrapping paper and pushed it out of sight. It was time to go to bed. He went into his bedroom, but was hardly through the door before he came back out again and stood looking at her.

'Goodnight lady,' he said.

He spent many evenings shaping her fingers to rest just so, then reshaping them to a fist. The arms moved less stiffly now; he could guide each of them smoothly from hand-under-the-chin to offering-to-shake-hands. When he exercised her through a motion it would become easier and smoother, until at last he could simply give a nudge in the right direction. But the skin was still wrong. It had a flat monotonous sheen. When grasped it bore the imprint for too long. She was a doll – a headless doll. He sat beside her and massaged each of her arms. Gripped her like she was suffering from frostbite. Caught each finger and counted little piggies. Took her wrist and moved it in circles, like playing with a puppy's paw. And with little thought to it, cupped her breasts, feeling them take form under his palms. He worked his way down, delineating the ribs beneath the skin, urging the life heat to emerge. The flesh tightened and became resilient beneath his guiding hands. Each tautness encountered, each curve under his fingers seemed almost right, familiar, but not quite there yet. He lay behind her, stretched out arm alongside arm, leg alongside leg, wishing form to borrow from form. Stroking and clutching each curve until at moments it seemed perfect.

A blemish. No, a speckled bruise on her underarm. Terrified, he turned it to the light and gently rubbed it, but it was deep in the skin. He sprang up, ransacked his cabinets for skin cream. Antiseptic maybe, diluted in five parts water. Cold or hot? He stopped, poured the mixture down the sink, finally realising there's nothing much can be done with a bruise except to leave it be.

The body lay crooked where he had left it. He straightened it to a sitting position and thought about throwing a blanket over it, to keep her warm perhaps, or because it pained him in the gut, like it pained him one time he'd seen a run-over dog at the side of the road.

One large piece remained among the packaging. He had shied away from unwrapping it. Working swiftly, he steadied the head against his chest and pressed it onto her torso, in a trembling panic thinking it would never find the right position, hearing the obscene creak of cartilage under his palm. Then, whispering in her ear, hugging her close, he ran his fingers along the join, wishing the nodular line away. He held her firmly, not daring to let go, urging strength into her. The flesh must respond to his warmth and his wishes, it must heal where no harm has been done. He held her so long his own neck became stiff, and he couldn't help but stretch himself.

She was pretty, like a woman sketched in a children's storybook. Her dark hair fell down in a zigzag over her forehead. The locks looked sharp in outline, yet were like feathers to touch. Each time he saw her he wanted to smile.

Even so she was little use for anything except sitting with arms folded, staring ever more sharply right and left. The exercises continued; methodically every evening, arranging her in a dozen different postures, bending and unbending a thousand times.

'I got a package through the post,' he announced to his workmates. It was a Friday night drink. 'This thing in kit form.' His friends often talked about their construction projects, cars or kitchen extensions.

'What is it, some cabinets again?' they laughed.

'No.'

'What is it then?'

He should have foreseen this question and had his answer prepared. But it had been a long time since he'd been out talking with people.

'It's a kind of a hobby thing. Like a model boat.'

Fran and Duncan nodded. 'That can swallow up all your spare time.'

'You're right there,' agreed Eugene, 'the hours just fly by.'

'Did it come by courier?' asked Fran.

'I don't know, why?'

'How were you at home to take the delivery?'

'It was there when I got home. The landlord has a key.'

'Eugene.' Fran looked at him in distaste. 'You can't let him walk into your house whenever he wants. You have to stand up for yourself. God's sake.'

Eugene maintained a dignified silence. His affairs were of no concern to other people. Fran had no right to make personal attacks just because they had gone to school together many years before.

'So when will it be ready to sail?' Fran resumed in a normal tone.

'Another month at least. It's going fairly slow.'

'Take your time at it. If those cabinets you made were a ship, I tell you, they'd be sitting at the bottom of the ocean by now.' They all laughed. Fran had a sharp local wit. 'It'll be a definite case of 'God bless all who sail in her' with this ship.'

'Give it a chance,' said Duncan, 'sure we'll be round with the champagne to launch her.'

'Indeed. I'll let you know. Any cause for celebration. How is your own ferry workers' dispute going?'

'The problem is, they're presenting their case with all this workers' rights guff. If they dressed up their argument as a business proposal, they'd be fine.'

'That's it,' agreed Fran, 'No-one wants to hear a diehard socialist.'

'Exactly. Even to call it 'a workers' dispute' is to turn people off. It's a re-negotiation of their contract. They're making a mistake by putting up the banners.'

'Would you look at this –' Fran tipped his head towards Eugene. 'Eyeing up the lounge girl he is.' The girl was placing bottles and glasses one by one on her tray. There was much to be learnt from her movements.

'No,' protested Eugene, 'I just thought for a second I knew her.'

'Where would you know someone like that?'

'Go on, admit it, you were eyeing her up. The slinky black dress.'

'That's just the uniform.'

'Go on, admit it. Sure, aren't we all looking at her?'

Several weeks later he had forgotten what the flat had been like without her there. The exercises had become a comforting routine. But that evening when he ran his hands across her neck and breasts he noticed a rim of dust on his fingertips. He backed off, horrified. The ugly secret was exposed: she was just an object. He dragged her into the bathroom and splashed up a foam.

'You have to begin to do things for yourself,' he told her. 'What more can I do? Do you want me to shake you?' Her skin bloomed pink among the white suds. 'Can't you see I shouldn't be doing this?' he said as he patted dry between her legs. He held her hand, just the four fingers, and helped her back to the settee. She slumped there, alarmingly naked. A sense of emergency gripped him.

The taxi took him to the late-night shopping centre. He filled a basket with camisoles and slips, brassieres and sweaters. There was no embarrassment at the checkout; he was too preoccupied for that. Too much time had slipped past, it could never be regained. She had lain naked for weeks – it shamed him now, what she might think of him. His mind played over the image of her draped along the couch. Retrospective desire swelled in him. A new fear seeded and grew as he sat silently in the back of the taxi home.

On one knee he knelt before her, guiding a slim foot into the underwear. Faced once again with the practicalities of muscle movements, the nervous desire he experienced in the cab dissipated. Genevieve, as he had begun to call her, was easy to dress. He did not know anyone else with this name and did not know why it had occurred to him. Eugene. Genevieve.

'You're looking good today,' he told her. Things were different now that she was dressed.

'You're looking good today,' she replied.

And so each evening he would talk through the things that happened that day, beginning with the bus stop and the traffic jams, the river that runs through the city and the morning cafés. There are four different types of coffee, he explained, cappuccino and latte, espresso and americano.

'We can go out right now, you can see for yourself,' he said. She turned her face away.

'And have them all laugh at me?' she said.

'They don't know you. But we'll go out when you want to. You'll get bored here soon enough.'

'I like it here,' she said. 'And anyway, I know a lot about what's going on outside. In here it's fine. Why would I want to look at people I don't know walking up and down a street? To see them drink coffee maybe?'

'Suit yourself,' he said.

'I will,' she said.

Yet when he came back from the kitchen just a few minutes later she was unaccountably livid.

'How can you live in this mess?' she said.

He looked about him. It was the same as always. Cleaner, in fact, because she had straightened the items on the table and sorted his letters into neat piles – indifferent as to whether they were bills or fast-food leaflets.

'What mess?' he asked, following her eyes. And then he

saw the scrunched up wrapping paper spilling out from the gap between the settee and the display cupboard.

'I'll get rid of that,' he said, pulling the pulpy papers out.

'You don't have to do it right now.' She had shrunk to the corner of the settee. He pushed the papers back and moved a chair in front of them.

'Please, let's go out soon. I'm making it sound more boring than it really is.'

'What am I to talk to them about?' It was not a complaint. She was excited about meeting his friends for the first time. A hum emanated from her all evening. Partly it was a song winding in and out of tune, partly the incessant small noises an anxious person makes. 'What if they ask me if I prefer Beethoven or Wagner? I haven't listened to any Wagner.'

'They won't ask you that.'

'What if they ask me about places in the city that I don't know?'

'Just give a silly answer, make them laugh.'

'You won't leave me on my own and start talking to them about me? They'll be looking at me . . .'

'I won't leave you on your own. Whenever you want to leave just give me a sign and we'll go straight away.'

'Why aren't you putting on good clothes? They are your best friends. You should show them some respect.'

'You're right,' he laughed and chose a yellow casual shirt he had not had occasion to wear.

'I'd like to bring them a present. Flowers would look silly, wouldn't they? Maybe some chocolates. Tell me about them again. Fran and Duncan. Fran the civil engineer. They are important people, your friends? What about the friends that they have, do they become your friends too?'

'Sometimes they do. After a couple of years or so.'

'Years? And will your friends become my friends too? I mean not in years, but soon.'

'Yes, definitely.'

The taxi driver responded readily to her chat. She was still talking about friends. It was an important topic to her. The taxi driver was charmed. Close friends should meet once a week, he maintained. Three or four times a year for what you might call acquaintances. Now that's a word that should be used more. Generally they had a few pints, but someone that you only meet in the pub is never a true friend. The driver was certain on this point. To be a friend with someone you had to have relied on each other for something. Or worked together on some dodgy business.

'I'm unusual,' the driver said, catching her eye in the rear-view mirror, 'in that all my friends do totally different things. Usually if one schoolfriend becomes, say, a solicitor, he loses touch with all the ordinary pals left lower on the scale.'

'That's horrible,' she said.

'Horrible, yeah. But that's not the way it is with me.'

As he held the car door open for Genevieve, the driver threw Eugene a wry smile.

The pub was dim inside and milling with people. He had wanted to suggest a restaurant for this first meeting, but hadn't dared. It would have made too much of the occasion. It would only have made Genevieve more nervous, he told himself. As it was she had fretted for hours. He hoped she wasn't dressed too stylishly for this place. The boots she had chosen were tall with silver eyeholes. He was a down-to-earth person, and hated ostentation of any kind.

'Genevieve, this is Duncan, Fran.' He clapped his hands together. 'Let's move to a table.'

'See,' said Genevieve with a large wink, 'he makes you all to follow.' Duncan and Fran laughed at the cryptic comment.

'So you are Fran? Eugene said you were a wit. I hope you're not planning to give me lessons.' They were in loud guffaws by the time they reached the table.

'Me and the lads are just getting to know each other,' she explained. 'I tried my elephant joke on them.'

'And it worked,' said Duncan. 'Jeez Eugene, you've been keeping this one hidden away.'

'Eugene doesn't like to share me,' she said.

'But what's your opinion on this?' said Fran.

'I am going to have an opinion on everything.'

They laughed knowingly, eyes flitting from the girl to Eugene, watching to gauge his reaction. This quick wit and forwardness amazed him. He was too surprised to feel anything like jealousy. His confidence grew. She could handle herself well in company and there were no awkward moments. True, she asked the waitress if they could meet the next day. And at one point she lost interest in Eugene and his friends, as though they had nothing to do with her, and she turned to talk with the people at the next table.

'Where do you come from, hey, Genevieve?' Fran asked, drawing her back. She sighed.

'I had a feeling you in particular would ask that.' More laughs. 'So I prepared an answer for you – am I doing well Eugene?'

'You're doing very well,' he said blandly.

'I'm from a place you don't want to go to.'

'And where's that?' said Fran.

'Not telling,' she said in a bored voice.

'Eugene,' Fran said ignoring her, 'tell us where your lady friend is from.'

'Ask her.'

'Well I'm asking you. Where is she from?'

'If she wanted you to know she'd tell you.'

'Don't start this mystery crap. It doesn't suit you.' Fran had had enough of the joke. 'So we're waiting.'

Eugene did not want to spoil the atmosphere by being irrationally stubborn.

'She's from Croydon. She moved there from Russia with her parents when she was eight.'

'Ah, I thought I saw a touch of the Kremlin in your features.'

'That must be where your absurdist jokes comes from,' ventured Duncan. Good humour was restored. Genevieve remained the focus of attention, but the conversation managed to veer away from her a couple of times. Fran was getting involved in politics at local level and had new experiences to relate.

A moment of frankness broke through when Eugene and Duncan were at the urinals.

'She's a very genuine person. How did you get a girl like that?' His eyes betrayed a disarming envy.

'Oh, just by being polite.'

They laughed heartily.

'You impressed them,' said Eugene, 'you were the star of the night.'

'It's easy to play the fool.'

'No, Duncan said you were a very genuine person.'

'He said that? There's still something I don't like about him. "Girls only want a rich guy", he said to me. There's a reason no girl would go out with him.'

'I thought you got on well with them. You laughed with them all night. And now you suddenly turn against them?'

'Don't you notice the way they are? Do you not see? Fran only meets you so he can show his power to control you.' She began to cry bitterly. 'How can you stand to meet them week after week?'

'We don't have to meet them again.'

'And when I look at Duncan I can see it's only a matter of chance that he's not a rapist or killer. Things could have turned out completely differently for him.'

'They're my friends,' he said, 'I've known them all my life.'

'They are nothing people.'

The strangeness, the ruthlessness of this judgement made his heart beat tight and shallow. A few months previously he had held her in the first evenings, fearful she might come apart into separate pieces. She was close to nothing herself. She could be dismantled again into a nothing person and no-one would know. She might not even object – the subject had not been brought up.

'Leave them alone,' he said.

'You should find better friends.'

'We don't have to meet them again,' he said. 'They're just basically decent people.'

She lay in bed beside him, curled against him like she would burrow into him. He could not sleep; a motor was running inside. There was one point on which his experience bore more weight than her lacerating insight. His years – quiet though they had been – must have counted for something.

'Genevieve,' he nudged her awake. He did not feel bad about this: she had done the same often enough to him. 'You are too harsh on them.'

'I don't want to think of them,' she said.

'Everybody's like that,' he whispered. 'You just haven't met enough people.'

'It's not so.'

'They're no better or worse than me.'

'How can you say that, after what you've done?'

He sat up on one elbow. 'What have I done?' he asked. He felt something extraordinary had happened during the nights when he first held her. Something which he should know because nobody else ever would.

'Nothing,' she said quickly, embarrassed.

He too fell silent, touched by the silliness, the shamefulness of that cardboard box, pieces wrapped in paper, the resilience of fleshy parts.

Greetings, Hero

Part I

We stood in the foyer of the multiplex. I ran my eyes down through the starting times, calculating how long we had to wait among this humid throng. Gauging the length of the queue against the quality of the film. Wondering if there was something else entirely different we should be doing. It was a rare day: it had not yet rained.

The high skylight of the atrium streamed light down on Stan and me. The ragged row of pale freckled faces clashed with the metallic lines of the balustrade. This place was too clean for these people. Too clean for me.

'I see Silent Michal,' said Stan.

This had to be another of Stan's artistic whimsies. He

was proud of his bizarre dreams. *I picked up a lettuce leaf and saw the face of my brother in it. In a dream my mother was speaking to me in Latin. I opened my mouth to protest, but the words came out in German.*

And now another whimsy: Silent Michal materialising in a multiplex in Dublin. This is a person I last met six years ago in a shoeshop in Grodgoszcz, Poland. Though "person" is not the right word – it sounds like one more standing in a queue.

Stan had vanished into the milling crowd. I cast my eyes around to locate him. We had invested time in that queue, and I counted out a minute before ducking under the rope.

There he was at the entrance, explaining something to a thin man whose face was a cubist artist's dream. Flat planes and angles, a jagged fringe of oiled black hair. A mouth cut in wood. The thin man looked down blankly at Stan, leaned towards him, shook his head once. Tolerant enough to bear with Stan's convoluted excuses for a case of mistaken recognition. But Stan kept talking and the man kept listening. I could hear him as I approached. The staccato rhythm of Wielkopolska Polish.

'Geoff, can you believe it? It's Michal here in Dublin.' I held out my hand. Michal took it, no flicker of recognition in his eyes. It was him, without a doubt.

'This is a big surprise. How do you like Dublin?' I said in Polish and continued with the usual banalities. He replied with a long distance yes or no. *Nie*, he did not know Stan was also in Dublin. *Tak*, he had found work.

Stan stood to one side, smiling with pride at his protégé. Generously allowing long pauses to deepen and develop between Michal and I.

A few questions later and I was conscious of imposing on Michal. I looked at him, stared at him frankly. His eyebrows stood out over his eyes, but just a little. His cheeks were sunken in, but just a little. It takes decades for a face to resemble the person who inhabits it. For now he was a thin, sallow-skinned European with the attitude of one listening to an urgent whisper. An earnest student with halting English, who pauses before each sentence. Always one heartbeat too long, but perhaps he is a meticulous learner. His neat dark hair and open shirt did not mark him out from the thousands of others in this multinational city. There was even a flush on his cheeks from the blustery climate.

I suddenly realised. I of all people should not try to impose the old personality on him. We were in a different country now, thousands of miles away, several years later. I should not hold any presumptions.

'Did Stan know you were here?' I asked.

'Nobody knows.'

'But we found you,' I laughed.

He grimaced and rocked back on his heels. He directed a smile to the bright skylight.

'What are you working at?'

His head and shoulders shrugged derisively. After the usual five-second lag of course. 'Nothing much.'

'Waiter? Cleaner? That sort of thing?'

'It's. A secret.'

'That's OK. We all have secrets. So!' I rubbed my hands. 'Were you about to go to one of the films?'

He dug into his pocket, drew out a wad of credit-card

sized rectangles, and sorted through them. Stan and I leaned towards him.

'You're a club member?' said Stan. 'Your English must have gotten pretty good if you can understand films. Do you understand what they're saying?'

'Yes, most of it,' said Michal.

'This is just amazing,' I said. 'Last time I saw you in Grodgoszcz you didn't have a word of English. And now a few months in Ireland and you've got fluency like people who have gone to college for years. You've got a degree in English for nothing! What made you come over? Did you come over with other Poles? Is life in Dublin any different?'

He exhaled. Paused. Inhaled.

'It is. The same.'

'The same as Grodgoszcz?'

'No.'

'So what do we do now? Go for a coffee?'

Michal pursed his lips. Frowned at the cards in his hand. I could see his Polish ID and several months of wage slips.

'A pint, perhaps,' he said.

Stan nodded sagely. Michal strode ahead of us out through the glass doors. Left us standing. Staring at his long shadow on the immaculate tiles.

'This is unbelievable,' said Stan. 'It's a massive transformation. And the way he talks to you Geoff. Words, words, buckets of words.' He raised his arms. 'Did you see the way he was the first one to suggest we go somewhere! This would never have happened before.'

In the years since my return I had gotten used to hearing stories of old friends in Poland who had become lost to drink, or who six years on were still living with their parents in a shoebox. Grown used to Irish friends working seven days a week, then moving to the distant suburbs never to be seen again. My own life was nothing to boast of either. I'd been caught in a rut for four years.

And now here was someone whom time had not corroded. He had consumed time and become stronger. He had dropped himself into a different environment and emerged a new person.

As we trooped up Parnell Square I realised Stan had directed hardly a single word at Michal. He was content to observe us and release the odd smile.

Lanes of traffic were caught in a gridlock extending down Dorset Street. People wandered freely among the cars. Coloured flags waved, cheers erupted and died down. The pubs had spilled their human contents across the pavements.

'Who is playing today?'

'A county called Wexford,' said Michal. I looked along the road at the sea of fans cascading down the road. Cars were abandoned, double and triple-parked recklessly. The air was warmed by the jostling and cheering.

'We should go to the match too and cheer,' I said.

'It would be appropriate for this extraordinary day,' said Stan. He lowered his glasses and squinted against the wind.

Michal, Silent Michal. How did I first meet him? But "meet" is hardly the right word either.

It was in a cellar bar called Pod Aniolem – the sign of the Angels – in Grodgoszcz, a small industrial town of 240,000 inhabitants where I worked at the local college. I was drinking with Stan, Romeo, Stepan, other names gone from memory. A long unvarnished wooden table, weighty beer glasses with handles, plates of bread with smalec, coarse-grain salt crystals sprinkled over. Light-golden beer with a raw whiff of alcohol off it. Polish beer hits you in the high nasal passages.

A pitcher is set down in front of me with a clunk. The waitress squeezes by at my back. The door opens. A draught of air flows around my ankles like water. It is winter. I don't remember the summers much.

One more beer inside me and I felt I was making contact with this place called Poland. I was moving towards an intuitive grasp of what it was to be a Pole. Suffering patiently for decades – that bit I could understand..

Despite the five beers, I sat up alert, ready to focus my attention. This was my constant state when I was learning Polish. Waiting to pounce on a few phrases and make an apt reply. Thinking, this time I will make effective communication. This time I will break through the barrier. I bought into the idea that each language is a code to its own vision of the universe. If I listened long enough I would break through the code, and break out of the insular mindset that closed me in.

I had never learned a foreign language before.

There was another at the table. He sat straight-backed but with head slumped forward. He was part of our group – I had seen Romeo pass him the pitcher – but he did not talk to anyone. He had a long bony face, dark eyebrows, and the stringy build of a marathon runner.

Romeo was standing now, eager to convince the whole

table. 'There was me and The Teacher and Silent Michal there for the weekend. The queue for tickets went all the way back to the level crossing. It spread across the slip road and held up the traffic. Chris and me and Silent Michal here. We slept out on a bench with the drinkers and dossers. Shared a blanket with them. And when we finally get to the ticket office they say they smell drink off us and tell us we look drunk. We'd slept under the stars all night. Under the beautiful stars. Even Michal here. Drunks came up and talked to him. He listened to all their problems. And I swear no-one waited longer than us, me and Silent Michal.'

This way of invoking someone as witness impressed me. I watched the same Michal closely. He held his hand to his jaw and rubbed it as his name cropped up three times in succession. He uncrossed his legs and drew in a deep breath. The conversation moved on and he relaxed, took a long sip from his beer.

'We call him Silent Michal,' Stan told me. 'He's an old friend from school.'

'Is he a student or what?' I asked.

'No, not a student. He works in the family clothes shop. Here in Grodgoszcz. We know him from way back. We're used to him.'

We had our backs to the bar, taking a moment away from the table. Stan nudged me, tilted his eyes. There was Michal, joining the queue for the bar. Rubbing the coins in his hand. He was calculating if he had enough money for a pitcher. Mouth stretched to a straight line. Eyes to the floor, like his neck had lost its muscles.

'Clothes shop, yeah? What does he sell, shoes?'

Stan laughed, easy-going. 'You should drop by, get yourself a tie for work.'

We waited to watch Michal order. He raised his head and said "four" just like anyone would.

When we got back to the table, Romeo was laying it out large. There was something bugging him.

'These Westerners talk to everybody as though they've been friends for years. It's hey Jack, or hi! call me Pat. And you don't know each other from FUCK.'

He was speaking in English, maybe for my benefit. I rose to the bait. 'People like it like that. It just makes it easier for everyone to get on.'

'It's BULLSHIT. That's what it is. A big pretence.'

'But why does it annoy you so much?'

'You talk to the boss in the same way you talk to your best friend. Like there's no difference. A universe of equidistant humans. In Poland a stranger is *pan* or *pani* until you get to know them. You know where you stand.'

The one Romeo had called The Teacher pushed a pitcher in my direction.

'Where did this come from?' I asked.

'Michal.'

I tilted my glass toward Michal but there was no chance of catching his eye.

'Then my brother came back from an interview with a Western company that's setting up here. Name a moment in your life when you were proud of yourself, tell us how you helped around the house when you were a kid. Unbelievable questions. What's up with these people? Who can answer such questions? I'll tell you who: whoever is docile enough to answer gets the job. 'In this company,' they told him, 'we like staff to have fun together in after-hours activities. What ideas do you have for events we could hold?' Do you know what he told them? Remember this was the last question. He was getting on great up till this point. A nice job in quality control is in the balance. German level salary. He's got twenty seconds to come up with something. So what did he tell them? *Communal mushroom picking.* Bam!'

Stan pulled me away. We squeezed along the back of the bench. The cellar brickwork curved low overhead. We went through to the next section. It was closed off on quiet nights like this, chairs were upended on the tables. Stan brought me to an alcove. 'See,' he said. I could see nothing but I could smell the dry rot. He reached up and switched on the full lights like he owned the place.

I remembered his talk of the carvings then. They were supposedly famous, amazing, a national treasure. The pub was famous for them, even Germans came from Germany to see them.

They were stacked like timber waiting for a skip. Stan took a couple of images out and set them leaning against the wall. They had the appearance of sacred icons. Not religious themes, but simple town scenes carved in relief. A queue in a meat shop. People on a tram. A bum drinking from a bottle of wine. Carved in a faux medieval style, but there was something horrifying about it all.

'Is this it then?' I asked.

'His mother is Russian,' Stan whispered. He made a yak-yak gesture with his right hand. 'He needs to let off gas every so often.'

'What?'

'Romeo,' he clarified, 'Romeo the Great Slav. Don't let him annoy you Geoff.'

'Doesn't bother me, I like Romeo. I thought his name was a joke at first. Must be an advantage in life to have a name like that.'

'True,' said Stan. 'I'm just plain Stanislaw. But inside I feel I should be Socrates. Or Michelangelo.' He waited to see if I would laugh. Stan found it hard to hold down a steady job. He survived on the odd translation passed on to him by Romeo.

I ran my fingers across the rough chisel cuts, trying to achieve a closer contact. The farmer, the writer, the merchant. I was overwhelmed with nostalgia for a past that I had no claim on.

My stomach lurched and I knew another beer would make me vomit. I needed to get out fast. I needed to avoid the whole *just one more* charade.

Each stone step upwards was a hazard after so much beer. The blast of cold air quenched my attack of the sweats. The slanted roofs opposite were so white that when I looked away I couldn't see anything else clearly for several seconds. Minus ten degrees. I could tell by the way it hit the tips of my ears.

Stan came out the door after me. He had obscure fears for me, a foreigner in a remote industrial city with a reputation. Then Romeo emerged too, and Stepan, and half the pub dragging billows of steam into the night. I insisted I was fine, spent ten ludicrous minutes arguing that I was fine, until finally I got sense and walked off.

The air was brittle, making a crystal of every glimmer. The snow and ice of the past month had been tramped down to a plate of armour. Under the afternoon sun it would get slippery, mushy where it was trod, and then freeze solid again at night.

My block was three tram stops away and then a short distance up a side street. There was no tram at this hour so I walked in the centre part where the grip was best. The city felt compact, even though it had a substantial population. I could see where the last blocks ended and darkness beyond. There were few out on the streets. Pod Aniolem was one of only three late-night pubs.

I didn't take the turn to the right. I walked on past the last tower block, past the blank walls of the co-op farm, out the road by the frozen stubble fields. Straight roads taped on a flat landscape. I wanted to walk until I felt enveloped by the cold. Out there where only my heart beating fast and warm would keep the life within me.

The city became a ruin of light behind me. I was on a road lined with spindly hedgerow. A snowplough had been down this way. The waist-high ridges pushed to each side had a grey crust on them. When I stumbled against it the surface broke and caught my ankles like a trap. I shook the crystals from my socks and tramped on. The snow was squeaky underfoot now, and I knew the temperature must have dropped further.

My only fear was a car might pass. The driver would be certain to stop and ask if I needed help. I didn't want that. I tried to compose a plausible answer, a light-hearted parting shot even.

I thought back to when I first came to this place, during a midwinter thaw. Roads like gashes of wet black in the snow. Everywhere an ugly juxtaposition of filth and white.

Whenever I think of the town, I am looking down at it from a height. I see it all in one piece: the apartment blocks in four distinct clusters on the northern edge, the long green roof of the railway station, the little square space at the centre of town. The vegetable oil factory – for which the town was famous throughout the province – recognisable from its stainless steel ducts. And beyond it a few rows of pre-war wooden houses. I can picture the town laid out like a map in a book for children.

There was good reason for this. Every friend I knew lived on the seventh, tenth or twelfth floor. The higher the floor, the cheaper the rent. And my friends were invariably smokers. That meant we would stand for hours on a landing looking out the window. I knew that city well from ten stories up. Down on ground level I huddled inside my coat and pressed on with small steps.

It seemed to me that the road I was on was curving in a huge orbit back towards the glow. I had the notion that the surest way back was to keep plodding forward. On and on, hay foot, straw foot, hay foot, straw foot. I kept my hands pressed to my ears.

A car whined and drew alongside at a walking pace. I waved cheerily. The driver reached over, flicked open the door. The car jolted to a halt with the door swinging.

'Hello there, hero,' he shouted. *Witaj, bohaterze.*

'Hello there.'

'Well are you going to just stand there?'

I kicked my heels together, shook out my scarf. Just as I stooped to get in the door my left leg seized up. This took me by surprise. I couldn't explain "cramp" in Polish. I gripped the roof and swung down onto the seat. He pulled off with the door still open.

Then he rattled on about night-life and girls.

'Luxusowa,' he said, and hammered his knees.

'That's some place.'

'Pod Kogutem.' He kissed his fingers.

'Pod Aniolem. That's where I was.'

'Nice place.'

'Chimera.'

He whooped and made gestures of gripping large objects. 'You know good places. That's the brains of a quantum engineer,' he said. It was easy to slot into the conversation. The driver didn't ask what I was doing, out on a country road, on a night so cold most people would think long and hard about making the five-mile journey to town. He kept the car chugging at a stately pace. I could hear the little puff-puff of each piston keeping us going. As the headlights pitched and rose they threw garish images of snow ridges at us.

He stopped talking and concentrated on the road. He scrubbed a rag at the frosted windscreen and passed it to me to clear my side.

'Is here fine for you?' The car slurred to a stop.

'Yes, the old square is fine.'

'There's your place.' I climbed out of the car onto the bare cobbles of a market square. The paths swept neatly and the snow on the grass unblemished. Three lamps glowed on three corners. All else was black except the orange letters above the hotel porch. Hotel pod Aniolem. The glow lit up a fleet of some half dozen company vans parked out front. *Quanto Engineering* in dynamic letters.

Even as the car had slowed, with the windscreen all frosted, I'd known we couldn't possibly be back in Grodgoszcz. Now I made a guess of how long and how far. Ten or fifteen, maybe twenty kilometres away. A distance not to be measured in numbers. The important thing was this: I knew I could do it. I knew I could make it back. The car chug-chugged out of earshot and I too was utterly dependent on a small engine inside.

I walked to the opposite side of the square and scouted down the side streets, just to feel I had made contact with this village. Then I set off in the direction the car had come from. I passed pre-war wooden houses with steep-pitched roofs. Rows of concrete sheds on the edge of town. Then a field of beets, probably sugar beet, with the leaves shrunken and the round root protruding from the earth. Why had they not been harvested? The field seemed to go on forever, the kind of field you stare at through the window of a train because the rows of crop glit by so evenly you have to blink and focus your eyes.

But when I thought again about the field it was a long time later. I had covered several miles, and now there was just a wasteland of weeds or maybe it was hops or something I didn't recognise. Each time I turned my head a slice of cold air got at my throat. I felt neither warm nor cold, but knew that if I stopped for a couple of minutes my muscles would find it hard to get going again.

Narratives of Elizabethan voyages ran through my head as I went.

I tried to commit to memory the details of what I saw. Then a long argument with myself on the topic: what is the value of remembering all these details? To what ultimate purpose was I storing up these images of the frozen fields? What good would it do me? And not a single car passed.

Some time later I became aware I was moving on a trajectory which would take me farther away from the city, or where the city should be. I kept hoping the road would twist back to the right for surely it must go towards the city, where else could it go?

I lifted a foot across a blue-white ridge and stepped onto the endless field. The furrows and ridges had a deceptive regularity. At any step I might put my weight on a shadow where the plough had cut a deep crevice, or a ridge might turn out to be a curl of frozen snow. The stark black and white confused my eyes. I walked with high deliberate steps. A twisted ankle could leave me stranded in that field. On and on, guided by the orange glow against the clouds. When the mist rose and obscured the glow, I got scared that maybe I had taken on too much. I had no way of knowing how tired I was or how much energy I had left. Maybe one tumble and I would not be able to get up. Then much later again, on my left, a big pink orb so weak I could look directly at it.

The trams were rattling when I reached the outskirts. A grey pall hung over the city. People stood at the stop and smoked. Their faces all looked like they had been smoking the same brand of unfiltered cigarettes for twenty years. Do no pretty girls have to get up at this hour?

I had never thought so many people had to get up so early. A couple of years of rising in the dawn would be enough to wear anyone down to assimilation. The cure for all wanton thoughts. The cobbled noise of trams on rails made me jittery. I felt it coming at me from every direction. My eyes rested too long on things. They were staring back at me, the people. Perhaps because I am walking down the street instead of waiting for the tram. Down the broad concrete street with the hard rails sunk into it. It is sunny because there is snow. This city is. A blotch on a map. I am entering the city in triumph. See, I return. See, this city is within the measure of my stride. The people with leather faces all waiting. The cure for all wanton thoughts. They stare because I am still walking with a high step like I did across the frozen fields.

I sat with my feet in a basin of hot water and when I coughed the phlegm came up cold in my mouth. It was some hours before I felt anything, some more before I felt sleepy.

I had got my wish. And was I satisfied?

Yes. I believe I was satisfied.

I was English tutor at Grodgoszcz City University. My title was 'professor', but that was just for the wages office. The week before term began I found a typed sheet in my pigeonhole. It listed the times and room numbers of all my classes. I met with the students, asked them what they did last year, then discussed with them what they wanted to learn this year. When I suggested to the head there might be a better way of organising things, he told me this was academic freedom.

It diminished the professor title somewhat when I had to ask the students everything: dates of public holidays, expected exam format, where to get previous years' papers. They would negotiate the length and type of homework assignments and an extra day off on a long weekend. Poland has the longest weekends in the world. One time a weekend went on for nine days until the government declared it over.

I liked to go for random walks around Grodgoszcz, even after many months there when it had no more secrets to yield. It was big enough to have 'suburbs' of high-rise flats. Concrete hulks with jutting balconies like vertebrae. Tracts of scrubby waste land between them. A kid pushing a tricycle along, a girl in a plaid skirt – the merely human stuck out. You wanted to wave in recognition, *hey so you're here too?*

The outside space is hostile. The very first week I asked about all the half-built houses on the outskirts, abandoned heaps of gravel in front gardens, grey blockwork left unsurfaced. Expanses of pitted earth like bulldozers had gone to war with each other. But up close you saw that these buildings were years old, that they would never be finished. Outsides didn't matter.

The workload at college wasn't heavy. I could do as much or as little as I liked. Nobody gave me a syllabus to teach, nobody checked my timesheet. There was no such thing. But I tried to do my job well. I brought stacks of English newspapers from Warsaw one time, and we would study these. Occasionally I would run into a student in a bar and would wince when they called me professor.

Like all shops in the town it had a plain front with small glass panels forming the window. Five crumbling steps up to a door with a handle, like an ordinary house door.

I hadn't expected the Lycra skirts and luminous popsocks. Green and orange were all the rage. Racks of camisoles, teenage disco-wear, multi-coloured jeans. Yet he was alone in the shop – no mother or sister to help him.

'How did everything get so fucked up?' I asked in slang Polish. He laughed through his nose. 'You remember me from Friday night?'

He lifted his head a fraction. 'Of course.'

'This is a nice shop you have here.'

He shook his head, exhaled derisively. Kicked a chrome support. Tapped his foot and then stood with his hands behind his back. Just for a second he looked the part.

'You sell women's clothes?' I picked up one of the tiny stretch-Lycra tops popular that year. Pushed my knuckles against the thin fabric.

'Yes.'

'You give women advice on what they should wear?' I folded the filmy garment and put it back.

'Sometimes yes,' he said.

'Interesting job.'

'It's OK,' he said.

The clack-clack of sharp heels coming up the steps. Late twenties, oval face with small mouth twisted to a pout against the cold. She clutched her coat at the front, two fists together. Sure-footed on the cracked and icy slabs. I busied myself examining the rack of casual shirts.

She spoke rapidly and breathlessly. Michal considered

a moment, replied in a couple of words. Then he selected
a few pairs of stockings from under the counter. This one,
perhaps that one. I caught the few words he said. I never
had a problem understanding Michal's Polish. She handed
over some money, caught my eye and smiled. I nodded, said
hello. She took two packs, chirruped pretty, pretty, pretty,
and left.

'Do you have any special offers?'

'Yes. We have shirts.' Four for the price of three, office
standard. I sorted through them, trying to select four
different patterns. I asked about Stan and Romeo, when he
had last met them. I asked whether he had been to the new
M7 mall everyone was talking about, whether he was losing
business to it. At last he breathed through his nose in gasps
and shook his head, as though we should both finally admit
I was making conversation for the sake of it, and we should
stop the farce.

'I wouldn't say content,' said Stan. 'You know he got accepted
into university? The really tough matriculation exams. But
he gave up in second year. Now he just works as a shop
assistant.'

'Didn't think you were such a snob,' I said. 'It's a good
job. A difficult job too. I'm sure he has to keep the accounts,
buy from the wholesalers, all that stuff.' I could not imagine
Michal doing these things. I could not imagine him selling
stockings to women either, yet I had seen it.

'His mother used to run the business. She's not in good
health so leaves it up to him now.'

'Does the place do good business?'

'It has its loyal clientèle I concede.' Stan was playing with his college-book English again. I had dropped by to his tenth floor room. He shared a two bedroom apartment with a student. He himself was no longer one. He had completed five years 'but without collecting the degree' as he put it.

A drop-out, the rest of the world would call it. But he had indeed finished all courses and passed every exam he had chosen to sit. He'd missed the deadlines for doing repeat examinations and now was stuck in a limbo.

Stan had been sitting on his bed drinking a Turkish coffee when I called. He apologised and folded his bed, stamping down the quilt into the bottom half. The bed-sofa creaked and snapped and completed its transformation. He pushed a chromed rack of suits to the wall. Now we could stretch our legs under the coffee table.

'Are you comfortable Geoff?'

I leaned back. Stretched my arms extravagantly to emphasis the spaciousness. 'This is a great place you've got here.'

He fetched a couple of beers from a crate. When I first met him I was bothered by this habit of cracking open a beer at any time of day.

'You know him a long time. Was he always the same as he is now?'

'Always.'

'Even at school?'

'He was always Silent Michal. He would say only what he needed to say. We used to go drinking together. I mean in secondary school. We would skip a day and Michal would suddenly want to jump on a train going east.'

'An adventure?' I said.

'Yes. He always was the one to come up with a plan. And when he had an idea, that was it. We had to carry it out. There was no other way. It was quite scary sometimes.'

'How so?'

'We would be just drinking from a stupid bottle of workers' beer. Then he would get the idea for "an expedition". We had to stand at the foot of the Sudety. Or we had to buy a bottle of buttermilk in some particular town because that's what some rebel did in 1921. Or we had to go to a particular war bunker and sit inside it. And we had to do it. There was no evasion.

'So one day we ended up five hundred kilometres east in Sandomierz with no money for a ticket home. I remember why we went there. We were drinking at the back of the school – this was also a sort of joke of his. He could tell his parents he was "at school" because he was technically still on school property. That was one of his principles. It is better to say nothing than to tell a lie. And so whenever we skipped school it was only to stand by some fucking grass mowers – old rusty harvesters left there – all sorts of junk. We could have been down in Pino's bar playing pool, or back in my place playing music because my parents were working all day. But no, we had to stay all day in that shitty place. It began to look like a dosser's hideout with all the empty bottles and empty toilet rolls.'

'Toilet roll?'

'Yes. We stayed there all day. Anyway that day we were talking about what a shit school it was. And he says, we'll go to the place where the founder was born. Are you serious,

I said, you hate this fucking school. No, he insisted, we must go there, the founder was an idealist, not his fault it all turned out shit like this. It was better to go there than to go to school. More noble. Like we were not just two kids bunking off school to go on the piss. We had a higher mission.' He smiled wryly.

'Michal talked a lot more back then by the sounds of it.'

Stan squinted into his memory. This was not something that had occurred to him before.

'Maybe he did. With just me and him, maybe he did talk a bit more. When we were doing nothing for hours he had time to say all he wanted. And when he had a few beers the words would come out more freely.'

'And what would he talk about?' I felt on the track, closing in on something.

'Just. His "teachings".' Again an enigmatic smile.

'His teachings,' I repeated. I had an intuition of some of it. A refusal to engage in bullshit. A thought-line aimed at the essential.

'So we got to Sandomierz at five o'clock and just walked around. It was like a place where legends come from. People gave us food just because we were so amazed at the cathedral.

'There is this weird tree, down on the avenue to the cathedral, and it has dangling fingers. The whole tree crawls forward and back in the wind. The drunks all sit on one bench, ten in a row. The tree makes a move toward them. Oh whore, they say, oh mother of whores, watch out for the whoring tree. And they scatter to the safe end and squabble. Then the tree calms down and they go back to their places. Ten minutes later and again the same drama, oh whore, that thing will crush our bones. This is what makes Michal laugh.

'We bought two cans in the Monopolowy. No, bottles. There were no cans back then. Then we set off on our quest. Sandomierz has more than a dozen old churches. A lot of graveyards. We went to the first church we saw and the founder's name was on the announcement board, a big arrow pointing up the side path. They must be pretty short of famous people. Of course this was only what Michal had expected: that we would be led there, we would be given a sign. We stood over the grave and knocked back the beer. Our "pilgrimage". Pretty fucking sick.' He clicked out the side of his mouth, smiled bleakly.

'But you don't think it's sick at all. You think it's cool.'

'I'm still – loyal.'

'Sandomierz.'

'A beautiful city. It looks even more beautiful when you are stuck with no way to get home. We had about forty zloty left. Old zloty. That's enough for two buttered bread rolls. But of course we had to spend it on a cup of black coffee. In some café bar where the drunks hang out. The woman asked us where we were from. This is where Michal is beyond the bounds of all society. This is where he simply closes up. If he doesn't like a question, he doesn't answer.

'Hey, tall man, will you speak to us? said the woman. I've figured you out, tall man, you're a spy amongst us.

'She was joking. Of course. Everyone in the bar was staring at us, thinking what kind of smartass city guys are these, maybe they need a lesson in manners, and I shouted at Michal, go on to the railway station we have only ten minutes before the train. Go go go. I'll catch up. Go.

'But Michal doesn't want to play along with this deception. He stands as still as an Easter island statue. I swear, the last thirty seconds in that place was hell. All these workmen shouting at us that we are morons and assholes and Jew boys .'

Stan shook his head and drank lovingly from the bottle. 'You don't know him. On the train journey home – because we sneaked on – he was thinking a long time. It wasn't just the normal Michal silence. Something was on his mind. "I am a spy," he said to me. "That's what the woman said." This was the outcome of the trip, that this was revealed to him. Even today, if you talk to Michal for long enough, at some point he will say, "I am a spy". So if you hear him say it, you will know it dates back to Sandomierz.'

'Sandomierz.'

'Yes, Sandomierz. She put milk in the coffee. Like we were little boys. That was our last money so Michal's next mission was to get a cup of black coffee. He had the idea that we might find road workers on a late shift and ask them. It was bright until later, and I remember I just didn't care how we got home. It wasn't the time to worry about that. Now was the time to worry about black coffee. I remember the crows in the trees following us around.'

'What were the crows a sign of?'

'The crows were just crows. We got coffee from a man sitting out in his garden. He was happy to give us a cup. So now I had nothing but coffee and beer in my stomach, and no food since breakfast. But that's another of Michal's principles.'

'What is?'

'Food is an animal necessity. Eat only because you have to.'

'Why?'

'He thought eating was degrading. He was disgusted at the whole process of chewing and swallowing like an animal. He wanted to be above the animal side of things. He wanted to be pure thought.'

'Where did he get his ideas from? Where did he come up with that notion?'

'It's just him.'

I was exasperated. I felt an obscure indignation that he had no right to his ideas. I wanted to pick apart his origins and find out that his father used to beat him his mother was an informer his mother's father was a Nazi collaborator – something, anything that would explain him. I wanted to pin him down and find there was a reason. He had no right.

'I see you still stick to the principle of eating only when necessary.'

Stan never kept any food in his room that I could see, nor cooker, nor cupboards. Just an electric kettle. In the four hours I'd been there he'd offered me coffee, tea, vodka, and Fernet. The beer was not offered. The beer was placed in front of me.

'Are you hungry Geoff?'

'Maybe a little.' It was more curiosity than hunger.

He jumped up and slid open a cabinet drawer, took out a tin of pulped tomato. He selected a pot from the windowsill. They had been there all along, but hadn't registered with me as pots.

'Follow me.'

He led me down the corridor to a communal kitchen with garish yellow walls. I felt like crawling into the space beneath the cookers to get away from that light. He opened a cupboard and took down a cardboard box with a crinkly plastic lining. He shook the box to shift the contents to one end and scooped out a portion of pasta shells.

As the pot simmered on the gas, we leaned against the wall and did what the residents have been doing for decades: picking holes in the friable plaster. Some were gouged to a depth of three inches right to the concrete wall. We lit up cigarettes and rested them in these recesses between pulls.

I ran my fingers over the scarified surface. 'This is beautiful.'

'Yes, and practical too. See the way the holes are shaped to hold the ash. This building used to be a workers' hostel for the vegetable oil factory. See the political slogans here.' As he decoded the inscribed acronyms, any trace of embarrassment at his living conditions changed to pride.

'With sunflower oil and paprika you can make a meal out of anything.' He sprinkled these two ingredients into the pot of pasta and let it simmer a while longer. We took the food back to his room. I told him everything was fine as once again he tried to create space around us. He had several rolled-up kilim rugs. But the biggest extravagance was a chrome suit rack, presumably from Michal's shop.

When we finished eating he washed the pot in the kitchen and set it back on the windowsill. He carefully opened the window behind and took in a bottle of spirit alcohol. I watched the delicate procedure he now performed. He decanted the last tarry inch from the coffee pot into a glass, added a couple of drops of cake essence, and poured in a shot of the sub-zero spirytus alcohol.

'I got a bottle of whiskey as a present once, and a small glass of it was great for clearing my mind and making me focus. Now I use this instead.'

I took a sip. It was smoky sharp with a sweet linger. 'This is your own invention?'

'We are masters of ersatz. What do you think? It gives you no dizzy feeling, just pure concentration. I use it whenever I have to stay up late studying.'

But you are no longer a student Stan I wanted to say.

My plan was to make the pretend professor title do something real, at least this one time. I wore a suit and tie to work for a week beforehand. I checked with the departmental secretary before knocking, to see if it was a good time. She frowned, checked a schedule sheet, and informed me the professor might be a little stressed but I was not to be nervous.

'Hey Geoff buddy,' the head said when I walked in. 'Look at this photo of me standing next to Her Majesty.' He flipped a yearbook over and showed me a double page spread. The academic staff were formally arranged at the front of the building, with a frail grandmother in a wide magenta hat at the centre.

'What's this, British propaganda?'

He hooted with laughter. 'I thought that might rile you a little.'

I had spoken to the head only once or twice before. He had received his PhD from Columbia University and come back to Poland just after communism fell. Whatever board of trustees ran the college must have been impressed with his American degree, and made him head of department. With me and the other native speakers he behaved as though he were a grad student on Erasmus. He would fire out phrases like "no shit" and "hang out".

I scrutinised the photo. 'Is this pasted in?'

'No. Her Majesty paid us an official visit.' He pronounced "*her majesty*" with ironic relish. 'And for the first and only time our little town got a front page mention in The Times of London. I can dig that out too if you're a doubting Thomas.'

This was all good fun, but I needed to get round to the purpose. I spoke about the relevance of practical experience in language training, and how it was great that the department was increasing emphasis on this. 'Sure,' he agreed. But already a troubled look crossed his face, and I could see he resented being ejected from his role of American grad student.

I talked about a former student of the college, a guy called Stan, who did translation work for an international company and had even interpreted for millionaire American business clients. 'There should be some accreditation for people like this. Some way for him to complete a degree building on that experience. In other countries colleges are more open to mature students.'

These were significant points I was raising, the head said, it was good to get such input from staff, and I was fully right to bring up the topic. The zarząd were currently revising policy. There would be new developments soon, maybe even by next term. But the government didn't allow grants for mature students – you got one chance, and that had to be taken within five years of finishing secondary school. There were no procedures in place for what I was suggesting.

I had drawn out the man whom the secretary told me not to be nervous of. He didn't make me nervous, but I knew I could not make him go back to being the carefree grad student.

'If your friend can work out some way of paying just one year's fee,' he concluded, 'arrangements might be made. I believe so.' I was to let him personally know if and when an application was lodged.

He had switched to Polish now. A balance in the room had shifted and I was now a subordinate appealing to someone far up in the hierarchy. Yet it felt more real.

I played Stan's own game against him; told him not to worry about the fees, if the application was successful the money would follow. Is this Stan, a person who worries about money? You can pay with butterfly wings and tell them it's thousand zloty notes. The power of belief. You can get a loan from Romeo's boss at HP. You can play the clarinet on the streets.

We established a routine for our intensive form-chasing sessions. It involved a progression from beer to fortified coffee, set to a soundtrack of Gorecki's symphonies. At the beginning of the evening Stan would assure me all efforts would turn out to be futile. But he believed in the absolute necessity of making the effort. The nobility of it. Transcripts from the college, attendance records, letters from HP stating he was a professional interpreter who would benefit from academic accreditation, tax returns, employment contracts on headed paper Romeo had swiped from the office, residence registration forms.

The lady in admin told me there was no such thing as an application for a mature student. I told her the head of department himself said it was possible, and she could ring him to confirm this. She said she did not have sufficient authority to personally ring him.

Stan however never got dismayed at obstacles like this. The ends of his mouth would curl in an infuriating smile each time we encountered a setback.

'Your subconscious is secretly hoping for failure,' I accused him.

'But if it's my subconscious then I'm not aware of it.'

When we slit open the envelope (he saved any official post for our sessions) and saw the bill for college fees inside, I thought, this is it. We have succeeded, and this is the final stumbling block. I made enquiries into taking out a loan. Romeo might be able to advance a few thousand.

A couple of days later a registration requirements list landed in Stan's letterbox. He handed it to me with a smug smile. I scanned my eyes down.

'What?'

'Read it again.'

A confirmation that he had completed his military service, or alternatively an official letter stating that he would not be called up for the next four years.

It was a well-known secret that the Polish military didn't have enough money to pay for the upkeep and training of every young male in the country. In certain regions, only

about two-thirds of school leavers were called up. Those
who excelled at sports or science were sure to receive their
number in the post. Others took life month by month,
knowing their chances of being called diminished with each
passing year. Until the magic age of twenty-six, when you
were no longer liable for service.

Stan had been useless at sports, and achieved only a
grade 3 in science. Besides, he was presumably still on the
military's books as a student. If they kept such books, for the
methods of the military were shrouded in secrecy. Stan lived
in near-certainty that he would not be called, and wanted to
do nothing to call attention to himself.

'Who could personally hate you? Who would want to
punish you? A secretary in some administrative building?' I
marvelled at Stan's paranoia, the product of an upbringing
in a dysfunctional society. He was afraid the authorities
would call him up out of pure spite and nothing more.

'There are no plots against you Stan. Let's face it, you're
insignificant.'

All that winter and into the spring I used to call by the shop
on Mickiewicza every week and buy a pair of socks or a shirt.
Michal would raise his head slightly at the sound of the door
chimes. Seeing it was me he would let it hang again, then
twist to each side as though looking for an escape. He would
exhale windily, then lift his head a fraction once more to say
dzien dobry. He said it like it was a word he and I knew from
some childhood storybook.

He told me Stan had written him and said he was happy
in the army. This surprised me. The letters I got from him

contained a litany of complaints about Russian-made alarm clocks and seeing live fleas for the first time in his life.

Maybe Stan had meant happy in some deeply fatalistic sense shared between him and Michal. Because I knew his family weren't happy. They had spent a lot of money on doctors' fees to get Stan diagnosed with weak kidneys and a pigeon chest. He got a medical cert with category D: in the event of a real war he would be called up along with men aged over sixty. But in an unusual move the army also insisted on their own medical procedure. It was at variance with the doctor's report, and the resultant legal wrangle dragged on for long enough to delay Stan's deployment by three weeks. It seemed to all appearances that they really were out to get him.

I would browse unhurriedly along the clothes racks, taking my time at selecting whatever I needed. Two hours could go by easily. And Michal was not totally silent; he said a lot, it just took him much longer than anyone else. He might remark on whatever item I was holding. *These are from Romania. This pattern is dyed in, not printed.* He loaned me history books and novels. He gave me advice on where to go for a weekend trip. He taught me the basics of the cash register. More than once I kept the till while he unloaded new stock out the back. I wondered if Michal's defining characteristic applied to his letters too, and pictured them, ludicrously, as sheets with long blanks between short sentences.

Michal would occasionally meet up with Romeo and the others at *The Angels* bar, but I kept away. I hadn't been there since the week after Stan got called up. Stepan had taunted me about being a know-all and a blundering Westerner. An ugly blundering Saxon he called me. I took this to be irony of a kind I knew how to handle. I retorted with a few street Polish expressions I'd learned.

Bad mistake. He slapped me a stinger on the cheek. Just in case I was in any doubt what it meant, he slapped me again and drew up his fists. Someone shoved me in the back and I put up my hands. Again a slap. Possibly it looked to the outside like I snapped, but I made a deliberate decision that there was no way out of the situation. I might as well do my best. I swung punches at him and kept my guard up. He dodged and weaved and I caught him with a glancing blow. I was throwing hard ones, and I thought if I got him with just one he'd hit the floor. Just one would demolish him.

Too late I realised he was only making a demonstration of me. He got in three or four hard punches to my face before I fell in a heap. And all the time a tag end of me thinking, *this isn't you, a pub brawler.*

When I visited the shop during the spring mid-term an estate agent's poster was pasted on the windowpane and the display behind was bare. Michal had said nothing and given no hint of any business problems. There was nowhere to go with my resentment. I could have found out where Michal lived and called by, but that seemed too drastic a step.

My time in Grodgoszcz was drawing to an end. Now that my Polish had become more fluent, I constantly had extra things to do at the college. I was asked to be on exam committees, attend meetings, and sort out accommodation problems for the new foreign teachers. Then I heard that from next term there would be no salary bonus for foreign teachers, except for during their first year in Poland.

The smell from the vegetable oil factory began to bother me again. It dried out my throat, made me spit constantly. It was always there, even ten stories up when I opened a window. It was a smell to burrow back into. You knew it would be there for you, familiar and obscurely shameful.

Stan's letters to me contained a litany of complaints about Russian-made wind-up clocks and seeing actual fleas for the first time in his life. His unit was now stationed in the Masurian lake district, where the mosquitoes were reputedly as big as geese. The days were passed in long marches and in learning how to drink. He was reaching out to new horizons, he wrote, in his ability to drink.

Entirely missing from these accounts was any resentment, or hint of bullying. I had underestimated Stan and his abilities to adapt. I found it hard to reconcile what I knew of him with the image of him standing before a drill sergeant. It occurred to me, briefly, that maybe he was not telling the whole truth, to save me from feeling guilty. But that was just ridiculous; his letters had enough griping in them.

I was wandering through the market, as I often did. I liked to look at the huge variety of fruit and vegetables on offer. One woman was selling eight different varieties of apple. I wanted to try them all. Soon, I thought to myself, all this will no longer exist.

Maybe the traces of a black eye made me look like the kind of guy who'd be interested in bootleg goods, because several times a seller whispered to me that he had vodka and cigarettes at a very special price.

Romeo shouted to me from across the street and came over. He began a bullshit conversation about a local block of flats that had recently been demolished, and how the construction company couldn't get official supplies of explosive so they bought some off the mafia. We chatted for a while and we went back to the seller and asked to taste a sample of his vodka. He gave us a decent measure each and explained it was produced in a proper factory to high quality standards. Romeo bought a bottle and we chatted some more, as though getting beaten up was just shit that happened and not worth mentioning.

Part II

When the news reached me that Stan was coming over my first thought was *not you too for fuck's sake.* The cafés were full of foreign workers. Whenever you saw a building site worker without a sneer, you could bet he was Polish. Or possibly from the Baltic states. You could spot the quick determined way of moving. You noticed the wide-apart eyes and lack of irony.

And Stan would be yet another trawling the streets looking for work in a café or hotel. I feared he would sink into the ordinary. Whatever that might mean.

My parents told me the news when I made my weekly phone call. Stan still had their number because I lived there for a few months when I first came back.

'Flight GA one six two six two eight. Write it down so you won't forget it.' My parents treated the news of this arrival with an eighteenth century gravity. The esteemed friend from the lands beyond the Vistula.

'Is it rye they grow in that part of the world? Will you be needing a lift to the airport?'

One by one the faces lit up with a smile. Sometimes gazing straight at me, which gave me a little jolt. The arrivals display said the last plane landed was from Barcelona, but the people coming out did not look like returning holidaymakers.

I sat back on a seat opposite the arrivals corral. Stan had no euros and no mobile phone. He wouldn't be going far.

I saw him dragging a fantastic caravan of tartan bags lashed together. It glided along behind him. He was heading for the lounge.

'We'll leave the bags at home first Stan,' I said.

'Geoff! I'm still trying to imagine I'm here. And yet I really am here.'

'What's this? A hovercraft?' I tilted the larger bag to see underneath.

'I'm a "constructor". I used the wheels from an old skateboard. But hey, you got here to meet me! You're here!'

I insisted on dismantling his trolley-train and carrying the bags by hand.

'Jesus, I thought the luggage limit was forty kilos?' The straps dug into the flesh of my shoulder. A diet of soft white bread and soft spongy burgers. I had been tougher in Poland.

We struggled out to the cutting wind. Stan raised a hand to shield his eyes. 'Is there a taxi?'

'There's one there. There's another. But we're going by bus.'

We tottered towards the bus stop. People were throwing disapproving glances at the oversize tartan tote bags –

identification of the new immigrant. Stan tightened the strap around the largest bag and dragged it after him like an anchor. He needed it. He was so thin the wind might blow him over if he let go.

A half hour later our bus was trundling past the native version of the blocks of flats which blighted central Europe. Excited voices cut through the damp air. The bus made several unscheduled stops as teenagers jumped off at traffic lights. When pulling off from the next stop, someone caught up running and banged on the door to get the driver to let him on.

Stan in a Dublin bus: laughter bubbled up in me at the idea. I had been mistaken. Ireland was a puny challenge to the likes of Stan. Someone who was born and reared in apartment "N" of block "M" in an industrial town no-one has heard of is in no danger of sinking into the ordinary. Whatever that might mean.

He stretched out his legs in my North Circular Road bedsit. 'So this is your home?'

'This is it.'

Stan stroked his fluff of a beard, looked about him at the four walls, the plaster bulging with the damp, the sickly egg-blue paintwork, the iron-framed spy window looking over the back yard, the rumples in the carpet.

'It's good to be here. This is a real nice pad you've got.' He wasn't being ironic.

'Yeah, we're just fifteen minutes from the city centre.'

'A good place to commute from if I get a job in a city centre office.'

I tugged and worried the strings of his baggage, prodded the bulges and felt tins and bottles.

'Just cut it with a knife. I won't be putting it together again.'

I slashed the strings. The contents spewed across the floor. I took up items one by one. Cigarettes galore, potato starch, dried dill, Krakow kielbasa, kabanosa, stomach vodka and cherry vodka, rye vodka and potato vodka. Then a layer of woolly jumpers and ironed shorts. And underneath again; jars of beans, mocne beer, packets of soup, instant noodles made in Vietnam, long-life rye bread, more instant noodles. Dozens upon dozens of instant noodles. At the very bottom a layer of cartons of UHT milk.

He spread his hands. 'I didn't want to be a burden. I won't have much money until I get a job.'

I picked up a kielbasa and cut a chunk off with the knife and chewed it. You could buy kielbasa in any of the dozen Polish shops around, but it had been a long time since I'd eaten any.

'It's good to see you're doing well Geoff.' I snorted at this. 'You said you were a teacher in some school?'

'A few hours a week. It's summer now so I'm not doing much.'

'So your job will start again next month?'

I scratched my nose. 'Maybe. Maybe not. Who can tell the future? It's an unwritten book.'

He jumped up, pumped with animation. 'Exactly. We must make the future. We have to reach out and grasp hold of our lives. Don't let the monkey hold the wheel. Those fucking monkeys with their little monkey hands.'

The slapped-on plaster and creaky floorboards quickened his soul. The bare pipes running up the walls gave him solace. He bounced out to the toilet cubicle with its iron-framed window set ten foot high. A metallic creak and rattle of chain, then a gush that trailed off to white noise.

'Interesting sound,' he roared.

The bastard. I could see right through him. He had thought to find me a career-drone, speaking the language of opportunities and investment. From reading the newspapers he would have gotten the idea that I must be earning thirty, forty, or fifty thousand, just like everybody else. He had imagined I would tolerate an old friend from a distant poor country. Now that he knew I had nothing he felt comfortable about sponging off me.

He rubbed his hands. 'I'll make us a proper Polish dinner. We'll have a feast of kielbasa and ogórki. You know I have an optimistic feeling in my soul. Even though the air is damp, it's like charged with energy.'

'You can feel a dampness in the air?' It seemed to press on me quite a lot recently. I longed for a day of dry air.

Stan paced the room. 'I think I will be able to get a job pretty soon. I feel like I'll walk down the street and see a sign Jobs Here. And when I walk in the door the boss will say Your name's not Stan is it? And I'll say, that's me, Stan the man and I'm ready for action. I could do anything here. I could work in publishing. I could work for a magazine.'

'Right.'

'I could become a male model. I read in a magazine that Irish men are too shy to become models, and that all the models in Ireland are foreign. That's an amazing fact. I don't claim I'm good-looking, but people don't realise you don't have to be. I'd say I have a good chance. I have no objection to wearing a leather jacket and posing for photographs. Stanislaw sports an autumn tweed jacket. Stanislaw in this season's Ralph Lauren shirt. Yeah I don't go for the pissed-off look, there's too much of that. It's more generic thinking man stroke artist.'

This kind of talk was going on for about ten minutes with me just hmming along and turning kielbasa under the grill. Then I tuned in to what he was saying. *What am I listening to? Why am I listening to this?*

'Stan. Stan. You're not a model. You're not a fucking model. You're not even fucking gay. Models come from acting college, or they get the job through gay connections or whatever. You're talking pure bullshit. I can't fucking listen to this. Your dream job, and this is the godshonest truth, will be to get into Starbucks rather than McDonald's.'

I expected him to say *okay, okay* in a back-to-earth way. The elated look on his face hardened.

'What's up with you?'

'Me?'

'Seriously.'

'Seriously what? What are you saying?'

'I have a list of addresses, phone numbers of agencies. My plan is simply to try them. This is boom boom city. A lot of big advertising agencies work here. You just have to be slim and have a tan. Can I not even try?'

'Go for it then. Grand.'

'I will. Fuck. People really do get paid to model stuff. These guys in magazines and adverts, they're actually real. I mean even Michal got asked to be a model once.'

This seemed utterly implausible.

'Really and truly. The supplier asked him to be a model. It was for the suit factory in Szczecin. We need someone for this new line, the rep told him, do you want to come over on Saturday for a few hours? He was the right height, the right figure. Simple as that. They were going to pay him. Real cash, plus a suit of course.'

'And what did he say to that?'

'Nothing.'

We stepped out onto the street. Stan had a document folder of CVs ready for distribution. I asked about how things were back in Grodgoszcz. I asked about his time in the army, delicately enquiring whether he encountered any of the infamous bullying.

'Bullying? Of me you mean? It was like going back to school, except I was five years older.'

'And when you got back to Grodgoszcz?'

'Grodgoszcz won a Picot light bulb factory in a European competition. The milk bar has a Picot pizza now. And the town hall is lit up like a light bulb factory. And I had to move out of my apartment for a couple of weeks while they renovated the building. The windows were all ripped out and an extra skin of blue glass plates put on the building. The whole thing looks like a rocker launcher. And then the rent went up.'

I tossed out names and places. "Angels" was still there, but now it had five other pubs on the square to compete with. The paving stones were still not completed. Customers

and tourists had to walk across compacted sand. A foreign teacher, perhaps my replacement, had started a fire in his room by accident, and the upper floors of the Dolphin block had to be evacuated. Wanda at the Black Sheep café now organised talent nights and had speakers rigged up outside. Stan related all this news in a quick monotone.

I felt a tug of loss at my gut. Not exactly nostalgia. I didn't want to go back and live there again. But I still knew that city better than the one I was in now. Tram routes, shortcuts, shops, and familiar faces: a complete set of skills to live in that city was preserved in my brain, and all of it no use. It would fade away in a few more years.

We had now reached the intersection where the carbon-monoxide winds of Phibsboro blow. I stood and lost myself to the flow and hum of traffic. A beer shop, Stan shouted, you said there was a beer shop close by.

A woman behind plate glass folded clothes into neat piles. The clothes looked too ordinary. Chunky-knit jumpers, pleated skirts, pale blouses. Like a misplaced memory.

He feels more comfortable, Stan was saying, in a place where things are not perfect. In a city where shopkeepers paint their own signs above their shops, where neon tubes flicker, where countertops do not meet seamlessly with the wall.

We took refuge in the charity shop, and browsed through the cardboard boxes of books and kitchen utensils. Stan was on the hunt for a bargain, though he had no money with him. I bought a stainless steel soup ladle to pay for our time there. When we left I noticed a small sign pasted in the window. Help wanted.

We passed three more premises displaying a staff wanted sign. Stan took it as an omen of good fortune, on his first day too, not to forget the number 48 bus that slowed down with a man singing out of it: *Stop me if you can me name is Stan, sure I'm your man.* I didn't spoil the moment by telling him the name is Dan.

And Michal?

Times had changed; new chain stores were springing up, a huge shopping mall opened on the outskirts. There was a free bus out to it every hour. The shop had become a relic, relying on suits, shirts, and Sunday best. Besides, Stan said, as you can imagine, Michal himself ...

I remembered the way Michal stood to one side in an unobtrusive silence while his customers picked out their wares. It might be that though he was averse to one-to-one communication, he could make a connection with the dozens of anonymous customers who drifted into the shop. It might be that they returned for that special atmosphere of tranquillity.

But it seems even in Poland the laws of the market operate the same way as everywhere in the world, or at least now they do, and a business where the shopkeeper never speaks to his customers will be doomed. Michal ceased to turn up at the Angel's. Many of the old circle had in any case emigrated – none, as it happened, had had to do military service. Michal stayed in his room and read books about megalithic tombs. He was learning Japanese, or so he claimed. He would help out at the family allotment, planting beans and potatoes. His older sister occasionally brought him groceries.

When Stan got home from the army he took him out once or twice for a drink. Then one time Michal said he was busy. Another time he had to get up early the next morning.

'I got the hint. I knew I would meet him again when he was ready. That's the way it is with Michal – you can meet him after several months and resume a conversation. If anything bad had happened to him I would have heard about it, I'm sure.'

We sat on a parapet, our backs to the traffic on the Finglas road. In front of us cars crawled bumper to bumper on the forecourt of a shopping arcade. The drivers cast glances left and right for a vacant parking space. We were sitting at the end of a four foot gap between parked cars. Drivers gauged the gap with their eyes and looked angrily at us.

'But hey, my first day in Ireland and we're talking about Poland?'

Stan lifted his head. Though he wore no glasses he was always squinting and blinking to get an eye-grasp of things.

'Where is this place? Is it somewhere historic?'

'Does it look historic to you?'

Stan flicked a glance at me, unsure of this sarcasm.

'Only messing,' I added quickly. 'Look, we should really go to the city centre. I'm being a bit too anti-tourist by bringing you to this kip.'

Stan jumped up decisively and checked out the window display opposite. 'A lot of anti-sun lotion here,' he called over. He looked up at the small sky. 'It seems to be working. And what's this green thing?'

'It's a postbox.'

He pressed himself against the postbox. 'I had a toy one,

it was like a teddy bear to me. I thought they were supposed to be red?'

'The English ones are red. Don't you know where you are?'

'The buses are green too instead of red! This place is like England with a different coat of paint.'

'Let's go on,' I said. I was getting bored. But the window displays along the strip exercised a magnetic attraction on Stan. He went from one to the next, standing slack at the plate glass with his hands under his armpits.

'This is the beer shop?'

'Off-licence we call them.'

We pushed through the glass doors and a breath of warm air went down the back of my neck. An electronic bell tinkled distantly. I drew in a deep breath of filtered dry air. It made me feel keener, lifted a weight from me. Cooler air flowed against my hand as we passed the chilled section. Transparent bands of plastic hung down to keep the cold in.

Cans in metallic gold and blue were stacked in staggered tiers. Signs with prices were placed apologetically at the bottom. Someone designed each of these arrays, lavished them with love and attention to detail. Someone came around after a customer took a couple of cans, and thought about how to rearrange the rest to a harmonious new order.

In the wood-shelved wine section the bottles stood close to the front edge. Two bottles, then a space before the next brand. Enough to give a feeling of abundance, yet without appearing cluttered.

Stan held his arms outspread. 'This is the bounty of the West.'

A shop assistant polished bottles at the counter. My voice emerged unexpectedly loud when I asked for his recommendation of ales. I cleared my throat and tried again. He came down to the ale shelves and guided us through the selection of brands.

When we did our drinking in Poland, Stan and I, we used to buy the cheapest trashiest booze, stuff sold from crates under the counter because no decent shop would publicly display it. Jabol laced with sulphur dioxide, a whiff off it like an abandoned corner of the fruit market on a warm day. Czekoladowa too – described on the label as "domestic wine with a chocolate flavouring". We would buy this shit with a straight face, asking the assistant politely if he stocked the "jabol wine". Our gateway to spaces of mind detached from the mundane lay directly through what was most sordid. We cherished it because it was common and despised. Our drunkenness was esoteric because it was profane.

I paid for the bottles of ale at the counter and Stan asked the assistant if he would mind opening them. The assistant did so without comment. We went back to our place on the low dividing wall. Stan sat with poise and lifted the bottle to his lips. He did not notice the wary glances of afternoon shoppers. I always admire people like that.

'But you never checked to see if he was okay,' I said. 'You talk and talk about him as if he's this famous friend of yours but in the end you just left him to rot in his room.'

'What are you talking about? I knew from his older sister he must be okay. He used go for a walk on Deptak, people had seen him. Sometimes I wanted to call by and I had to stop myself, no don't do it Stan, that's exactly what he expects you to do. It wasn't worth making a contest out of it. And then – this was maybe a full two years later, after I'd spent a few months working in the sellotape factory in Warsaw – I heard he had left that flat and was in a new place. That was when I began to get worried. I stood on the street outside and threw pebbles up at his window. Nothing, no answer.'

'Did you not try knocking at his door?'

'Of course.'

'Did you not shout through, it's me Stan?'

'Not "shout". A loud whisper. Enough for him to know it was me. I heard the floorboards creak so I knew he was in there. This was being dramatic – hiding behind the door and not answering. This is like a television movie, not like Michal. Should I stand there whispering through the keyhole? Should I kick the door in?

'I was pissed off with him. I went back out and waited at the end of the road. Like a TV detective, leaning against a wall, smoking. I had work, translations, people to meet. My legs were dead from waiting. I went twice to get more cigarettes. He had to come out some time. According to his habits he would come out for a bread roll before the shop closed. Unless he'd been out already early.

'It was a good place to wait. There was actually a tap in the laneway beside me, so I had water to drink. With my liver problem I have to drink plenty of fresh water. So I waited.

'He came out of the building. Walked by me and I started walking with him. Hmm, seems like you want to be alone these days, I said. Hmm, what makes you draw that conclusion. Hmm, well I knocked on your door several times and you didn't answer. Hmm, so what made you suppose I was inside. Isn't it obvious I was not at home?

'But at least he was speaking to me. He told me he was considering joining the monks, he'd written off about it and even had an interview with the chief monk of a monastery at Kolnierz. But, he said, in the end he concluded the idea was too impractical.

'Since when have you become a practical person Michal?

'Everything I ever do and have ever done is completely practical, he says to me. Or do you have an example to the contrary? No? Then we are practical people. That is why I have decided to become a shepherd, he says. He had found a farmer in the Bieszczady who needed a shepherd. He had printed out his CV and sent him a copy. By registered mail. A letter came back, inviting him for a job interview in a café in Smolnik. He was due to go in five days time. He had been busy for the past two weeks preparing himself for the trip. How? I asked. By reading about sheep, he answered.'

Stan kicked the green post box. A passer-by threw us a second glance. Such people as Silent Michal, walking the streets among us. And nobody would ever know. The world opens up within, universes within universes, vortices within vortices. There is as much of the world as you wish to understand.

Stan wanted to get another beer. This was no time for beer, I argued. Our heads were lucid and full of dry air. Beer makes us sink into the generic. It's spirit and coffee we needed. At home we had stomach vodka and rye vodka, potato vodka and ice vodka. I steered around him as I talked. Pasted on the letterbox was a hand-scrawled page torn from a copybook. *Polish good worker. Handwork experienced. I do anything. Please to call me. 084 727 5463.*

'So he actually got a job as a shepherd?'

'He wasn't at home a week later, or the week after that. I moved back to Warsaw to work in a branch of Romeo's company. Romeo's Translation Services. You were right. The name gave him a good start in life. All these foreigner businessmen love him. He goes out to dinner every evening.'

'Romeo? The Romeo who hates these shallow Westerners?'

'The same Romeo,' affirmed Stan. 'And still he calls them "the suits". Hey Romeo, what's different about *your* suit? He is the reason I came here to Dublin. His mission of being a better businessman than the *real* businessmen began to wear me out. One day he took a huge book from the shelf. I've been reading this book on management practice, he said. Stan we must set goals for ourselves. Stan we must have a vision.

'Yes, I have a vision Romeo. I see the door opening and beams of light coming through. I see myself walking through the door. I see myself getting on a plane to Ireland. I see myself telling you to stuff this job.'

'It's good to hear,' I said. 'I mean about Michal. That he found something to do.'

'I don't know about that. He was seen back in Grodgoszcz a few weeks later. I don't know what happened.'

'Shit.'

'The last I heard of him someone had seen him rummaging in a second-hand clothes shop for a pair of shoes. Always dress ordinary, that's what he used to say. Always have polished shoes and a white or blue shirt. The idea was not to look any different from anyone else. He would be careful not to forget to shave or go to the barber. He doesn't believe in trying to look bizarre or grow his hair long. That's all there is to say, I didn't see him since. I thought maybe he just wasn't coming out, but then his sister said she hadn't seen him either. And whatever he's doing now, I'm sure he's keeping to his teachings.'

'His "teachings".'

'Michal will not deviate.'

'What the fuck for? He's a one-man sect all to himself. It's like he's preparing himself, but for what? What's driving him?'

'I don't know Geoff. Don't kick the wall for fuck's sake. Jesus, I came to this place thinking I needed to sort myself out.'

We got out of that place. The frantic exhalations of the traffic unnerved me. The thought of so many going by made my stomach weak. Poland had never felt as crowded as this. People there occupy less space.

We made our way towards the city centre. A coffee in a nice café, Stan reckoned, was what we needed. Just sit down and *be* in the centre. His first trip abroad, except for a school excursion to Prague when he was twelve. His first flight ever. He talked about seeing the ground fall away, the rush of acceleration, and how several people vomited. I'd been on many flights and never seen anyone vomit.

We stopped somewhere on Camden Street. A simple café, a couple of wrought iron chairs outside, a small selection of cakes in the chilled display. Stan enquired about the cheesecake – raspberry or lemon – and whether it was home-made. Who did he think was paying for all this?

Stan sipped his coffee and looked approvingly at his surroundings. He noticed hot chocolate on the menu, and wondered if this was true hot chocolate, like they serve in Warsaw, or just something made from a powder. He observed the waitress keenly as she wiped a table. When she set the cheesecake in front of him he asked her if she thought there were any jobs there, and how much the pay was.

A couple of weeks of Stan in the flat began to annoy me. It was not the extra presence, nor the extra expense. It was the mild ironic smile. Each evening he would recount his failure to find even the most humble work. He would describe the streets he'd traipsed, the CVs that got soaked in the rain, and the rise and fall of his hopes. There must be some job out there waiting specially for him, Stan. And then, just when his spirits were at their lowest, he'd encountered a homeless man begging for coins, and suddenly realised there is always someone who has it worse.

The reality was, Stan could get a flight back at any moment and resume his work as a translator. Romeo would be able to throw him a few jobs to get him going. Or he could get a position in the civil service through his brother.

I listened also to his occasional stories about his family history. Stan's remote ancestors had been nobility. His great grandfather had been intelligentsia. He had been an engineer, a member of the Sejm, friend of artists and writers, and a newspaper contributor. He had come to a tragic end in the war.

Back in my time in Poland, I used to listen to these stories in that cramped room on the tenth floor. Stan and I drank our beers and at a certain point he rooted about in the cardboard boxes on top of his wardrobe. He brought out a couple of old books and pointed to his great grandfather's name, right there in print. Then another newspaper clipping, preserved between the pulpy pages of an old textbook. And a photograph of six men in high white collars, hand-captioned: Lublin conference 1929.

Stan would show me these scraps with a shy pride. These relics of an era more real than the present. For after came the obliterations of war, and then communism and the making small of everything. Life was levelled to something makeshift and modest. Life was what happened at a family grill party when good kielbasa was available. I looked at these clippings without comment and passed them back. To show that I understood their significance, and for my own reasons too, some weeks later I would ask to see them again. He would root them out from the box and we would pass them to and fro, and I would feel that pang of dignity lost.

Now in my North Circular Road bedsit, Stan's allusions to his great grandfather seemed less and less endearing. This great grandfather was an irritating third presence. Stan did not constantly talk about him, he didn't need to. He was there in the background, to be invoked as validator. Maybe Stan only mentioned him once a week, maybe less, I wasn't keeping count. But sooner or later the great grandfather would be mentioned and Stan would smile his indulgent smile.

Fuck you and your intelligentsia great grandfather, I

thought to myself secretly. And then one night after several beers the words spewed out aloud, in the form of an ironic joke: 'Fuck your great grandfather, it doesn't matter who he was. You are what you are.'

'He's here in my soul,' Stan pressed himself on the chest. 'Get a grip.'

'I feel I can look out at the world through his eyes. I don't mean reincarnation, that would be silly. But I know that we are very alike. His time on earth is gone, and now it's my time.'

Stan and I walked the tourist beat most days and did the rounds of all the historical pubs. We met up with some of my old Clontarf friends and held a couple of parties. It took a lot out of my bank account, but I hadn't been saving for anything concrete, just saving by habit. A couple of weeks of this, and Stan reached a big crisis. He wanted to go back, Dublin wasn't for him, his English was crap, the only jobs for men were on the building sites, and so on.

The problem was his CV, I told him. It needed to be the modern format with a photograph. He also had to ring companies directly, and not simply post out queries.

It's always easier to sort out someone else's life.

Stan filled in dates of a career in admin and sales. Sales of what? Language   solutions, that's what. The Warsaw company where Romeo worked would be the reference. If a potential employer rang they would be talking to Romeo himself. And Stan's degree from Grodgoszcz University, he could finally award himself that. Grade 2.1, because that is what his exams entitled him to, and no higher. It took a lot of work, that CV, and we were justly proud of it. We were certain it would work. Not a mutually reinforcing shaky certainty; I simply couldn't imagine anyone having a more suitable CV.

Within a week Stan was offered a job in a Rathmines bar. He started at eight each evening and his taxi home at two or three in the morning was paid by the job. It was good for him to work nights, Stan reckoned, because it meant he didn't drink anything through the whole week except Sunday, when he got off early and had the next day free.

That was how things stood when Stan and I ducked into a Dublin multiplex to see what films were on. There had been intermittent rain for a whole month. *It's Silent Michal*, said Stan and disappeared into the crowd.

I held out my hand and he took it like an object. The chiselled planes of his face matched well the angled panes of glass around us. There was a scent of damp people, and outside on the streets purple and gold were waving. It was the day of the big match.

I stopped at the door of the first pub we came across. Michal tightened his lips, a pained expression crossed his face. We moved on until he stopped outside a place on Dorset Street. The brick on the façade was the colour of dog biscuit. A faded handwritten sign read *City and Country Pub*, and there were photographs of footballers in nineteen-fifties shorts and Brendan Behan astride a bicycle.

Stan ordered three pints of stout. The bare timbers of the bar were tar-black from decades of tobacco smoke. It was one of the few pubs left which still had bare floorboards.

'The calm before the storm,' said the barman.

We took our pints to a partition and set them on the ledge. A glass case with photographs of the rare auld times faced us. Stan nodded, expressing his satisfaction with the authenticity of the place. In Grodgoszcz he used to avoid workers' pubs, and would only visit classy places. We spoke to Michal, or rather mainly I spoke. This is what we found out over the course of half an hour:

He had been in Ireland for over a year.

Nobody in Poland knew he was here.

His job involved a uniform.

He did not know any Poles in Ireland.

He ate once a day.

He detested Brendan Behan.

When he first arrived he'd worked on a mushroom farm.

That was in a town called Cahir.

Enough. I felt like I was turning a halogen beam on him. Michal reached into both his pockets, searching through the contents. He took out a wad of payslips, a Polish ID card, cinema membership card and other cards. I thought he was about to spread them in front of me and say: 'Here, look through all these if you want to know so much about me.' Instead he extracted a ten euro note and laid it flat beside his pint.

'Do you like this place?' Stan asked.

'Yes, I live close,' he volunteered.

'Where exactly? Gardiner Street?'

'Close to there.'

There was a distant sound of surf crashing. The barman checked the clock. 'I don't bother with a television in here myself. Never have.'

'What time are they due out at?' I asked.

'I think that's them I'm after hearing. Stick your head out the door like a good fellow and see.'

I looked out and saw a thickening horde of purple and yellow and blue down by the canal.

We downed pints and emerged out onto Dorset street. A mass of bodies wrapped in colours moved against us. Earnest hearty faces, all flushed with heat. The low August sun glazed the street with orange light.

We veered down a side street, walking with long strides. But they were coming at us from all angles, up Fitzgibbon Street and Charles Street. We sped up and dodged through, keeping at right angles to the flow.

The crowds thinned abruptly at Fairview. The sea was surely within a stone's throw, but there was no view of it from any point.

By the fifth pint Michal was talking in complete sentences. Alcohol had always freed his tongue. Not in the sense that he started trading confidences – he simply spoke longer sentences.

He had worked at the so-called shepherd job in Smolnik for a few weeks and then left. It was not a proper job, it was a stupid situation not worth talking about. For several years afterwards, life went on as normal. Occasionally he got a few days security work at the Picot plant. He gave up drinking because it made him feel sick the next morning. So without alcohol, he said, you meet people less often. You know, he added with no particular emphasis, I don't need to meet people in the way that other people do.

Stan told him of how he had worried, how he had occasionally walked by Michal's flat at night to check the light was on. Michal was not pleased to hear this. He twisted his head from side to side. He had not shut himself away, he insisted, in no sense or form. He had gone regularly to the library, to the shops, and made a trip to the giant M7 shopping mall.

'Which, I hope, will satisfy you,' he said drily.

Then it was the year 2001 and the Internet arrived in Grodgoszcz. It arrived at a basement premises below a solicitor's practice. Kids would gather there, maybe a dozen inside browsing the Internet, an equal number on the pavement above discussing what they had seen and how to download music. You paid your five zloties, put your name on the waiting list. A sign hung at the entrance: maximum two to a seat.

News of this Internet café reached Michal in his room. It came as no surprise to him. He had read about the Internet years before. All the information of humankind would be connected and instantly accessible. Every place in the world would be the same; there would be no more countries, no more divided regions, just individuals communicating with each other constantly. The things that one person wrote could be instantly shared with the whole world. There would be no more suppression and censorship.

Somebody told him there were special sites on the Internet where you can look for jobs, any job you like, anywhere in the world. Michal decided to try it out. So one day – maybe two years later – on a quiet weekday morning Michal descended the steps to the cellar and handed over his five zloties. He sat in front of the Internet, learned how to move the mouse, and typed in the words *shepherd job*.

He took down names and phone numbers on a piece of paper. There was a job in the Czech Republic, in the Karkonosze mountains. He thought about this for a long time. In the public library he found a boxed set of cassettes for learning the language. He borrowed it and took it home. The language made new demands on his tongue and lips. Completely different to Polish, he insisted, though many individual words are almost identical. Each language is different because the people have different perceptions.

'What do you mean?' I asked. But Michal was not about to explain. He had gone to the Karkonosze and worked there for several months. Not as a shepherd, but as a forester, fixing fences and cutting out dead timber. He learned how to drive a jeep and operate a chain saw. No, he did not live in a wooden cabin. Every evening he returned to an apartment block in the mountain town. He got free meals at the local state-run meat factory. As things turned out, he never needed to speak much Czech.

This was a lot of talk to coax out of Michal all at once. He looked as though his throat was sore. There was a natural pause in the conversation, and we let it stretch. It felt strange to sit there beside him and know he was indifferent to us. It didn't feel good.

The idea to come to Ireland was a long time fermenting. Michal had long known about the early Irish hermits. The sixth century monks, St. Kevin and St. Tassach, and St. Gall. There were no books about them in Polish, and his English improved in leaps as he read about them in English. And had we heard of this man Subi or Swoob? We borrowed a pen from the barman so he could spell out the name.

'For this reason I decided to come to Ireland.'

'You have to realise though,' I said, 'Ireland is just an ordinary modern place these days. There are no hermit monks any more.'

Michal stretched his neck back like a horse, then his head slumped down almost to his lap. He rubbed his eyes with his hands. A hiss escaped from him.

'Do you think he's an idiot?' said Stan angrily.

'No, no. I meant like that's so long ago it's the same as if it never happened. It's got nothing to do with Dublin today.'

'Do you think Michal is a halfwit? Jesus Geoff, I thought you knew better than that.'

Michal remained slumped over. The barman flicked a glance in our direction. His senses had long become attuned to spotting signs of trouble. He exchanged a discreet murmur with the assistant barman. This was a pub in a mixed local area.

Time to leave. Michal straightened up adequately as we pulled on our coats. I said goodbye loudly to the barman and we were out on the street in the rain.

The match crowds had dissipated. We were not on any main road, and I couldn't tell in which direction the centre lay. Stan insisted on a taxi, and said he'd pay, no matter how much it was. He stood out in the road waving at any car with a light on top. We got wetter and wetter, and at some point Michal waved goodbye and began to walk off. We shouted after him, and stood in at a doorway and made arrangements to meet again.

'This thing about becoming a shepherd,' said Stan, 'all these years it was to me just a crazy idea. Something that was typical of Michal. Now I see that's it's just common sense.'

'That's exactly what it is.'

'He told me he was a practical person and I didn't believe him. But he sees what kind of person he is. So he makes his decision.' He sliced the edge of his hand on the table. 'A perfectly reasonable decision.'

'Except he's going to find it hard to get a shepherd job in international tiger boom town Dublin.'

'We can help him,' said Stan. 'I mean not necessarily a shepherd job, but work out in the countryside on his own. There are serious things we can do, ask your country relatives, contact people, look up the job ads. Is there no place in this world for someone who just wants to be a fucking shepherd?'

'Apparently not.'

We leaned against the stone bridge and stared at the lock. The water level was high that day. An oily scum mantled the surface and floating cans clumped together. No barges ever passed through the locks, but sometimes the water was low and sometimes high. Perhaps some organisation liked to open and close the gates periodically to keep them in working order.

Isolated remnants of the match crowd slapped each other on the backs and pissed into the rushes. Not as big a match as the previous week, but this area was close to the stadium. This was where we had agreed to meet Michal. Initially we had suggested the pub the colour of dog biscuits, but Michal didn't want to wait in a pub. The canal lock was directly across the road.

A plan formed in my mind. I would type out an English CV with fake agricultural experience. I would ring the forestry service office and see what jobs were available. We could coach Michal to answer questions the right way.

I said, 'We are two of the few people who know him and can help him.'

'Nobody in Poland even knows where he is. We are the only people who know him.'

And then I felt a hollowness inside, falling into myself, with nothing to grip on to. I wanted to be able to laugh at how eccentric Michal was, at how fascinating it was to know someone so incontrovertibly authentic. To see him only from the outside.

'I know him,' Stan insisted. 'He overdid things. He needs to stock up on silence.' We drank our pints in the pub opposite. 'This is how Michal's mind works. He'll be here next week at the same time. This is how we used to meet in Grodgoszcz, Friday evening, the electricity substation.'

We went to the door and looked across at the canal until the barman growled at us to either come in or go out, like good fellows.

Most evenings I called by and played 3D games on Stan's new Apple Mac. It felt like making a trip to the future. It's not *mine*, Stan stressed, it belongs to the company.

He had had a stroke of good luck. One of the companies he'd spammed with his juiced-up CV had rung back. 'You tell us,' they'd said, 'what kind of job would suit you best.' At the interview they told him it was their devious policy to ring candidates out of the blue, and that how the person reacted to this unexpected call told them more than any CV could.

He moved out of my flat and into a one-bedroomed apartment on Jervis Street. 'There's no rush,' I told him. But way the rental agency worked was to give you only twenty-four hours to decide. Apartments were being snapped up within hours that summer. People were in love with the idea of thin-slicing. As soon as Stan requested a viewing, he was as good as hooked. I gave him a loan of the deposit and we drank a bottle of vodka.

A couple of days later we drank another bottle while standing on his foot-deep balcony looking down on Parnell street. We took turns spotting night-club people, working people, teenagers in track suits, and winos, and a Chinese man who came out of his restaurant every hour to sweep the section of pavement outside.

I sniffed the air. 'You can't get any more central than this.' Down below, a man stumbled on the step coming out of the chippy. He lost a few chips, or maybe a battered sausage, and he went down on his hunkers to see what could be salvaged.

'This moment Geoff, right here, is success,' Stan said. He had on his whimsical expression. 'Not the fake success of fat bastard businessmen making a million. But this is success, here and now.'

'I know what you mean Stan,' I murmured.

'Always chasing, chasing. And then realising that that moment years and years ago, that was the high point of your life. But now I have that moment and I know it.'

'This is it Stan. This is it I suppose,' I murmured.

'Hikikomori,' Stan stated. 'This explains everything about Michal.' He thrust a torn newspaper page into my hands. '*He spends his days reading newspapers, watching sports and thinking. "Maybe I think too much," Yenji admitted, his eyebrows fluttering nervously.* He lives his life locked in his room. It's a recognised phenomenon in Japan.'

I took the page and sat on the bench. We were at the appointed canal lock for the fourth Friday. This time the water was at the low level. We planned to stay for an hour then have a pint in the pub opposite.

Stan snatched the scrap back from my hands. 'And look! he only eats once a day. This is Silent Michal.'

I wondered how Stan could be so trite. How could he – who knew Michal for so long – imagine there was something to learn by classifying him to a type?

'See that. *His mother takes a plate of food and leaves it outside his door.*'

Stan lifted his arms in a eureka gesture. Kicked the green bench beloved of the winos. They sat on the one at the next lock gate up. They looked back down at us and gauged our street-toughness.

Stan was elated at his discovery. He wanted to write a letter to the newspaper, tell them this hikikomori phenomenon doesn't only happen in Japan. He wanted to send a personal letter to the journalist. The drunks on the bench a dozen metres further up elbowed each other and skewed around.

I didn't bother to argue with Stan. I didn't know what arguments to use, I just felt a wave of disgust. I folded up the article and told him I'd read it later. It can surely do no harm to read it, I thought to myself. It would be strange indeed to prefer not to read it.

Two of the drunks were shuffling down towards us. *Where are yis from, who's that fella, is he a foreigner, here I'm talkin' to you,* and so on.

'Yous can have your fuckin bench,' I said to them. 'We're going now.'

'Fairies,' the toughest one wheezed triumphantly. 'If you know what's good for you,' growled the second.

Stan was already doing his fast pace away.

'Do you want your bench or not?' I said. I stood my ground, aware of the twenty foot drop to the empty lock at my back. 'Do you have a problem? I said, do you have a problem?'

They grumbled some more and I walked off, up the steep ramp to the pavement and over the bridge. The exposed bottom of the lock was littered with cans and angled wires and shopping trollies.

'He'll be taking long walks at night when it's quiet. Until four in the morning. Then he'll sleep well into the afternoon. He will take a trip to the Skellig Rocks, I'm sure of this. He talked about them. He'll hitch a lift. He'll stock up with a supply of rye bread from Lidl. He can live a long time without money.'

These narratives of Michal's current movements and state of mind grew more elaborate each time we met. I couldn't tell what purpose there was to these stories. Stan would relate them with a whimsical grin.

'He'll follow the trail of the ancient Celtic monks.

Michal is hardy, he can sleep in a hayshed. I've seen him sleep in the open air in a frost, with just an army blanket over him. He'll walk around the old ruins and absorb the atmosphere of history. This is what Michal does. He'll pick vegetables from farmers' fields and boil them.'

'Maybe he'll sit under a rock and live off fresh air.'

Stan chose to ignore my irony. We still met up at the lock gate every Friday, each time without counting how many weeks had passed. It became our weekly meetup spot, and we might only stop a few minutes and then go into the city centre, or rather back to the city centre, and have a few pints with Stan's workmates.

Stan peered down at the curds of green on the water. 'Are there fish in this canal? Could we bring a rod next time?'

'For fuck's sake Stan.'

It was a reasonable job, and reasonable to want it. My degree was a long time ago now. My career path had been unsettled for a few years, it was time for a job with responsibility and prospects.

This is the attitude I had practised for the interview. The three faces sat opposite me across the table. I had no fear, no embarrassment now. These three men and their three bottles of mineral water had their allotted place in the world. My replies pleased them. Their scepticism was allayed, they could see my head was screwed on the right way.

The chief security officer ran through the schedule of duties. I would have to remember a long list of telephone numbers, would that pose any difficulty? And I would have to greet all kinds of people at the gate and say hello by name, even the director himself. No problems recalling names and faces?

Only a few months before my inner self would have cringed like a pinched worm. And they would have spotted this, these beefy-faced suited men, they can tell when someone is faking it. They might have no inkling what else goes on in a person's mind, but they can latch on to that.

Here, he said, is the map of the route. Each hour you have to turn this electronic key. And here is the location of the phones which link directly to the garda station. One week of night shifts every three weeks. Are you comfortable working night shifts?

They had no interest in knowing who I was or what I thought. They just wanted to know if I could do the job. And equally any of the three men opposite could be anyone at all inside, as wrathful as Kaczynski or as silent as Michal.

I felt I had reached an understanding. If you will allow me to play the security guard, then I will allow you to play the man in a suit with no rancour and no envy.

'It's nothing too complicated. Not for someone with a degree,' he finished. I could not tell from his tone if this was heartiness or irony.

'Tell me,' I said, 'what age were you when you first met him?'

'We were five or six.'

I was at a loss for how to picture this.

'What was he like then?'

'Our parents knew each other. I remember my mother saying, go and play with Michal. And my father saying, let him play with whoever he wants to. There was some social awareness going on there, Michal's family being shop owners. I don't actually remember if he was silent then.'

He unfolded a compartment from the wallet which he had begun to carry with him everywhere. 'I have a photograph of him.'

'What, here with you?'

I took the creased rectangle from his fingers. The colours had a greenish tint, a broad white border around the image. Communist Poland was always a decade behind in technology. The tacky patina stuck to my fingers. Six smiling teenagers, arms arranged awkwardly at their sides and on each others' shoulders. It was hard to single him out, but there he was, grinning, big-jawed, looking straight into the lens. Head straight.

'We used to skip off from school. We were too young to drink then, we'd go down to the fortifications at the lake. I remember once he said to me *I am a decadent. All I want to do is get through life annoying as few people as possible.*'

I felt queasy and wanted away from this sodden canal air. It was pointless to keep coming here.

'Why are you carrying that photo around anyway?'

'No reason.'

'You do have a reason.'

He took the photo back. 'His parents were ordinary people, they didn't understand him and just accepted it. They did their duty and fed him and clothed him. Michal was sure about that legal point. The flat belonged to society, you know, the apartment was assigned by the communist authorities of the time. He had a legal right to live there.'

I pictured him as a spider, feeding and growing in a

room on his own. Eyes of haematite, dark glinting facets. The angles in his jaw. Feeding and pacing, his long tight-jointed legs, from the window to the bolted door. Inhaling and exhaling through his nostrils. Taking the world in through the eyes.

'He won't change. There's no helping him.'

'He doesn't need us to help him,' said Stan. 'He just needs us to believe he's for real.'

I went up to the desk in the multiplex and told them in a Polish accent that I'd lost my loyalty card. I might have lost it two weeks ago, I said, and gave her Michal's name. You last used it three months ago, she said, and told me the film I supposedly had seen. She said she could issue a replacement if I brought in my passport and a passport photo. Then she checked with the girl working alongside and said that actually no, a replacement wasn't possible since there was only two weeks left before the expiry date.

I felt like I had uncovered a terrible truth, and wanted to tell Stan immediately, contact the gardai, finally get things moving. Somebody out there must know what had happened to him. Then I got home and made tea and checked my rota for the next day and it all seemed less significant. I told Stan anyway the next time we met up, and we agreed we should do something. At the very least contact Michal's mother.

Stan got hold of her number and spoke to her on the phone. She hadn't heard from Michal in over four years. She said it was good to hear that we had run into him, that this was happy news and brightened her day. She said if we met him again, to tell him to ring her, that his old mother would welcome a call.

One time I tried to broach the question, of how he actually did it, to leave no trace behind. But Stan spun another of his shadow-fables involving a winding road and cottage, black coffee and a herb garden. Michal was becoming a talisman to hang in the hallway, to bring out a frisson when you touch it occasionally and whisper, *I believe*.

Stan flew regularly to Warsaw for meetings. He got a good laugh out of being introduced to his Polish counterparts as "Stan the Dublin promotions man". After listening to their shaky English for a few moments he'd launch into colloquial Polish. The change in atmosphere, he said, was always amazing. But it wasn't wise to keep up the ruse for too long. A couple of sentences about the weather and it was laughs all round. Stretch it a little further and these businessmen would treat him with suspicion for ever after. Fear and dread of The Spy runs deep in Poland.

I called at his apartment the night before he moved back to Poland. We were going to hit the town to mark the occasion. We planned on going through the trendiest pubs in Temple Bar.

Several packed boxes stood at the end of his bed. Stan said he'd be back in Dublin in a couple of months to bring home the rest of his things. I offered to keep the boxes at my place. Why pay rent for an empty apartment for a couple of months and maybe even longer? Anyway, it would take the luggage allowance of a half dozen flights to bring all that lot back to Poland. 'Let's get a taxi and bring it to my place.'

That was how I found out he'd bought the apartment some time ago and was keeping it as an investment.

There was one time at work I saw a manager carrying filing boxes and books from his car into the building. When I saw him coming out the doors a third time I approached and asked if I could help. The back seat and boot were crammed with boxes. It wasn't a small car either.

'I can hardly ask the secretary,' he confided. When we were done he tried to slip me twenty euro. It was an awkward moment; he just wanted to say thanks and instead I was waving off his money like he was trying to buy me.

The next day he stopped the car and chatted to me through the window of the security hut. He asked if I needed a laptop at all, that he was dumping one from the office that was only a couple of years old. I was delighted, of course. After that he would occasionally drop things off: table lamps, digital weighing scales, even a set of kitchen knives. Other managers too began to give me things; spare samples from their product range or unwanted executive gifts. I got a side of smoked salmon from a manager who didn't like fish.

'Cheers,' I'd say, without overdoing it on the thanks. People don't like it if you thank them too much. Some of the stuff was a hassle to carry home, I don't think it occurred to them that I didn't have a car. No, it didn't occur to them.

I stayed in that dive on the North Circular for too long, putting money aside each month for a deposit. The neighbourhood got more run-down with every year. Each weekend night I could hear music hammering until the small hours. The guards frequently turned up in several vans to break up these house parties. Heroin addicts became a common sight. Something attracted them to that stretch of street. My flat was only a ten minute walk from the Phoenix Park, the largest city park in Europe, and fifteen minutes to the centre in the opposite direction. That should have set it in one of the most sought-after neighbourhoods. But Dublin is a strange patchwork of so-called good areas and scummy areas, and reputation trumps reality.

From the moment I dropped a mention that I was "in the market" the managers never left off the subject. Every time they slowed down for the barrier they'd nod and ask how the search was going. The house buying was like something I could have in common with them, we could talk about it on level ground. I got sound advice on mortgage rates and recommendations of solicitors. After all that talk, I would have felt a right fraud if I hadn't finally made a decision.

It has no balcony and no view like Stan's. The complex is only about ten years old, but already feels like a building from a different generation. The main door buzzer doesn't work, the corridors smell of damp carpet. Some of the residents haven't pay the maintenance fee in years, as I found out much later, and the management company has cut back on services.

I get on best with the managers. Data-entry clerks and office assistants are always too ready to show their authority. Not that there are many of those, it seems to be mainly managers in this place. Product managers, marketing managers, brand managers, communications managers, all the variations. You'd wonder who actually does the hard work if it's only managers doing their managing. I hear there's a Polish manager with one of the companies. I haven't met him yet but I'll give him a surprise when I come out with a few words in Polish.

I have seen him! Today I saw him, the hermit of Grodgoszcz, the one who holds his silence. I was strolling through the Jervis shopping mall in the city centre, trying to make a Saturday afternoon pass quickly.

Burrowing through a crowd of thousands saps the vital energy. I read somewhere that each new face costs a toll of stress on the nervous system. Friend or foe, our subconscious is forced to make instant assessments. So many so quickly left me exhausted.

A tightness in my head, pinch of warm blood at the backs of my eyes. Twice-filtered air with the taste of carpet. A multitude of women pecked at the racks of clothes and discarded half-open packs to one side. Reducing the place to a comfortable level of disorder. I thought of peasant women at an outdoor market in some place I used to live.

I took the escalator and a humming rose from the metal step and the walls around me. I was cocooned inside my hangover and the buzzing sound wove textures around me. It was a good place to be.

He smiled at me, a thin man with tanned bony features, and raised his eyebrows. This perplexed me. If I were that way paranoid I would have imagined he was testing my reaction. Then I noticed he was staff, and thought maybe he wanted to sell me something. He turned momentarily to one side, to lay down a jumper he'd been folding.

'! Michal', I said, the "Silent" swallowed back down my throat.

'Geoff, it's good to see you.' He swung his hand down slow and gripped mine. I stared in incomprehension, unable to connect this figure with the Michal of memory. It was the neck. He held his head straight now. I had never seen his nose and eyebrows from this angle.

'You work here?'

'Yes,' he said lazily. A metal rectangle pinned on his shirt read *Floor Manager*.

'That's pretty good,' I said.

'It's okay.'

'It's been a long while. Michal.' I thought my perplexed tone said enough, but he just nodded. 'Where did you go to? Were you here in Ireland?'

'Most of the time, yes. Not doing much. Then I started here.' A short Chinese girl glided behind us and prodded him. She walked on a few steps and swivelled around. Turned her black droplet eyes on him. He held an open palm towards her. She let out an indignant sound and moved on, her feet paddling her forwards. Michal voiced a string of twangy syllables at her retreating figure.

'You speak Chinese?'

'Vietnamese actually. She's trying to teach me.' She called back some equally twangy words and was gone.

'Is she your girlfriend?'

He pursed his lips, his cheeks forming flat facets, let his head drop in a flicker of the old Michal. 'Yes, she's my girlfriend.'

'How did you end up here?' I raised my hands to comprehend the clothes racks and display aisles.

'I have always worked in a clothes shop.'

I had to laugh at this. An evasion by telling the truth.

'But hey – what about Stan? How is he?' Michal asked.

'I haven't heard from him in ages. He's back in Poland now.'

'Yes, so I heard.'

'You were talking to him?'

'Not recently. You know he lives in Warsaw now. He seems to be a big cheese in his company, goes on flights abroad all the time.' Michal laughed softly and looked back at the customer service desk. A queue was forming.

The ordinary way Michal spoke had nudged me into replying in an equally everyday tone. I was slipping into the easy rhythm of casual conversation, the kind of boilerplate chat you can exchange with anyone. But this was Michal before me, the man at the bottom of the canal.

'You seem different now. More talkative.' He did not visibly react. 'You were *different* when I last met you. When you disappeared. Lost contact.'

He nodded slowly, creased the planes of his cheek with the knuckles of one hand. A brunette in the shattered black-on-white pattern passed close by. She muttered something about the hectic pace.

'I am different from that time. Yes.'

I felt that I should stop, that I had no right to push at the bounds of sense like this.

'You wanted to get away from everybody. You were keen on something like a shepherd job.'

He released a nod of acknowledgement. 'I didn't believe that people had anything inside.'

There is no possible response to words such as these.

Since I was not going to speak, he did.

'What are you working at yourself?'

'I'm a security guard at Ovis distribution.'

'Are you ... happy doing that?'

'Of course. Why wouldn't I be?'

He shrugged, shook his head. 'The Vietnamese are a great people,' he remarked, apropos of nothing. 'The only third world country to defeat a superpower. What they had to live through. Their history is amazing, the stories I've heard from them.'

'Have you been there?'

'I'm going in a few months. I have to learn more of the language before I go. It's a crazy difficult language, it's got six tones, you know?'

'You're going there for a holiday?'

'I might stay a while. Maybe a whole year, see how it goes.'

'Will you work in a clothes shop there?'

Michal laughed. 'So many questions. I don't know. Maybe I need a change from clothes.' Another staff member passed and exchanged a speedy communication of article numbers and thumb jerks. 'They'll be on to me. Listen, how about meeting up for a pint on Friday evening?'

'Grand,' I said.

'How about TP Smiths across the road? About eight, would that be all right?'

I took the escalator back down to the crowded streets.

At the back of my mind I felt that I had been on some important business which the encounter with Michal had interrupted. I wandered round for a while, wondering what that might have been. I stopped at a bookshop and bought a book on the history of the Vietnam war from the Vietnamese perspective. The day had split in two and I no longer thought about my headache or what had gone wrong the night before.

On the night shift later I drank too much instant coffee and saw shadows subside from the corner of my eye. The executives waited for me to hand them the right keys and their eyes seemed to focus on the steel pen in my pocket. Perhaps they thought I would stab them.

I took out the pen and hid it in the bottom drawer, and when I closed it the timber edge took the skin off the side of my thumb. I took out the pen again and made a time chart stretching over the last few years. I tried to fill in a significant event that occurred in each month. I could make a continuous chain of seven non-empty boxes before I was stumped. Stan had left Dublin just before Christmas. Two and a half, three and a half years ago. Then it was close on a year before that when we met Michal in the cinema. There were long blanks in my chart. I pinned the sheet on the noticeboard in my hut and during the night I filled in extra events, but they were mainly bullshit things like training sessions at work.

For three days I woke with the enigma and breathed it, and at night grappled in loops that wound ever further from sleep. I didn't try to solve the enigma, I didn't know what questions to ask. I simply felt out of sorts, couldn't concentrate, and tried to think what might be bothering me, and thought again of Michal. I sat in my hut and read the book on Vietnam, and thought of myself, and how I seemed to be outside of all histories.

At work I made several small slip-ups, but nothing that any manager noticed. For three days it did not occur to me to ring Stan. The idea came to me during the night watch, and seemed an overwrought thing to do. The years that had elapsed formed a barrier between us. I could not imagine contacting him out of the blue.

But it's normal, my reason told me, to ring an old friend, even if you have not heard from him for a long time. In the daylight I became more confident that this was the right thing to do, and that any barrier existed only in my mind.

I rooted through the presses at home where I throw my bills and junk mail. I found a letter from him, but it had no telephone number. His address was on the back of the envelope, as the law requires, but he had surely moved several times since then.

There was one possible route to get in contact with him. I looked up Romeo's company, and there on the company website was a profile shot of Romeo with his phone number underneath. I carried out a ridiculous array of delaying actions – cups of coffee, dialogue rehearsals, practising Polish idioms – before I finally lifted the phone and dialled the number. Romeo stuttered with amazement to hear me, I don't know why. His English had improved greatly, he had a pitch-perfect American accent. He wanted to talk about the state of the economy and the number of Poles in Ireland,

and Irish coming to Poland. I was not prepared for such a high-speed exchange of information.

He was no longer in regular contact with Stan, but gave me a couple of numbers to try. Finally my search was reaching a conclusion.

'Geoff, is it really you?'

'It is. Listen Stan. You know who I met? Silent Michal.'

'Yes?'

'He's working in a department store. Kind of assistant manager.'

Silence.

'And he's getting on fine, he was talking to me for a long while, he has a girlfriend, he goes on holidays abroad ...'

'He talks more freely now, yes?'

'He does, yes.'

'I can tell you something about Silent Michal.'

'I'm listening.'

'Some time ago, back in Ireland, he saw a television programme about a doctor who cures people with communication disorders. Very rare disorders, and he was some sort of genius in dealing with them. Michal sat down and wrote a letter to this doctor. He addressed it to the hospital mentioned, in the states, Colorado actually. The doctor wrote back, he actually wrote back to Michal's address in Dublin, the doctor who'd been on television. And he told him I can't diagnose you or assess you, but here is the name of a Polish doctor who works in the same field, that he had worked with this doctor and so on.

'You see Michal said in the letter he was studying at college in Ireland. You know, he was ashamed to be a Pole working as a cleaner in Ireland – as if the doctor would give a damn who or what he was. So he said he was a student temporarily in Ireland. Some of this he told me back in Grodgoszcz, some of it I heard from people.

'So, Michal looked up the address of this Polish doctor. Didn't send any letter, didn't ring him in advance, he just got on a flight to Warsaw and straight onto an overnight train. Eighteen hours travel non-stop. He got there in the middle of the night and slept for six hours on a bench. This was Szczecin, it's full of parks. He woke up at seven, had a shave in a fountain, combed his hair, and knocked at the door. He had all his savings in his pocket, just in case. A little kid opened the door, stood there looking at him. And Michal said, *I speak very little. Would the doctor be interested in me?*

'That's how it began. The doctor did some tests on him, booked him into a hospital, Michal stayed a while in a hostel, then more computer scan tests in Warsaw, back to Dublin, then Szczecin again. He had a device put on his head to record brain waves while he talked. Actually I don't know about the money situation – maybe there was no charge because it was a test of brand new treatments. They located the problem. It was something related to autism, completely different, but that's the best comparison. There's a structure in the brain, and people with the normal version want to talk with others, but Michal had a faulty version. They did some brain treatments and he began to be able to chat like normal. As normally as anyone else.'

There was a silence as I waited for Stan to say something conclusive. But he had finished.

'Good news,' I said.

'Good news,' Stan replied.

I fried a few chicken skewers and ate them with bread and tomato. It was best to be there just before eight in case Michal was on his own. TP Smiths wasn't a good choice of pub; it gets crowded on a Friday evening.

I sat on the floor with my back against the sofa and ate. Music for the news headlines came through the wall from the apartment next door. I hated listening to the news through the wall. A couple of phrases would come through clearly and get my attention so I'd start to listen, but just as it was making sense the words would lose their edges to become a fuzzy mumble. It was better not to hear it at all.

When people hear what my mortgage is it sparks off a big drama of indignation. *Fifteen hundred for a one-bedroomed apartment?* They go off on a political tirade patched together from the latest newspaper opinion articles. *You're being sacrificed instead of bondholders* and so on. It can be nice to feel such a participant in the life of the nation. I'm a minor *cause célèbre* among the execs who like to stop for a smoke before going inside. If they saw the size of this place their indignation would pop a blood vessel. It's a three-quarter size version of a typical one-bedroomed apartment. But in Ireland no-one knows the actual square-metre size of their apartment. People view an apartment and say things like *it looks a bit small* without imagining there is a way to measure the size.

The clock approached ten past seven. I closed my eyes to get rid of the pain behind them and opened them again and it was a quarter past. Tension is another experience and another existence, and also worth living through. I dared myself to go and not to go and couldn't think of anything much until the hands crept up towards eight. It was too late then. If he was on his own he'd have left. Or he could be with workmates, regular Friday evening drinks. They stay on until closing time.

It wasn't until eleven that it was definitely and finally too late. I washed the plates, sat down to read for an hour before bed. But I'd missed my evening walk and didn't feel the day was over. I went down the stairs quietly and headed for the Phoenix Park. I stuck to the gas-lit path along the main road. At night the deer wander all over the park into the areas they avoid by day.

It was late when I got back, only five hours sleep to look forward to. But the kind of job I have, sometimes it's better to be half asleep. The time passes more quickly, and I actually feel more observant, because I'm not thinking at all, only watching. And that's what they pay me to do.

Contempt

The perspective of evolution

At break they shake the lime dust off their jeans and troop out the gates. They are in jubilant mood. Drivers in traffic peer through their windscreens at these workers from all parts of the world.

The group of men splits up at the corner. Some go to the Centra, some for the pub lunch, and some to the chipper.

'No brains,' says Marcos. 'They spend their money on booze and now another ten or fifteen on lunch every day.' Marcos always brings a flask of coffee and bag of apples. He buys bread rolls and cheese slices in the shop.

On this day Ruben goes to the Centra with him. They

sit back against the ledge outside. The concrete is dirty and sticky with dried liquid. Junkies and drinkers will take their places here later in the day.

Marcos digs his thumbs into the sides of a bread roll and splits it. He stuffs ham and cheese into the gap and squeezes the roll flat.

'No brains,' he says. 'They smoke dope all day and don't think about what they're doing. They drag timbers from the partitions without stripping the wires first. It takes hours to pull them apart. It's no wonder Bungalow treats them like morons. You have to tell them to do every little thing.'

And yet Marcos laughs with them at all their silly jokes. He chats and laughs and they slap him on the back. He copies their accent and their curse words to amuse them.

'In my country if you don't have brains you go zilch.' He flipped the flat of his hand downwards. 'You need brains or you go extinct.'

In recent weeks Ruben has begun to regard the building site from the perspective of evolution. Some survive, some adapt, some fail. Other people don't constantly have such trains of thought, he feels sure.

Ruben is thirsty after the cheese roll. He goes back inside to buy a litre of mineral water. A young man – Indian or Pakistani – stands behind the counter. He smiles when any customer approaches. Then his face goes blank as he wipes the counter and keeps himself occupied.

It's an easy job; he's inside out of the weather. You could feel envious, but only for a few seconds. Then contempt takes over.

'Pakistani,' affirms Marcos back outside. 'Those guys have brains.' But he doesn't say it in a tone of admiration. 'And you? Where are you from?'

Volunteers to a discipline

Three pallets, making a total of forty-eight bags of plaster, have been dumped onto a gravel heap. The bags have to be brought up to the sixth floor. If they queue a request to the crane it could be available within a couple of hours.

'Fuck the crane,' says Ruben. 'If we stand around waiting they'll only find some bullshit sweeping for us to do. If we do the bags we can do it at our own pace.'

'I don't know,' says Marcos, 'Maybe I'll stick with the sweeping.'

That leaves just Ruben and Eoin. Twenty-four bags each.

Ruben curls a hand around a bag, takes a breath. In a single motion he slides it onto one shoulder and straightens up. The bags have changed from a hundredweight to fifty kilos with the metric system. Fifty kilos is slightly heavier. This strikes Ruben as something of an anomaly. So many other things on the building site are becoming easier and safer. There are all sorts of regulations on training tickets and hard-toed boots. The gates to the site are covered with bright warning signs and lists of hazards. Yet the weight of bags has increased.

After a few round trips he has found a rhythm. Eight toddler steps to the doorway. Then the ascent. Two flights of stairs; a pause leaning against the door frame. Then another two flights, a pause, and the final two. He moves the last few metres in an extended fall, letting the bag tumble heavily on top of the others. The floor is clean and dry; it doesn't matter if the bags split. The drop area is alongside the stairwell. The adjacent rooms are bare, open to the wind. The glass exterior has not yet been put in place on the upper floors. The building is still a skeleton, held erect by six spines of reinforced concrete. Yellow and black warning tape flutters between the pillars.

Each time he makes a drop a plume of lime dust shoots up and engulfs him. He staggers out and gulps at the clear air. He can take as much time as he wants to catch his breath. He is out of sight up here.

He and Eoin each work at their own rhythm, but occasionally they meet at the top floor. They keep up a nonsense dialogue about the dangers of lime dust. 'I take off my socks at night. And in the morning they're standing up looking at me. My socks scare me.' And then: 'Did you ever notice the way the dust sets into little stones in your eyes? And then you have to pick them out?' And: 'Did you ever hear of dermatitis? That's the word I was looking for.'

Theory of mind

'Would I fuck,' says Eoin. Everyone has seen them lugging up the fifty-kilo bags of plaster, so they can afford to take a break for a couple of minutes. 'My ass would I prefer. Learning to count other people's money, that's all.' They

The black and white hero stops the wrong blonde on the street and gets a slap on the face. She falls sideways with laughter and then pushes herself back up straight, as though his leg is part of the couch.

The divisions of man

Robustus have wide chests and short legs. A red blush rises readily to their cheeks. They talk about football over mugs of tea and tip their heads back to drink to the dregs. The sound of their own voices makes them ashamed. Their eyebrows are bushy, and their pungent morality repels him.

Gracilus are slim, but graceless actually. They lurch along, ever watchful for who may harbour ill will against them. Lantern jaws, veins on the back of the hand, a runny nose: these are their features.

The first type is descended from forest dwellers, with a body evolved for dragging carcasses and turning a spade. The second loped with the wolf on the plains.

Marcos and Bungalow are Robustus, Eoin and the Chinese fellow are Gracilus. Since he started on this building site a month ago, every new worker has fallen into one or the other category. He hopes that someone soon will break the pattern.

Padding

'So they come around in white hats, we were all told to stop work. You, you and you come up here. I thought, this is it now. Jesus. Maybe I should pretend to speak no English. Where are you from? the man asks. Portugal, I say. OK, so name the most famous beer in Portugal. Me? I don't drink beer. I drink Coca-Cola. OK then. Tell me your favourite football team in Portugal. I don't watch football. Tennis. Golf, I play golf. He's fucking messing says the other guy. Fookin messin. It's true I play golf. What, he fuckin thinks we have no golf? All right then, all right he says. Tell me eight cities in Portugal. Eight? Lisbon, Oporto, Faro, Seville, ehh. Not Seville. Fuck it. I should have made cities up.' Marcos break into shakes of laughter. 'I should have made them up. Those Dublin guys didn't know any cities in Portugal. They know shite. They caught me out. OK, says the man. Now you tell me where you are really from. Which is it, Romania or Albania? Romania, I said. Do you know this boss is paying you below the legal minimum? Yes, I heard that. OK. What he's doing is illegal, it doesn't matter whether you have a visa or not. So the man was not police. He was from some organization. Someone called these guys in. One of the Irish workers, when they wanted to pay him the same amount as what we get. You tell again that you're from Portugal, and it will all go zilch, we can't help. And then he goes and asks the others, where are you from, where are you from. And they say Portugal, Portugal, Portugal. Because they are afraid. And he says, I can do nothing for you. You're pissing me off, you can all fuck off.'

Marcos grins like a schoolboy. The girls behind the sandwich counter love him. But today Marcos has a big problem. He has to arrange three weeks off in September.

He needs enough time for visits to cousins, a trip to the mountains, and a couple of weddings.

'September? That's three months away,' says Ruben.

'Sure. Time goes by quickly.'

Marcos tells about a slaughter festival out in the country, boar hunting, home-made log cabins built on patches of abandoned land. This is a man for whom the months on the building site fly by. Then for three weeks he will resume his real life.

It must be such a relief to be able to regard each day as mere padding of minutes and hours. The only obligation is to get a laugh out of it, make time pass quickly.

Things are different for Ruben. The days are not accumulating. There is no real life waiting at some future point. The burden of each day weighs on him.

Like a martyr

Ruben mounts the unplaned timber steps to the cabin door. He knocks and a voice calls him in. Every step, every scratch and sniffle, takes on a woody tone inside the small cabin.

'Take a seat, take a seat,' says the foreman, whom the workmen call Bungalow. 'Don't mind the mess here. As long as we have order on the outside, that's what matters. Here, here's your envelope. What I meant to say was, keep the helmets on whenever we have the architect or anyone from the company. See! You don't have it with you now, do you?'

'It's in the toilets, I can get it.'

'Whenever, whenever. Wear it as much as you can. Listen. It can be hard work here, but you can pace it out. Call in the crane, that sort of thing. No need to be lifting everything by yourself. Do you get me?'

'Yeah.'

'You do, do you? There's no need for anyone to be killing themselves, that's all I'm saying. You're taking on every bit of hard work out there. Like a – like a martyr or something.' The foreman laughs, but stops when Ruben does not share in the laugh.

'I don't mind work.'

'Well fair play to you. You're a happy man. Grand. So. There was something here.' He searches among the papers on the table. 'You can do a training course in crane operation. One day a week. You have the Leaving Cert, don't you? One day a week for six months and you're a qualified crane op. We cooperate with this crowd, we have an arrangement.'

'No, I won't bother.'

'Your wages would still be the same.'

'No thanks.'

The foreman nods slowly, as though nothing could surprise him any more. An immense Gantt chart, illustrating the project schedule, stretches behind him on the wall.

Big problems

Marcos's shoulders heave in chuckles before he can answer.

'I told him, look. Look, I said. I need three weeks off

in September. No, he says, no way. It's for family reasons, I tell him. He looks at me. What family reasons? OK, it's like this. I'm getting married to a girl in my village. Then you should see him! He jumps up from the desk. Good man, good man, he says and shakes my hand. Good fuckin luck to you.' Marcos repeats this with gusto. 'Good fuckin luck to you. And then he gives me a look and says, hey, you told me you were not back in Romania for two years. And now you want to marry someone you haven't seen in two years? My family arranged it, I said. And he was all suspicious, Jesus, he's not stupid. Even though he's called Bungalow. But I just kept talking. I never seen this girl, I tell him. Not as a woman. The last time I saw her was when she was going to school and we all used to make fun of the girls. We used to sit on a ditch and shout kiss me kiss me. And then my family sent me a photograph of her and I said OK, she's very pretty, I'll come back and marry her. That's the stuff, he says, and he's slapping me on the back again. He's jumping around the room. That's the way to have it. Show me the photograph, he says. Is she hot stuff? Will you bring her over here? No, I said. My money here will buy us a little pig farm. When I work another year.'

Marcos stops to laugh again, cradling his lunch roll to stop the filling from shaking out. 'Oh Jesus, I'm in the shits so deep. Fair play to you, he says, give me a look at her. You must have a photograph of the sweetheart there in your pocket. And I said I'll bring it in tomorrow, no problem. And now I have to find a photograph. Fuck.'

'You can cut one out of there and hand it to him.'

Ruben indicates the top-shelf magazines just inside the Centra doors. Marcos leans over to see what he means and bursts into laughter. People stop on the other side of the street. 'There are often Romanian girls in them,' Ruben adds.

'And the wedding ring too, when I get back. Jesus, I have big problems. What about my Irish girlfriend? I can't be seen with her. Big problems, man.'

Trust

On the way back from lunch he crosses the Luas tracks at the back of a furniture store. It was here he met the Latvian girl some weeks ago. She was carrying a large olive rucksack with orange braids trailing from it. She approached him to ask if he knew of any jobs.

'Jobs?' he replied, puzzled, 'what kind of job?' It was nine o'clock on a Tuesday evening on the outskirts of the city centre. All offices and shops were shut. She said a few words in a foreign language, then changed to another language. He shook his head, I speak only English.

'You can try the job centre in the morning.'

She took out her map and he pointed out where they were, the line of the quays, and the direction back to the city centre. She knew nothing. Not O'Connell Street, not the Liffey. Nothing.

'Do you have a place to stay? You can stay in my place, I have a spare room.'

At the next pedestrian crossing she got a few steps in front of him and he watched the neat bud of her rear swivel.

If he'd seen it earlier he would never have asked her home. But there she was now, walking with him. Coatless, dressed in a pleated skirt that flapped about her knees. After some time he indicated that he would carry her rucksack for her. They walked under the overstretched arms of cranes and past red and white hoardings. Building sites all around. The dust underfoot was the same lime dust that he worked in all day.

Perhaps he should not be so surprised that she trusted him. People trust each other all the time. It's human nature. And he was, despite everything, a trustworthy person.

As she explained much later, she had been misdirected to that part of the city. She had expected to find a particular shop, a Latvian shop, which had a list of jobs in the window.

Back at the flat he made tea and toast. When he turned on the television she was content to look at it for the rest of the evening. She tuned into some foreign channel and watched it at high volume.

After midnight he went to the bedroom and pushed the bed over against the wall. Now there was a wide space the length of the room. He swept it clean and rolled out several spare blankets. He stuffed some T-shirts together to form a pillow.

I'm going to bed now, he said to her. You can sleep where you are on the couch or on the bed inside there. Whatever you prefer.

In his half-sleep on the floor he was aware of her in the next room. She had at last turned the television to silent but the flickers came through the door jamb. He drifted off thinking of a pornographic film he often watched. At

times during the night the cold woke him and he pulled in
a stray limb closer under the blankets. Once he woke up
filled with anxiety and sat up and looked at the bed. The
quilt was humped over. She was sleeping peacefully.

On the run

'What the fuck are you playing at?' Eoin lets his brush
drop hard on the concrete. 'Who are you trying to fool?'
    'Nobody.'
    'What are you up to telling me you're a Russian?'
    'I didn't say that.'
    'You're fucking Irish. Pretending to be foreign.'
    'I never pretended. To who?'
    Ruben is astonished at this attack from nowhere. All he
wanted to do was work quietly on the building sites with
no attention from anybody.
    'You distinctly said something about being Russian.'
    'Why would I say that when I'm not Russian?'
    'You fuckin said it. You let on to be. Your accent and
all. You've no Dublin accent. No accent at all. Where are
you really from?'
    'I'm from here.'
    'What fuckin "here"?'
    'This city.'
    'We all thought you were foreign. What's your second
name then?'
    'Why do you want to know?'
    Eoin eyes him cautiously. 'You're on the run, are you?'
he says quietly. 'You're hiding out.'

Eoin is being perfectly serious. And in a way, is he not right?

Sudden and absurd

'No,' he says. 'My name is –.' And he gives his name.

'Sure,' says Eoin, 'that could be any old name you're telling me. How come you're here on a building site? You didn't do this all your life.'

'How do you know?'

'I just fuckin know.'

'I was a student at UCD. I was doing economics and left it.' As he speaks he pictures facades of alternating plate glass and dolphin-green panels against a low grey sky. 'I just got fed up with it. Didn't want to work in an office.'

This is the truth as someone outside himself would see it.

'I knew you were a college kid,' says Eoin. 'You had that educated look about you, thinking all the time.'

'Fuck off, I left college years ago now.'

'A fuckin college boy. Getting your hands rough.'

'I'd fuckin work you under the table.'

Eoin stops and bursts into laughter. It rings out of him like a spirit of joy has squeezed his soul. Ruben laughs too, at the suddenness, the absurdity of it all.

How it is

If he had to explain how it is – and there is no one to explain to – he would say that he is only what he thinks.

He has stripped away things so that he is only the thoughts that run through his head.

His place of birth, the colour of his skin, the features on his face, his dead father, living mother, his grades at school, teachers half-remembered, the house he used to live in, this old city he inhabits, his money bundled in a drawer, the few people who know him – none of this matters. Nor what he will become in the future, or where he is going, or what his plans are.

Others – Marcos, Eoin – are folded into their lives. They do not fully own themselves.

But for him, being each moment only what he thinks, there is nothing to fall back on.

He is, he realizes, an impossible person.

Events in the day

The phone card habit started a few days after she arrived. She had borrowed the spare key and gone out with her coat on and a tiny rucksack on her back. An hour later he had gone out to get a litre of milk at the local shop. He saw her in a telephone box as he passed. She was talking animatedly while the rain streamed against the glass. He bought the items in the shop and returned past the phone box. She was still there. Her lips were not moving, she was listening now. She took the weight off her feet by wedging her elbows against the side panels.

The phone in the flat was blocked for outgoing calls, but could be used for freephone numbers. He went back to the shop and bought a call card, the kind that gives you a sixteen-digit code to punch in before dialling anywhere in the world.

When she came back he showed her how to use it. At this early stage she regarded him with an intensity that was not his due. Soon enough she got the card to work and was talking on the phone. She glanced warily at him and lowered her voice, though he could not understand a word she was saying.

To defuse her wariness, he decided to intrude as little as possible on her life. He would shut himself in the bedroom and read about the origins of man. He would cook himself some food without asking if she wanted any. He would never ask her to lower the volume on the television.

A couple of times a week he brought home a call card and left it lying on the table to avoid implications. She would tap the numbers and speak.

It did not seem to him there were enough events in the day to fill two hours of conversation. What kind of life is that, to do nothing all day and then talk about it for hours?

Her glance

She is writing a letter when he gets home, her eyebrows as sharp and abstract as the curvilinear script on the loose pages. She snatches the pages from the table and folds them over.

'I can't read it anyway,' he protests. 'I can't even read our address at the top.' He stops, conscious of the 'our'.

He watches her, head bent over the black letters. Do

Latvians write in Cyrillic? He can't tell from looking at the handwriting.

Although the language and script are foreign he supposes that she writes of very ordinary things. That the weather is bad, she is doing fine, she will get a job soon.

There is a contempt which rages, but it would never alight on her. How could it, when she can sit quietly for hours accepting his presence? Or at moments push him aside with a look that is the mirror of what burns him inside?

He wishes he could borrow the quick violence of her glance.

In the small hours

Later, he pushes in a DVD he has borrowed. It is another early Hollywood classic. She likes these films and can copy the accent perfectly. She replays the parts she doesn't understand first time. He repeats the actors' lines just to hear her shush him. Just to feel her elbow jab him.

The long days of lifting and digging have tautened his muscles. Every movement of his arms and fingers is accompanied by a pleasant feeling of tiredness. He feels invulnerable. The thrum of his bloodstream extends from his palms to his nostrils to the backs of his eyes. It tingles in his scalp.

She jabs him; he opens his eyes and sits up straight. Sleep falls on him like a grace when he doesn't wish for it. Later it will not come so easily.

Sometimes he looks at her rather than at the screen.

When his legs lean against hers for too long she kicks them away.

At some point in the night he moves to the bedroom and falls exhausted on the sheets. When he turns on his side his arm presses against something solid and it falls to the floor with a thud. He sweeps his hand to push the remaining things onto the floor: another book, his work jeans and heavy belt.

In the small hours she lies down alongside him. His hand moves across her stomach. She clasps it there. Some time later she curls against him. At times she is asleep, at time he is. At a certain hour they gain access to a place that will remain unacknowledged in the daylight hours.

'Do you think I am an object waiting for you?' she whispers fiercely in his ear. 'Do you?'

An object? How could she think that? Even when sitting still, unaware of him in the room, even then she glows with energy. She is the only thing in any room she's ever in.

Only with difficulty can he imagine her as an object. A fifty kilo sack, to be thrown over a shoulder or split with the edge of a shovel.

The photo

Rain starts as he passes the high railings of the King's Inns. On Brunswick Street the one-way traffic grinds slowly. Then a left turn at Blackhall Place.

Water runs in the gutters. The sky hangs low, drizzle drifts against him. If all that liquid were petrol, just one spark would ignite an apocalypse of fire.

Usually the concrete is delivered every morning ready-mixed, but today the lorry will be delayed until the afternoon. They are assigned to make a few barrowfuls to keep the concrete gang going.

Marcos opts to manage the mixer. He holds the open mouth of the drum down to take in shovelfuls of gravel. He keeps his feet well clear of the slurry that has accumulated around the base.

Ruben doesn't mind taking on the role of standing ankle-deep in wet cement and shovelling. It's tough work, but it warms his muscles. He begins to shake off the morning lethargy.

Building site rules mean they have to go outside the gates for their cigarette break.

'Here,' Ruben says, 'I got you a photo.' He shows Marcos a small white-bordered rectangle. He cut it from a strip of five that were tucked away behind some perfume bottles in the bathroom. A bad place to keep them: they were already curling from the damp. She had cut off the single one she had needed and forgotten them.

Marcos holds the photo and matches it with another from his pocket. Oddly enough, the two girls are broadly similar. In Marcos's photo the girl is smiling.

'Hey, which one should I marry?' says Marcos. 'Is this your girlfriend?'

There is an involuntary pause. 'No.'

'You don't seem sure.' Marcos finds this hilarious. 'Where did you get the photo then?'

'There's this girl. She doesn't have any place so she's

staying for a while.'

'Does she pay you sex instead of rent?' Marcos giggles at his own joke, but it's not his style; he's just copying the building site humour of the others.

An absence

She is not at home when Ruben gets back. He showers and dries himself, conscious of an absence. The feeling disappears when he gets out the pot to boil himself some rice. Lately he has thought of going vegetarian. He feels the contamination of meat, how it clogs his insides. He sorts through jars of ready-meal mixes and sachets of spice.

Again the feeling of something missing. He goes back to the bathroom. Her jars of cosmetics are gone from the mirror shelf. Her olive-green rucksack is not in its usual place by the sofa, nor in the bedroom. He opens the drawer he had indicated she could have to herself. A few tourist booklets and restaurant vouchers.

He opens the drawer next to it. His bundles of wages are gone. Each Thursday for the past ten or eleven months he had thrown in another envelope. Whenever he needed cash he opened one and took out a few notes out.

The significance drains from things, as though an artery in the world has been severed. His ribs tighten in around his chest, crab claws pinching at his heart.

He sits at the table for a long time. Does she not know he is bound by no law no taboo no conventions? Did she mistake him for some solid citizen who will duly report the matter to the police? Did she understand so little of who he is?

It is sordid, so sordid, to be dragged into a vortex of hatred over money. He always thought that money was of no concern to him.

The city is not infinitely large. There are only a small number of districts where a new immigrant from Latvia would live or work. He tries to picture her walking the streets, smiling, clutching a handbag to herself.

He feels himself moved into position on a chessboard.

Behavioural modernity

There is no direct correlation between the date of origin of anatomically modern humans and the beginnings of typically human activities. Creatures physically identical to modern people lived without symbolic behaviour, without art or ornamentation, or ritual or burial. Evidence of these behaviours appears all at once in the archaeological record: hafted tools, beads, ochre, cave paintings.

In some regions these traces subsequently disappear again from the archaeological record. Humans, however, continued to live there. They just changed to a less complex way of living. These purely biological humans endured for tens of thousands of years.

In the crowd

Where previously he could get through only a few pages

in the course of a week, now he reads forty or fifty pages at a sitting. When he thinks about what he has read, his thoughts lose the quality that make them thoughts and become a headache. At times he sees that such books are intended for college kids and coffee tables, and that he is reading them the wrong way, with too much seriousness.

He stands up from the couch and a needle of pain stabs at the corner of one eye. He goes to the sink and splashes water on his face. His skin turns slimy, frog skin and frog eyes.

The quays are bustling with morning commuters. He selects a person at random. He walks in the same direction, keeping well behind, watching her head bob up and down in the crowd, subjecting her to a blast of intense scrutiny. After that she can be allowed to wander ahead out of sight. He knows that even in a crowded shopping mall he will be able to scan the scene in one gulp and she will jump out from the field of vision. The angle of an elbow, the sway of a hip, the colour of her handbag. Any detail will suffice.

The woman surges forward to catch a bus. He breaks into a jog, and steps on right behind her. She rummages through her handbag and begins to argue with the driver.

'Sorry,' says Ruben, 'how much are you short? Forty cent? Here.' He drops the coins in the chute and the driver taps out a ticket.

The woman glances over her shoulder. 'Wow, thanks,' she says. 'That's very good of you.'

'I hate having to carry change with me all the time.'

'I know, I know! And then I always only have two-euro

coins and have to get the little scrap of paper back.'

'The thing you're supposed to bring back.'

'I don't even know where to go with them! I went to the shop and they wouldn't take them.'

'There's only one place and then you have to wait in a queue.'

'Wouldn't you just know.'

She was only a test, and now that test is over. He chats with the ease that others have, because for a moment of respite he is just another in the crowd.

The past

He takes up position on the steps of the old motor tax office on Chancery Street. The wide spaces relax his eyes. He can keep watch and yet remain unnoticed, just another dosser hanging around. There's enough space for everyone, the drinkers don't bother him.

But on this day there is some commotion around the courts. Gardaí on the beat pass every five minutes. People with banners gather at the railings opposite, blue and white vans pull up.

He leaves the steps and follows Abbey Street as far as T.P. Smiths, the heroin trail, turns up Jervis Street to Parnell Street, and stands outside the cinema. Then back again.

He has no feelings of hope or anxiety. He wishes only to put in his time keeping watch. Next comes a row of Asian restaurants. Chinese couples pass him, hand in hand, smiling. Of all the newcomers in this town, the Chinese are most at ease. They are born for city living.

He must keep walking.

He must make one more round and then he can relax. He will go back to the flat for bread and jam. Money is running low.

Someone is pointing a finger at him. He stops.

'Ruben!'

He stares at this intrusion.

'Ruben, it's you isn't it?'

The man is so certain that Ruben cannot help but agree. This is someone he used to know well. They sat at adjacent desks for two years. The name escapes him.

'I was just saying to meself that looks like Ruben. Very like Ruben.'

'Well. I'd recognise you too.'

'Of course you would. Jeez. Though by the look of you, there was a gap of ten seconds where you didn't have a clue who I was. Am I right? Eh? Am I right?' The man laughs. It is a familiar slagging laugh. They once climbed over a wall into the IDA premises and found several footballs and a genuine baseball bat. His name is – it will come to him later.

'Am I right?'

'Yeah, I just wasn't expecting to run into anyone.'

'What are you up to now?'

'Just around town. Shopping and stuff.'

'Here, you got into UCD didn't you?'

'Yeah. That's a while ago.'

'You must have finished by now? What am I saying, it's years ago.'

'Yeah. I left it.'

'You left? You mean you didn't finish?'

'No. Got fed up with it.'

'You mean you quit?' The man's mouth hangs slack as though this information from someone he has not seen in twelve years is of great concern to him. Ruben knows he can just walk on without saying another word. It is within his power.

'Sort of quit, sort of failed,' he says.

'Jays. I hadn't heard that. And you used to be good at school. You were one of the swots. You were. Old Quigley was keen to get you to go on to uni. The old fucker.' He laughs. 'You got into economics, didn't you?'

'Economics and finance, yeah.'

'Fair play to you. That was tough. Tougher than it is these days with everyone going on to college.'

'Hmm.'

'Though I thought you'd be running a bank by now, eh? I thought you'd be on Wall Street by now.'

Ruben concedes a snort of a laugh. Keane. The man's name is Keane.

'What do you do yourself?' Ruben asks.

The man unzips the top of his Adidas jacket. 'I'm wearing a shirt and tie under here. I look after accounts for a chain of petrol stations.'

'You're an accountant?'

'No-oo. Jays, some feckin economist you are.' He laughs scornfully. 'Account manager, you know? I chase down money that's owing and all that.'

Ruben is looking up and down the road.

'Here I'll let you go then,' says the man called Keane.

'Yeah, I was on my way somewhere.'

'Good luck so.'

'Good luck.' He raises a hand and walks on. He walks with a spring in his stride to show he is going somewhere. A Chinese man is sweeping the section of pavement outside a restaurant. He sweeps in a way no Irishman would sweep.

Her

And walking out from the department store, it is her. He veers away from the sight and goes into a nearby convenience shop. He stares at the magazines on the rack and replays the scene in his mind. Those two seconds as she emerged, looking left and right to orient herself.

She did not look like someone who deserved harm. He feels the attraction of the easy option: to confront her in the street, shout at her like a common drunk.

Minutes have passed. She must be well down the street by now. He edges out of the shop and looks up and down. She is nowhere outside. He reaches the end of the short street and doubles back. Time is passing. The radius of her possible location is dilating. He goes partway down each of the adjoining side streets. She might have gone into another department store. She might have headed directly for the nearest tram stop.

He completes a circuit and returns to the front of the department store where he first saw her. He has done all he could do. If he has lost her it does not matter much. What matters is to have made the effort.

She looked a very confident person as she emerged from the store. Not at all like when she had been in the flat with him, where she had not cared for stylish clothes, had worn no make-up, a slack and distant look to her face. I am not in your past, he thinks at her. You do not yet know who I am.

And there, gazing at a window display on the adjoining street, it is her. This time he walks slowly and tracks her from the corner of his eye. Something will happen soon, a conclusion will be reached. She strolls on, pausing at shop windows, pausing a moment where a busker plays a clarinet. Though the music to him is an arbitrary sequence of notes, to her it must be something different. She stops, stands in among the small crowd, listens closely.

Perhaps it will be sufficient to confront her with the truth of what she has done, so that it will no longer fester inside him. It's not punishment he wants, but to make her acknowledge.

She walks on and reaches the end of Mary Street, then on towards the old market area. There are people around, but not many. She walks past one narrow laneway opening, then another.

He swoops upon her.

'We have to talk.'

She looks at him, startled. 'What do you want?'

'This way.' He takes her by the upper arm to bring her down the lane. A convulsion passes through her.

'Let me go, you big fool.'

'Stop screaming. I know what you did. You. You thief.'

'I had to leave the house. Let me go. Let me go.'

Now she screams properly, a full-throated scream. He presses her against the wall.

Her hips, her narrow waist.

'Will you shut up and let me speak?' She twists her face away, refuses to even look at him. Another scream bursts from her.

He slams the side of her face to the wall. Her face stays there, under his palm, her scream choked off.

'You thought you'd get away with it,' he says. 'Just listen to me now.' And he begins to explain how things really are. How he lives ruthlessly and deliberately. But the words do not sound like his own, even now when the moment should be truly his.

He drops her and walks quickly away. The softness of her cheek is in his hands. The way her flesh yielded, and the surprising blood. He runs now, turns corners, reaches the wide streets. He needs somewhere quiet and turns down the small streets again. There is no one following, of course there isn't.

He crouches by a stone wall. It had felt like the beginning of an embrace when he had taken hold of her. Her arms, her soft side, her narrow chin. You big fool, she had said.

People glance at him and look away. He is in a laneway where many heroin addicts have crouched and vomited.

Other possibilities

In the moment when he confronted her there was only

confusion in her eyes. She did not have the look of someone facing due retribution.

He sees other possibilities now. She had Latvian friends. A man, or some men, might have been invited up into the flat. Or invited themselves up. She would have jabbered on about how she was going to find a job soon, and about this strange Irishman who shared the flat, his long hours on the building sites. They would have scanned around looking for what they could get.

She was naive. This was a girl who had followed a strange man home that first night. She talked to her mother for two hours on the phone every evening. Such a girl would not risk his vengeance. Someone else had come into the flat that day.

Fuck him, they would have laughed at her timidity. You owe him nothing, just walk out the door and keep walking.

What he is perceived to be

She knows where he lives. He must have understood this all along, but now the fact forces itself into his thoughts with increasing urgency. Someone might come for him, either the Gardaí or her own kind. Someone will come.

He packs his things into large tartan cargo bags. He packs all his clothes, even the grimy ones he intended to throw out.

He knows nothing of police techniques other than the usual procedures seen in TV and films. Perhaps it's ridiculous to think they will dust for fingerprints, take swabs for DNA. But it doesn't take a lot of time to wipe down every surface.

The books fit neatly into one bag, making a heavy block of it.

He harnesses himself with the bags and shuts the door behind him. He walks up Stoneybatter, which becomes Manor Street, which becomes Prussia Street, then right at Hanlon's Corner. It's slow progress: he has a cargo bag in each hand and another one noosed around his neck. He has to stop often to ease the pain.

The advert on the Tesco board just gave the house number, with no indication of its location along the road. As it turns out, the numbers don't follow the usual pattern of odd on one side, even on the other. It takes some time to locate it. It's a tall three-storey house with granite steps up to the front door. The door swings open before he reaches the top step.

'Are you the lad that rang?'

'I am.'

'Come on up.'

Ruben dumps his bags in the hallway and follows the landlord up the stairs.

'You have the whole package here. The cooker has an Xpelair, see you can switch it on. And you have the toilet and shower there. I'll get that cleaned up before you move in. Are you a countryman yourself?'

'No, Dublin.'

'Dublin? I was sure you were from up the country. You were saying you're working on the buildings?'

'Yes. Down off Arran Quay. Big projects going up

there.'

'Big money flowing into them. That's all Section 23 stuff.' The landlord talks on for some time, certain that here before him is a sound building-site worker who is exactly the way a building-site worker should be.

It is easy for Ruben to reply just as expected. It is easy to be fully and totally a building-site worker. Without any feeling of deception, he smiles and chats about renovations and damp-proof courses, big investments and the Polish influx.

There is absolutely nothing to prevent him being this building-site worker, now and forever more. The past is gone. It is time to become what he is perceived to be. Like every man does, like every man must.

The landlord accepts the cash deposit and leaves.

The wardrobe

The wardrobe door doesn't close properly. He swings it open and shut several times to see where the problem lies. The top beading is out of alignment. He prises it out with the kitchen knives, wedging first one blade then another in relay under the thin slip of timber, so it won't break. Then he straightens the nails and taps the beading back into the right position.

Then he thinks of the newspapers. He should go out and buy them.

This thing that happened

'Bungalow says he owes you two days,' says Marcos. 'He said that himself. All you have to do is come in and ask for it. He might change his mind, the fucker, and want to keep it. But he's not angry that you left saying nothing. He only gets angry if a chippie or tacker leaves and says nothing. Then he goes mad. So what do you reckon, will you give it another go?'

'Yeah okay. I'll call by in a few days and see.'

'Hey, it's nothing to me.'

'No. I need to get working again.'

'We have the craic with Eoin. The poor cunt.' He laughs softly. 'He's mad angry that he has to come on the bus the whole way from Darndale to Clondalkin. So he was forty minutes late one time, he comes in sweating and says he ran half the way –'

'That girl you were going to marry,' Ruben interrupts, 'how is she?'

Marcos looks closely at him for a few seconds. 'Jesus! That was a joke. Remember?'

'Oh, yeah,' Ruben rubs his eyes.

'Jesus. You even gave me a picture of her.'

Ruben stands up. 'Of course I remember. The passport photo, sure.'

'I hope you're not under stress.' Marcos laughs at the notion, a concept gleaned from Sunday supplements. 'Sitting up in this room all day.'

'Yeah. I need to get back to work.'

He thinks over the sequence of events again. This

thing that happened with the girl, that was an arbitrary interruption. He is not a violent person. But she had not treated him as real, or at least that was how it seemed when he came home that day. It was sordid, what had happened. He had been sucked into events. All he had wanted to do was to live without pretence. Now he feels that one single act swell in significance and begin to define him.

'Hey,' says Marcos, 'hey, what's going on?'

'Hmh?'

'What happened to you?'

'Nothing.'

'Something happened four, five weeks ago to make you leave the job.'

This comes as such a surprise he takes a moment to answer. 'Nothing happened. What could happen?'

'Okay. None of my business.' Marcos gets up. 'See you at the site if you're there.'

A hand on his shoulder

Things go on like this for some time: Ruben lying on the bed listening to the radio, Ruben walking into town. Maybe time alone will free him from the past. All he has to do is wait.

On his walks he begins to pay more attention to the various construction sites and the stage of development they are at. Money is running low. Soon he will need to walk onto a site and ask for a word with the foreman. There he will meet more people like Eoin and Marcos, make friends with them, begin again.

As he turns in his gate he hears a man's shout: 'Ruben.' He turns and they stand there for him. Three of them, with short neat hair and close-set Slavic eyes. They wait, confused perhaps by Ruben's blank expression.

'Ruben. You are Ruben.' It's an accusation rather than a question. The smaller man steps up close. 'You live here? Your ID please. Show me.' Pushes him on the chest. 'You live here, yes? You are Ruben. We know this.' Pushes harder.

He resolves their uncertainty by throwing a punch at the ferret-like one. It's a flat-fisted hammer swing, and catches the small man by surprise. His fists go up in a pantomime of a boxer even as he stumbles backwards to the ground.

Then the other two are upon him. They make short work of it, felling him with a straight punch to the chin. They shout words at him, the name Elena is in there too. They kick his ribs and break his nose. They kick at his chest, his stomach and his legs. The blows stop for several seconds. They push him over onto his back. One braces a knee against him, takes his arm, and snaps it back. The kicking begins again. A voice is raised. 'Is enough, is enough.' Even through the blinding pain, Ruben wonders why they are speaking in English, and realizes it must be because they are not all Latvian.

The kicking stops. They move off. He lies still, taking in a single slow breath, hanging on to a core of consciousness.

He hears their voices arguing. 'Is he breathing? You, go back. Lift his face.'

A hand on his shoulder. 'Hey. Can you breathe?'

The man tries to turn him onto his side. Ruben lifts his head up but instead of words a watery mumble comes out. He spits the blood out of his mouth and says more clearly: 'I'm alright.'

LOST AND FOUND

The missing something that had been niggling him all the way from the bus stop was not the litre of milk, nor a phone call to Edco – he'd already called – and whatever it was, it had slipped out of mind between entering the shop and leaving three minutes later. He paused outside to take a look up at the sky. A drizzle had started, not heavy, but enough to – and that was what was missing: his umbrella.

A feeling of frustration with the slow sponge of memory gripped him. These little incidents could only become more frequent with age. He racked his mind to reckon up other slips of memory over the past couple of months. After another pointless glance inside the shop to see if he'd dropped it, he shook the thought from his head. If something was important enough to him he would not forget it. Ergo, his umbrella was not very important to him.

In this windy city, umbrellas were a liability. The hallway amphora in his parents' house held half a dozen wind-twisted skeletons, not to rest in peace but to be put to use "in an emergency". Half an umbrella can still hold off the rain; far better to be dry. They might laugh at you along the street but you'd have the last laugh. And so on – parent talk. You never shake free of it, even in your mid-thirties.

But he had felt comfortable with the sleek black look of his umbrella. It was the unfoldable type – the foldable ones always turned their ribs inside out at the first gust. A solid one-piece umbrella, with a long gunmetal spike. The handle was dark varnished hardwood. He liked the feeling of buying a well-designed functional object. It was something neutral and stylish to carry into the staffroom on a rainy day.

Gone now, he reasoned, newspaper clasped under his arm where the umbrella should have been. He tracked back through his movements that morning. He'd gone to the city centre to take a look at the French newspapers. He'd walked – a healthy twenty-minute stroll – and just as he was starting home a bus came rumbling by. He checked his pocket for change and caught up with it running, jumped on, shaking out his umbrella, yes, he remembered, there was no doubt he had it in his hands then. He must have left it wedged at the end of the seat.

Less than useless to ring the lost property office, if such places still existed. The only thing would be to somehow find that exact bus. He wasn't too familiar with the bus system, but he was pretty sure the terminus was just a couple of streets down from where he jumped off. He'd seen buses parked there, three or four of them in a row. It was at least reasonable that the bus would park and wait ten minutes, then return by the same route, maybe even with the same driver.

He turned back up the direction he'd come. A few paces towards the main road and the idea grew in plausibility. The bus would be at the beginning of its route, and so almost empty. Chances were they don't clean the buses in the middle of the day. He broke into a jog, feeling energetic now, something concrete he could do. It was rarely he ran, rarely he needed to, and once he started he fell into a pace and it felt good.

There were a half dozen people waiting at the bus stop, so nothing had passed yet, and there it was down the long street, just turning the corner. A city-bound 8, though not necessarily *his* 8.

He let the other people get on first and pay their fares.

'Sorry, I got off this bus when it was coming in from town. I think it was this one. Was there an umbrella left on it?'

'Not that I've seen,' said the driver, still holding back the clutch.

'So I wonder if it's on it, I was sitting down at the back.'

'Go ahead and take a look.' The clutch hissed into contact and the bus pulled away.

He made his way down the aisle. It was a long, jointed bus. Hand over hand he proceeded purposefully towards the back where a young blond cherub sat with a brolly in his hands, daydreaming, the smooth handle pressed into his cheek, feeling the vibrations passing up through it.

'Excuse me, can I take a look at that umbrella?'

The boy shot up straight. In an instant his face hardened. He pushed the umbrella down below his knees.

'Why?' he asked sullenly.

'Because I think it might be mine. I left an umbrella on this bus about twenty minutes ago and it was very like the one you're holding now.'

'This is my one,' said the boy, looking straight ahead.

'I just want to see the label and then I'll know.' The boy didn't reply, just sat there, still a touch of the cherub about his fatty cheeks. Was there a blush there?

'It's *mine*,' he repeated.

'Yours?' said the man, as though to say, *I think very much not my young friend*, the kind of camp thing that his class had grown to love. Or if not love, at least they laughed. The boy remained tight-lipped, looking ahead of him, just a passenger sitting on a bus.

'What's your name?' says the man then, and already he has to control a tremble in his voice. The boy turns his shallow blue eyes on him.

'Boy,' he says.

'Do you know what job I have during the day? Do you know who I am?' he says, so the kid will maybe think he's a policeman or someone important. And the kid answers, at least he does that much, he's not cool enough to sit it out in silence.

'No,' he says.

Right, the man turns on his heel, goes back to the top of the bus. Get the driver to intervene, maybe his down-to-earth accent will talk some sense into the kid, or give the go-ahead to wrench the umbrella out of those chubby hands. Though he feels sick at the thought of a scene.

'A kid back there has it. The umbrella. He won't even let me see the label. A cheeky little brat. I should just grab it off him ... '

'Fucken hell,' breathes the driver and slows down the bus, but it's because of a bus stop coming up. 'Hang on a minute,' he says, meaning he'll get up and sort it out but he has to pull over first. The doors fly open, people are cramming out. And there's the little boy squeezing by, right by him in the aisle and not an arm's length away – he's really stupid enough to think he'll get away with it.

'This is him,' the man says grabbing the boy easily, without a struggle, smoothly and decisively, holding the shoulder and upper arm (was this within the bounds of the law?), but then he sees the umbrella lobbed out of the bus, clattering in the gutter among the people stepping off, and a lank blond youth scuttles over to pick it up.

An accomplice.

He thinks fast: what's he going to do now, bring the kid to the police? Smack him around his wet little mouth? Give him a short lecture on what kind a brat he is? Search his pockets for ID?

He lets go, and the kid zips out the door.

'See that? See that? They've just robbed my umbrella. Just like that.'

The driver leans over to get a hard look through the windscreen at the kid and the older one he's walking off with. 'Scum,' he pronounces.

'Little brats, I can't believe it,' the man says. They both

stare out at the two, and they're walking, just strolling away with the umbrella. *They know the way it works*, the older one telling the younger, *he can't prove it's his, keep walking calmly he can do fuck all. We're just minding our own business.*

The bus driver is still shaking his head. With one bound the man jumps from the bus and dashes at the two. They back off but don't run even though they've a chance, they're young and fast and in all honesty he just wants to chase them, he wants them to run off, to shout *thieves* after them; he's not up to a fight with the bony but hard-as-nails seventeen-year-old, maybe older.

And now things happen very quickly. He grabs the middle of the umbrella and the kid is still hanging on. The older one roars at the man, holding his fists ready, threatening to knock his head off, batter him to pieces if he touches the boy.

'I'm not going to touch him,' he says, forcing himself to show no fear, not in front of these kids. This teenager is not going to throw the first punch, he had his chance in the first few seconds. It's only an umbrella, things will not spiral out of control.

Yet his knees feel weak and his heart palpitates.

The teenager's ferret face is set in a scowl. Pale pock-marked arms. Blue shadows of letters on the skin. From the corporation blocks, most likely. There's no knowing what a youth like that could do.

The man pulls on the umbrella, swings the smaller one around. Like it's a game, the kid hanging on, legs about to lift in the air.

He gives this up and tries to talk reason to the boy. It's

only an umbrella, the kid doesn't even need it for God's sake, the driver can confirm he left it on the bus. But the kid is not interested. The older boy hovers between them, shouting *leave him alone*, bringing his face up close.

People on the other side of the street stop and look over.

'Get away from me big man. I don't want to show you my mickey.' And now he almost lets go in amazement, where the fuck did this spring from? Though he's still a stupid kid. His pretence is laughably obvious. The man tries again to talk sense into him, telling him the police are on their way; the bus driver had called the police on the radio.

'I recognise the label,' he says. It's true. He can see the brand tag at the snap button. The kid hangs on, keeping up his call of *let me go*, while the older companion ducks around them like a referee. 'I'll knock your fucking head off if you touch him, go on, hit me and I'll fucking box your eyes out.'

Someone is passing by. A young woman in tweeds and mid-high leather boots.

'Excuse me. Do you have a mobile phone? Can you call the police please?'

'I'm sorry, I don't have a mobile,' she says and looks from him, to the little kid, to the umbrella between them. She smirks. A grown man wanting to call the police over an argument with a twelve-year-old child.

'Thanks anyway,' he says pleasantly, and she walks on.

And so they circle again. The older boy has his mobile phone out, he's ringing a friend of his, he says, a tough older mate who'll be there in three minutes. 'Just three minutes and he'll be here to sort you out. You better let go 'cos I swear to god he'll fucken knife you if you're still here. He'll scar you.'

And the man thinks, that's where you've made a mistake, that's where the couple of grey hairs and the long trench coat fool you too much.

'Is that right?' he says calmly, 'is that the way it is?' then lets go of the umbrella, and turns to power a punch straight to the middle of the teenager's face. He hears a breathed *ugh*, the youth staggers back like a toddler then sinks to the ground between two parked cars. The man grabs hold of the umbrella again – the kid hasn't moved, he was just standing there staring. But the boy still doesn't let go, he's screaming *let me go, help, help*. The man swings him to and fro, whatever way he wants, round and round and the kid hangs on. He's not going to punch a child, no way, but the kid doesn't know that, he can't know that, yet he's still hanging on like a dog that comes back to the fight when its back legs are broken.

With a sick feeling in his stomach the man lets go.

'Have it,' he says.

The boy backs off. He doesn't run. He understands. The umbrella is bent, the metal shaft kinked. But the kid still stands there. He knows.

The man walks away as quickly as he can without running. The seventeen-year-old might jump up and fight back, throwing gangly fingers into his eyes, biting and kicking.

He steals a look back. The teenager is still sprawled on the ground, holding a hand to his face. The man stops in surprise. He has never punched anyone before, not smack in the fleshy nose, and he never expected the youth to crumple over. Like in a film. He walks away in less of a panic, but even so, when he turns the corner he breaks into a run, and turns the next corner again, and another, and keeps running.

Well that kid certainly has a strong belief in finders keepers losers weepers, the man thinks, but he's not really thinking that, his thoughts are slipping down a dark alley to a place that smells of piss and puke. Yep, I sure as hell wouldn't like to be that kid's teacher, he tells himself, as he will tell his girlfriend of eight years later that evening.

A week or more later he was rooting through a local bargain store. There were some things to pick up on the way home from his school. A set of cardboard folders, a roll of black plastic rubbish bags. Canvas jogging shoes on special offer, but he takes one look and sees they are cheap thin-soled imports and he puts off the idea. He'll get a good pair in a proper sports shop, go out twice a week to the Phoenix Park. Then he sees the bruised face, purple spilled out on the cheeks, a petrol-blue school uniform and a school crest. He lowers his head but then he thinks, what the fuck, what the hell do I care, what's he going to do, will he look for another punch in the snout? Cunt. And he stands tall where he is, taking a sideways look at the battered face. The discoloured blood had seeped under the skin and faded from purple to a livid yellow at the edges. The right eye was sunken in at the bottom of a fleshy pit. Well someone hit you with one hell of a knockout punch, he says to himself. The youngster looks up from leafing through the records, gazes absently in the man's direction, then his head jolts back down again like it's jerked on a string. The man half-whistles to himself as he reads closely the cover notes on one record then another. He edges closer down the aisle, working his way through the section of old vinyl records, until there's no way out, he's right beside the teenager. The man stands there and he's not even sweating, he can feel the tense heat from the scrawny youth, see the spotty back of his neck. At last the youth squeezes past with a mumbled *excuse me*.

THE LAUNDRY
KEY COMPLEX

I used to wear the same T-shirt and jeans for weeks, so it was close to the end of term before I had to go down to the laundry room. I'd heard his name mentioned with a snigger, and the instant I saw him I knew. I watched him pegging out his clothes, one by one, with measured spaces, as though the maintenance of civilisation depended on doing it just so and no other way. I stared at this paradox, knowing right away this person didn't belong here, didn't belong anywhere.

He closed the laundry door after him gently, to avoid disturbing the students who sat out along the corridor. Then he pocketed the key – that key which came to play such a pivotal role in his attempts to establish normal relationships. He stood before me, bulbous, six foot two, roundy soft muscles, an XXL T-shirt hanging off him like a sail. His long arms dangled below his waist. His predicament emanated from him like body heat.

'Hi there. I wanted to wash some clothes,' I said, 'so can I get the key when you're finished?'

He appraised me cautiously, then revealed the key on the palm of his hand. 'I see. But you know I am obliged to hand the key back at the desk and not give it privately to another person? I don't want to cause confusion in the system.'

'That's fine, of course, no problem.'

He sighed, appeased. His fist closed over the key again. The battle scars of teenage acne were still visible on his face (but he had survived, he was there, still standing, grinning). Beads of sweat stood out on the sides of his nose. He was an acid test, to bring out the forgotten schoolboy self: were you the tormentor or the tormented? Didn't you too feel the urge to dismiss him, to curtly say: *You know what? Forget about it.*

'I'd say you must be Simon then?' I said.

Simon hesitated, testing the tone of this question.

'Yes. That's me,' he said. 'How did you know?'

'When I was looking for the key everyone told me, check with Simon, he's sure to know. He's on the first floor. So when I saw you there, I said to myself he looks like a Simon.'

'Yes?' Doubtful again.

'In other words, I took a wild guess.'

Simon laughed at last, swaying back on his heels. It was a laugh to see him laugh; students sitting in the corridor looked up at us.

'I'm Eugene,' I said.

'Eu-gene,' Simon said, placing equal stress on each syllable, 'Eu-gene', a relentlessly equal stress. 'I will leave the key in at half past seven, so you can pick it up. Please make sure you sign it out in your own name.'

It took a few weeks for Simon to become confident of the absence of hidden irony in the things I said, and of my respect for the rules of the key. He was not wary on account of my accent – he had grown up in six different countries across three continents, the connotations of my accent did not register with him. We had this much in common: we both had wasted several years after leaving school, and had gained entry as mature students.

'Eugene. If you have no plans for Saturday evening, perhaps you could call by for a cup of tea?' One hundred and twenty kilos poised in imploration. Afternoon tea, how delightful. I gave a quick nod.

'Fair enough, I'll drop by, sure there's nothing else happening.'

The dorm we lived in lacked a study room. With four students assigned to each apartment unit, the quietest place to read was often the corridor. Students brought out their cushions and coffees and fluffy mascots. This block, for obscure reasons, housed an overwhelming majority of female students. They sat and read and smoked and read, the same book week after week.

I was a single honours science student, and didn't believe in this kind of studying. For me, study meant working through problems from the easy ones to the hardest. How many times could someone read the same page anyway? And what was the point of all that highlighting?

I picked my way along an obstacle course of stretched legs, fearing a hip might swivel, my eyes might falter, and I would kick one of those shapely ankles. I knocked soundly on the door, one two three. *Just a moment*, Simon shouted. A sound of water gushing, sniffles, a long pause. The door eased open. Simon, grinning, huge. I caught the scent of animal hides, spices, and red soap.

'So this is where you live?' I took my time taking in the spice racks on the wall, the three pairs of polished black shoes poking out beneath a cupboard, a cardboard box festooned with customs labels. He apologised and shoved the box to one side so I had room to sit at the coffee table. He cleared jars of pickles off the table and told me the story behind them. They had been mailed from Indonesia, where his parents lived, but had gone the wrong way around the world and been held up for months in the USA.

A poster showing scenes from Glendalough filled one wall. The colours had that saturated look postcards used to have until about 1988. I was sure that this poster had hung on his wall in some country where Ireland was a remote island shrouded in mist.

Because his parents lived abroad and this was his permanent home, he had been allocated a three-person apartment to himself. Even so, the clutter pressed in from all sides. A shortwave radio, wicker throne, a huge German beer stein, a free-standing rack of shirts.

'Haben sie Sauerkraut in ihren Hosen?' I tried. Simon laughed, shook his head, no he didn't speak any German, though he'd lived there for three years. 'But for some time I went to French school and had to speak French when we lived in Gabon.'

Simon brought in two coffees – made with a real coffee machine, from coffee ground only minutes before – and I took out a tipsycake from my backpack.

'Eu-gene,' he said, 'this is very thoughtful of you. You know I intended to go out for some cake earlier but there was a forecast of showers. If you prefer a sandwich I have some quality Parma ham and French mustard.'

'Eu-gene,' he said, and I wished my fingernails would grow to points so I could curl them into my palms. 'Eugene, are you listening?' and he touched me on the arm. I looked him in the eyes, staring into earnest pupils until I should either hug him or punch him.

'Eugene, people in this country are becoming more and more materialistic. I have lived abroad for all my life until now. In other countries people don't put value only on money, and friends are more important.'

'Yes.'

'People are becoming more selfish in Western society. Everything is centred on the *me*. It is an atomised society, people drifting from each other. The image of the human is only as a fixed centre of desires. You can see how there is little respect for the notion of community. This key to the laundry room for example. If one person gets it, they pass it on to their friends, and then it passes to someone else, and the register at the desk is useless, it has lost any connection to reality. I looked for the key once and was told that Lysaght had it in room 408. I went there and she no longer had it.

But please, I said, you are responsible for the key, can I ask you to get it for me? And she looked at me,' he whisked his fingers, 'like I was nothing, not a person worthy to speak to. Not even a person at all. I went to the room number she told me, and some woman there, older-looking than a student, maybe a post-doc, she said she was not yet finished. I said that's fine, I understand, I will come back later. But please, can you sign your name on the register downstairs so other people will know where the key is? And she looked at me like I was a hippopotamus. I said to her, it is important to have a system. Please, do this for the benefit of everybody. And she threw the key at me and slammed the door. I stood there in shock. Can you believe this? Then I heard a mumbling behind the door so I stood closer to listen. I was wondering, what is this noise? She was praying to God, saying please help me God, make him go away. Maybe she could see me through a crack. I was still standing there because I was in total shock. This is something extraordinary Eugene. Do I —' and here he shrugged with his whole arms, 'do I look like a monster?'

I laughed breathlessly, sprang up from the couch and grabbed a book at random. *St. Andrew's, Nairobi* was rubber-stamped on the inside cover. I thumbed my way along the shelf. Several pulpy schoolbooks in French, a volume entitled *Coming to Terms with Yourself*, a book of Yoruba mythology. The shelves told of a childhood spread across Africa, Germany, and Singapore. As a kid he must have played with black kids in Nairobi, clapped hands to Christian chants. Where were the traces of that in him? Where did he get himself from?

'Please Eugene, why do you walk around so much?'

I flopped back into the armchair. 'You do psychology? You have all the books up there ...'

Simon took off his glasses and rubbed his eyes. This constant rubbing didn't redden them, rather there was a bruised yellow pallor around the eyelids.

'There is something I wanted to tell you Eugene.'

Yes, but why can you not just tell it? Why this leaning forward, eye contact, total focus of attention?

Simon waited intransigently for my nod of assent. Then the terrible intimacy emerged.

'I visit a psychoanalyst.'

'Oh.'

'I am undergoing a series of therapy sessions.'

This was a moment unshackled from the ordinary. I did not want to say anything trite or ironic. 'What is he trying to cure?'

'It's a developmental problem.' He hesitated, but not from embarrassment. 'A problem of excessive self-image. There's a barrier that gets in the way of normal relations with people. I need to overcome this barrier.'

'And what is this barrier?'

'I can't tell you everything, it might interfere with the treatment. But what I need to achieve is the ability to cope with normal situations. There is a pragmatics of everyday life that I need to master. The aim is not to become normal ...' Simon frowned. 'But to be aware of the normal and have it as an option.'

'I see.'

'My problem is not a psychological illness as such. The

root problem – though problem is not the right word, it's
more a facet of my personality – is a feeling of superiority.'

The breath stopped in my throat and wavered. I could
not believe that humans could speak like this. Words were
not used like this where I came from.

'This is not a fully conscious feeling,' Simon continued.
'I am not walking around thinking the world should worship
me. Or that everything I say is amazing and ingenious. I
don't believe what this complex is telling me, it's just a little
subconscious part of me. With the analyst's help we are
dragging it into the daylight. Now I am more relaxed about
chatting with ordinary people. I know each conversation
does not have to be full of meaning. It can be little pointless
things just to be friendly. I have learned to isolate this inner
self and cut it off, saying no, you are trying to delude me.
In this way I can relax. I do voluntary work with the Anne's
Park restoration team. We have great fun, we plant rose beds
and lay out cobble paths. We're applying for real antique
cobbles – there's a big stock of them held by the city council.
They give them out for free if you can prove your project is
of historical value or artistic. And we make sandwiches at
home and share them out when we're working. There are
all kinds of people in the group, some very idealistic people.
And we have a barbecue party at the end of the month, and
bring along a bottle of wine and play music and have fun …
but to be truthful, Eugene – maybe I do think a little more
deeply than other people.'

I avoided the laundry room after that. I steered clear
of the first floor altogether. There was nowhere left for a

conversation to go now it had turned a spotlight around on itself. *Let's talk about being friends Simon, let's talk about how well we can talk about ordinary things.*

I brought my clothes to a launderette in town instead. The drying machine there spun for only four minutes at a time. I couldn't afford to keep feeding coins into it. That was the big advantage of the dorm laundry room. The place had extra radiators installed, and you could drape your clothes over them so they'd be crisp dry.

I was playing poker one night in Hamilton block with a group of students. We would meet up every Thursday night. One of them, a guy called Carnew, used to stare his opponent in the eyes and say *I know you think I know what you're thinking*. It turned out he was a psychology student. I asked if there was anyone called Simon in any of his lectures. The name launched him off on a conniving chuckle. I smiled to indicate I was in on the joke.

'Simon, there's only one Simon,' he said. 'He gets into endless debates with the lecturers about the foundations of psychology, wanting to go right back to the ego–id differentiation and restructure it.'

'He knows his stuff?'

'No, no, far from it. He always gets crappy marks for his essays. But it just washes off him. He gets the library staff to order specialised books for him. And he stops the lecturers in the hallway to argue with them.'

It was mid-term break that weekend. I went back to my home area. For two weeks I was renovating the parents' kitchen by day, and boozing with old schoolfriends by night. We talked about our schooldays and the way things were back then. The Christian brothers used to love the quiet and studious pupils – the swots. The academically weak on the other hand were subjected to scorn on a daily basis. Wasters, chatterboxes, messers, omadawns, cligeens, maggots, lord Muck, cretin, eejit: the Brothers had a colourful range of labels. Yet hardly ten years later, the messers and rogues were the ones who were doing well for themselves. Phil was running a restaurant employing three Poles, Mark was selling twenty cars a week at five percent commission. Funny the way things turn out. No-one would have guessed I'd be back at university ten years down the road, still no career in sight.

I was sitting at the open-air lunch area outside the science block when I heard Simon's unmistakable pronunciation of my name. He greeted me with no hint of awkwardness. We went for a coffee. He chatted about the recent spell of bad weather, the changed opening hours of the library, and a Louise Brooks season the film club was showing that week. I explained that there'd been several crucial deadlines over the past few weeks, and promised to drop by now that the pressure was off. He gave a wry smile as he stood up to leave, as though to acknowledge this had been a successful exercise in making small talk.

'You can visit him too,' he whispered. The odour of decadence is a blend of shoe polish and burnt coffee. Its sound is a heavy breath being exhaled. 'I mentioned you to him and he said you would be an interesting candidate.'

'How, when he doesn't even know me?'

'I told him about you.'

'Anyway, I have no psychological problems.'

'Don't think in terms of what problem you have. He won't even ask you if you have a problem, he won't ask why you are there. Think of it as a journey inwards. And Eugene. You will not feel better afterwards.'

In the days beforehand I practised a sort of double layer of awareness. An observer lurking behind the observer. I tried to track my thoughts to their first origins, and delineate the habits that bound me. The ready apologies, the instant checking of whether I had the right to speak, the indecision about what the correct thing to do might be.

My parents were ordinary people who saved coupons and shouted back at politicians on the six o'clock news. They spoke as though locked into a mutual pact to never say anything beyond the grindingly mundane. And each month when I returned home for a few days, I entered into that pact once more. I entered the pact and relapsed into it with a miserable ease.

'Going to visit turnip-head again? How can you stand him?' Eyes shining with derision. She was one of the girls who sat out in the corridor.

'I know, he's a terror,' I answered easily, hunkering down for a moment.

'Old Mushroom we call him,' she said. That was how I pictured Simon too: a fantastic growth you stumble upon in a neglected nook of a rambling house.

'Old Mushroom?' I laughed. 'A minute ago he was a turnip. He must be the whole vegetable soup.'

'Why do you go visit him?' She seemed to take it as a personal affront.

'He has good coffee, real stuff his parents post over from Indonesia.'

'You'd sit with a weirdo for *five* hours, just to get a really good cup of coffee?'

We set off that morning, big friend Simon and I, squeezing into the seats of the number 39 bus and rattling our way out to the distant suburbs. The house at the end of our journey was a detached house like any of thousands we passed. Inside the front room a half-dozen assorted souls were waiting, young and old, all unashamed to acknowledge that we are not as simple as we would wish. Who had all escaped from the insistent *I am what I am*. And I understood that even those who seem the most rooted, the bar stool tenants, the flag wavers who have never read a book in their lives, my own parents too, were all constantly circling a vortex of thought, and shied away from it with all the strength of their healthy instincts.

Now the analyst, our Charon, emerged. A disciple of some splinter Freudian school, he had fled the troubles in Yugoslavia and nailed his brass plaque to the wall in this implausible place. A mild man in appearance, with greying sideburns and a lozenge-patterned jumper.

'Next,' he called in a tired voice. And I felt the old childish tremor within me, the thought of a secret divine spark, my hidden hero self, and that it might be revealed and might shine.

UNFINISHED BUSINESS

I was bound to my decision; there was no backing down now. The place I had chosen was Nero's, in the regenerated docklands zone of Dublin 2. The bouncers smiled and stepped each to one side.

'Good evening sir.'

I descended white marble steps, flanked by bas-relief columns. Aphrodite stood in an alcove holding her robes to her stomach. Male and female athletes cavorted. To go by the name, the club should have had Roman themes, but the Greeks do a better nude.

A pulsating blue light escaping from the dance floor lent things an alien aura. The girl behind the coat counter looked up at me without expression. Oblivious to the rhythm. The interaction between her makeup and the vagrant rays of ultraviolet transfigured her face. She became a stylised icon of herself. Narrow, oval, inscrutable.

'Do I have to leave in my jacket?'

Her features jumped into mobility. 'No, not at all,' she said with surprise. Her eyes followed me, a touch dubious about a man who would ask such an odd question.

Claiming no advantage, not hiding behind my job or status, I stepped into the arena. Just another man out on the town to have a good time. The beat of the music pummelled me, literally, through the chest. My eyes flitted across the dance floor. I could not connect the excited, radiant faces I saw with the daytime girls I encountered at work. Eyes glistened, luminous pupils lit on me and moved on. Bare arms extended from lycra tops. Bare legs tottered on high heels. A quiver of loose calf muscle set me aflame. I passed along the edge of the floor, slashed a quick smile at one of them. Not a tentative smile, not a sleazy smile. Just a smile.

Fluted columns extended up to the ceiling. I leaned against one, drink in hand. It was early yet; only a dozen or so people. Foreign tourists most of them, with a few early arrivals. It occurred to me I looked too much a loiterer with intent – feet crossed, leaning at a rakish angle against the column. I became conscious of my sports jacket, the severe slants of its collar. I took it off and went back to the cloakroom. As the iconified girl inexpertly coaxed my jacket onto a hanger I studied my reflection in a side mirror. The unnatural frequencies of light brought out a rough texture on the skin. My eyelids lurked in a penumbra of blue. It was not at all ugly; it was rather a transformation. I too had become an iconic version of myself. I could be any age. My features stood out starkly, yet at the same time had become more universal, like the Graeco-Roman statues behind me. No-one would guess I was forty-one rather than twenty-one.

I thought back to the fear with which I entered such places more than twenty years before. The sweat that lined my palms, the fake grin I would assume. I thought back to my schooldays at St. Kevin's, the burden of my virginity, my incomprehensible expectations of girls. Given that they were an alien consciousness, they might well have an alternative method of seeing who I really was inside. Speech would become superfluous, there would be communication of a sort I could not yet envisage. They would coax out my secret hero self.

It was a different era back then. Ireland, early nineteen eighties. The boys' school employed only male teachers. Most of these were Christian brothers; the rest were a mix of spoiled priests and GAA sports zealots. The latter were the most fearsome and dogmatic. To this day I feel an anxious trembling at the sight of Gaelic football supporters massing with their cheers and chants. I think of frost-hard pitches, roars of scorning laughter, the whip-crack of wet towels.

The girls from The Holy Faith up the hill wore thick socks and ankle-length woollen skirts. When we reached fifth year, a small group of us would take the long route to school, so as to intersect their path. We would dare to throw a few words at them. 'Don't get pregnant today,' or such. One of our group had a sister in the Holy Faith, and this provided a possible point of contact. I used to hang around with this boy at the paper factory gates. Sometimes his sister and her friends would be there. But they stood some distance away, at the bus stop. We didn't slag them because my friend's sister was among them. There would be one who would always be there, looking out from under a black fringe, and I'd imagine she was my secret girlfriend.

Some boys claimed to have had success with girls. 'Scored' was the word they used. 'Did you get your bit?' they'd say in a knowing whisper. Before ever I made my first gawky approaches across the dance boards, I knew the theory: if the female sniffs out that this encounter is at all crucial to you, then you've lost already. Keep it light, keep it floating. A few cutting remarks, then turn away. Only when you reach a stage beyond caring, then you begin to have a chance.

I admired the girls from afar. In my sinful night frenzies, each became reduced to some aspect of how she had first entered my awareness. A small-stepped way of walking, a short-sleeved blouse, a reddened earlobe. Having no idea of female anatomy, I imagined entangled limbs, bodies squirming against each other like worms. I was not to know it, but my instinctive imagination was in its own way more accurate than the cryptic ideograms scratched on the toilet walls – passed on no doubt from one generation of schoolboys to the next like a gnostic script.

One boy pinned a Page 3 girl to the announcement board at school. He had cut the picture from the British tabloids, which at that time were available only at Dublin airport. The pulpy paper soaked the ink from his nib. It took a separate dip for each letter. 'Missus Lindsy' he wrote across it in spindly letters.

Mrs. Lyndsay was the secretary. She was a thick-limbed

woman approaching forty. Her bosom was indeed as ample as the glamour girl's, whatever about her looks.

Class was cancelled; an investigation was held. The boy was detected and suspended immediately. I saw both his parents at the principal's door, nodding gravely, fearful of this unwholesome turn in their son's development.

For two years I hung around at the factory gates from four until almost six. We must have been familiar figures to the motorists stuck in the eternal traffic jam. We smoked, we swapped cards, we horse-played. We built tower upon tower of sophisticated humour that became incomprehensible to anyone but ourselves. All the while I'd be casting a glance at my imaginary girlfriend, with her small round head and straight hair that ended just an inch above the back of the neck. Her eyebrows arched, fingers on her satchel, and the thousand tiny differences for which there's no accounting.

She became used to my glancing at her, and endured it without comment. In fact she would look back at me – we would stare at each other and wonder how this was possible, that there was no turning away in embarrassment, no acknowledgement, and then Eoin might call me back with a resumption of the wisecracking.

When I finished school I got a job with a surveying company. I spent a year in various bog holes across the midlands, holding the staff steady until the bubble was dead centre. Then they sponsored me for an evening course. Two years later I graduated, and crossed from the rod to the theodolite. The company posted me abroad as part of a team, to Namibia of all places. We were to do the setting-out for a tin mining operation. I don't intend to recount my life story here. Least of all do I wish to give the impression that having been in Africa makes me a more interesting person. I mention it only by way of explaining how it was that I got a girlfriend and got married without going through the intermediate stage of chatting up. Sharon and I had gone for dinner at the *Jardin des Plantes* in the corrugated town. The clock in the restaurant – I should have known – was running to a different time zone. When we got out, the company bus had already gone back to the mining station. My workmates had left a helpful message on the roadside notice board. *Back tomorrow some time.*

Sharon had only one room. It was a distant land, beyond the reach even of self-scrutiny. I was making love with her before I had time to ruin it by anticipation. Before even she was my girlfriend. In the eyes of the world I had made it.

Sharon was the outreach nurse at a local missionary. She would make the rounds of local schools to give health tests and injections. I began to stay with her at weekends. I would get a lift with any truck from the station that was going into town. I got to know some of the people working at the missionary and used to help out with fixing things. The priests and staff were mainly Irish with a few Italians in the mix. Oddly enough, none of them ever asked where I might be staying the night. Things work differently off in Africa I suppose.

A hum and throb filled the air. The DJ was getting into mood. He would catch the eye of someone on the dance floor, track them with his magic finger, then get them to pump their hands in the air. Groups and couples squeezed onto seats alongside me. I got up and stood close by the wall. It was not yet ten, but I wasn't about to procrastinate in another game of self-deception. A bouncy teen with eyes shiny as a doll's. Nothing porcelain however about the way she wriggled and wrestled with her friends. They held her shoulders to calm her.

A sharp-faced girl, Russian perhaps, stepped down to the dance floor. A dust of rouge on her porcelain cheeks gave her an untouchable aura. Would she ignore me if I spoke to her? Let her ignore me then, or let her speak, just as she wished.

A lady in yellow who stood very straight. The backs of her legs made a little quirk in her straightness. Her lips were pursed forward. Yes, she disdained to be here. Every moment mortified her. Her eyes took the scene in with a skeptic coolness. Yet she had come here, one among all the rest, and spent hours of effort on her lipstick liners and mascara. And there, laughing girl, water-teeth, glistening eyes, shoulder bared to the spot-light. A blessing that seemed to hover about her so that at one moment she was just a girl, the next resplendent.

I touched the shoulder of the woman standing next to me.

'Can I get you a drink?'

'Why?'

'Cos you're good-looking.'

She wrinkled her nose, looked at me skeptically. I held up the bottle and shook the half-inch at the bottom.

'Wow. You're direct. But I'm actually waiting for someone.'

'Oh. I can still get you something. I'm on my way to the bar.'

'No, thanks anyway. No, I should really wait for the others.' A pause. 'What about you? Are you here on your own?'

'Yes,' I said. 'Just back in Ireland for a few days – I work abroad.' This was a line I had prepared. 'Just wanted to get out, you know, hit the town, see what's happening.'

'Yeah, it's good to get out.'

Now that I had been talking to her for a few moments, the situation quickly normalised. I could have been talking to one of our receptionists about the valuation of a suburban warehouse. And although she was pretty, she did not have that unequivocal attractiveness which my mind was set on. It was nice to have an easy-going chat with her, but I needed to move on. Feeling validated by her final pointed *good luck*, I dissolved back into the crowd.

Sharon and I got married soon after we returned to Ireland. I got on well with my wife. We were friends as well as spouses. Everyone remarked at how we would actually *do* things together, like jogging or going to Spanish classes. Sharon, they said, is always bright-eyed and bushy-tailed at any hour of the day. The pair of you, they told us, get on like a house on fire.

And I suppose we did. I never worried much about our 'relationship' – we just got on with life. And yet, I never got over my shyness with girls, that minor cognitive seizure I would get when plunged into the company of a beautiful woman. Not knowing what to say – blushing even, me, a married man with a professional job.

The Christian Brothers' school casts a long shadow.

There were a couple of odd situations down the road. Not long after my marriage I was involved in a big project on the Western Bypass. It was a government contract; we all stayed at the Corrib hotel in a group booking. I ended up at the dinner table one evening with Carol from Requisitions. We lingered for a drink after dinner. We were talking about the "weekend" – which was just Sunday, as we were all on a six day week. Not enough time to do much more than have a lie-in. She suggested we go for a drive along the Shannon. 'To kill the boredom,' she said.

I'd always wanted to see the local landscape. Two months on the job and all I'd seen was the road from the hotel to the construction site.

'I'll drive,' I said, 'My car needs a good workout.'

We had an interesting trip down the backroads and through dolmen country. We got out of the car for a short trek across the karst landscape, where she squealed with exaggerated fear of the crevices between the limestone slabs. Later we stopped for lunch at a small fishing village. My beeper went off just as we got back in the car (mobile phones existed back then, just about, but there was no coverage way out west). Duty called. I pulled in at the nearest petrol station to phone back to base. The lads were working all night by floodlight – another sign of the changing times – and I had to be back before the five o'clock shift.

I met up with Carol a few times after that, either at dinner or at the bar. I treated her no differently than my male colleagues. That's the secret, I thought, of getting on with women. And in her case it was made easier as she wasn't one to wear make-up or skirts. Strictly practical jeans and chunky cardigans for her.

Then came the evening when I met her at the hotel bar as usual and she claimed I was an hour late.

'I don't want to continue meeting you if you don't respect times,' she said icily. There were a few more words about my being 'ultra casual'. She sounded like a character from a television soap opera. She hinted she was going to go to the cinema that evening with somebody else.

I saw somehow that I should explain I was married. But it didn't seem right to simply blurt out the fact. I could see awkwardness approaching like a train crash.

I chose a neutral question. I asked her what film she was going to see.

'Fuck. Off,' she enunciated with a round mouth, pushing the syllables out at me. I felt bad about the situation. The fact that she was so annoyed made me feel I must be at fault. For a while I thought it best not to speak to women at all, beyond what was necessary for work purposes.

More recently, my wife Sharon had a very beautiful friend from college who used to drop by to practice Excel spreadsheets. She had a delicate face and pert nose. When she spoke it was with such sincerity that her permed hair shook. It was strange to be up close to such a glossy-cover woman. She was full of jokes and slap-dash humour about the house; she never acted the little princess. But she knew she was beautiful. They always do.

This woman, Martina, and I worked in the same city area. We got talking about the difficulties of finding parking, local cafés and the like. The idea cropped up that we should meet for lunch. Phone numbers were exchanged. 'Keep her company,' Sharon said with a wink. She wasn't the jealous sort. I never gave her the remotest reason to be jealous.

Everything was wrong about this meeting. I made such a fuss discussing what time was convenient for me and for her, and what café was halfway between us, and my stressing that it was a busy time at work (not to give the impression that I would drop all committments at the chance of being with her), that a huge weight of cruciality had accumulated around the event before we ever met up. Truth was, I couldn't prevent a fossilised part of my brain from treating it as a date. That long-feared first date I'd never had.

I could see Martina through the windows as I approached, her slim form perched on a high seat. Already I was thinking about whether I should apologise for being too late (no), pay for both of us at the counter (if she only has a snack) or suggest meeting again the next week. Should I tell her (in a camp sort of way) she looks lovely today?

When she used to visit our house, my wife would fuss about her golden curls, her eye-shadow, her perfect bust shape. I would be invited – as a representative male – to give my opinion. So in fact many times I've whistled *sexy* at her, agreed she looks fantastic, watched her twirl and stretch a leg in my living-room. But all the time only as a sort of token male presence.

It's not as if I had any devious designs on her. Or even desire. I just wanted a chat at lunchtime, make her feel relaxed, have a laugh. To show – just to myself alone – that I was accustomed to the presence of beauty and could appreciate it with charm and poise.

I can't explain what went wrong at that lunch. If I was

able to, then maybe it wouldn't have gone wrong. I talked too much about my job, was frivolous in the wrong places. Then came a moment when I realised she'd been speaking for several minutes and I had no idea what she was talking about.

She stood at the counter to pay. I thought forlornly of saying "nice derrière". The kind of mock-daring compliment I might have made (as a token male) if she was in the living room with my wife. Now it was as remote and absurd as the green cheese of the moon.

Yet like a man who wallows in defeat, I offered to walk her back to her office. The very thing I had decided in advance was a bad idea. 'It's all right,' she said.

'No,' I insisted, 'I still have plenty of time.'

'It's really all right,' she said again. I went with her anyway, smiling and smiling. Because of my wife, only because of that, she kept up a strained politeness.

Later Sharon asked how the lunch with Martina had gone.

'Okay I suppose. But she's a bit stuck-up,' I said.

'Stuck-up?' said Sharon, puzzled.

So I launched into some explanation: she was snobby, talked about herself a lot, boasted of once being offered a modelling contract. This last detail was something I had overheard when Martina was visiting us, and it made my story sound more plausible. It would in any case be more plausible than the reality.

Martina didn't call by until several weeks after. She stayed half an hour, didn't say a word to me, and talked Excel sheets with my wife. That was the last time she ever called.

I saw now that my relationship with my wife had helped me conceal a pathological inability to relate to women as sexual creatures. Sharon had seen only hints of this chronic shyness in me, but she had suffered from the consequences. There was unfinished business in my life, and I resolved to confront it. For all our sakes.

And so I had taken a hard look at myself in the mirror. Not with teenage self-absorption, but with detachment. I was forty-one, hairline high on my forehead, though not balding by any measure. Eyes crinkled at the corners, but no more than Lance Armstrong – still at his peak. My wife had always said I was good-looking, and pressed her giggling girl-friends into agreeing. She was away for two weeks. She and her sister were taking their mother on a trip to Rome, on a dutiful family holiday.

No more cowering behind the petticoats of my marriage. A new aftershave, a haircut at the best men's salon in town. These were minor details to make myself feel created afresh. I scanned the entertainments section of the evening paper. Nero's Nightclub. *Experience the opulence from eight 'till late.*

Things were heating up, the beat was pulsing. I needed to be in there, part of it. Not standing at the edges. A girl looked up and caught my eye. I borrowed a gesture from the Caribbean DJ and bounced an imaginary ball to her. She laughed and took it up.

'Can I get you a drink?'

'You can if you want to I suppose,' she shrugged.

Her name was Fiona. She liked James Brown and Groove Armada. The music here was nothing special, she said, just commercial drum'n'bass, not the real thing. She named several bands I'd never heard of. I suggested we look for a seat while there was still some space.

We talked about a city café we both knew, where the staff squirted pressurised cream over every cake. It occurred to me how silly this looked. Order any cake, even the peanut crunch, and before you could say *scrumptilicious* they lowered a nozzle and tsssssh, it was buried in white.

She talked about her dancing lessons and asked if I was into any sport. I told her about my training for a hundred-and-twenty mile cycling race. I explained how we would take turns at the head of the pack, letting the others ride in your slipstream. In fact the race had been a few years back, but it would have made the topic rather pointless to mention this.

It was exhilarating to talk with her, with no boundary set on who we were or why we were here. All females had come to occupy a fixed place in my world. They were secretaries or colleagues, my wife's friends or my friends' wives. All possible pathways of a convberation were set in advance.

Speaking with Fiona was like – well, to use a pretty weak comparison, it was like two people sitting on a cloud talking. The conversation veered out and away from us. I glanced at her sometimes trying to fathom how it had come to this. Finally she asked me what I did. I talked about the surveying, and mentioned being in Africa. She asked if I'd been in any danger zones during the ethnic conflicts.

'No, I was there long before that. About ten years ago now.' She looked at me in some surprise. She paused, seemed to make a quick calculation in her head and reach a conclusion. I had said ten years because that was what it seemed like to me. In fact it was more like sixteen.

'So, you're an experienced man,' she said with a wry smile.

'Experienced in surveying,' I said. 'Not experienced in coming to a place like this.' There was a pause. For an instant I wanted to take her in my arms, rest my mouth on the soft dimple where her throat met her clavicle. The upsurge caught me by surprise, unbalanced me. I had a glimpse of the oily chaos in which I had floundered in my youth, pushing forward further into failure, knowing it and knowing it, overwhelmed by an excess of consciousness. Then the feeling was over, and I wanted nothing more than to make her feel at ease, to find out more about her.

She was preparing for a course in communication and languages. She talked a lot about the course and the famous RTE presenter who lectured there. It was some time before I realised she was applying for the course; she was still at school. Her Leaving Certificate was several months away.

I felt a calm sense of poetic justice. Time was balancing measures, equilibrium restored. It was a Holy Faith school too. They still existed, though greatly changed.

'No, not nuns any more,' she said. 'It's all lay teachers. Well, there are a couple of ancient nuns who still teach, hanging around like dinosaurs. They must be over ninety but when they get up there teaching, you can still see, they rule. They *rule*.'

'We had Christian brothers. Hellfire and brimstone. Do you still have to wear the uniform?'

'It's mad,' she laughed, 'the skirts we have to wear are

like something from Saudi Arabia. Even the teachers agree that they're way too long. We should refuse to wear them at all. Go into class in our knickers.'

'But still wearing the socks.'

'Oh yes, still with the thick socks on.'

When this kind of talk finished she put her hand to her mouth as though struck by a silent coughing fit.

'So where does the conversation go next?' I said, which set her off even more. Her friend came over to say goodnight. The man with her waited a few steps back from the table. I supposed she had just met him in the nightclub that evening, but I didn't ask.

As soon as her friend had passed up the stairs I looked at Fiona for about three seconds then put my lips on hers. I had not planned it, I was going with the moment.

'You're funny,' she said. I kissed her again. The sweet comfort of her kiss like a homecoming, her lips still for the first few seconds, then pushing out. The thrill of her breath, nose against nose like merry eskimos, then my hand on the jut of her hip. I framed her face in my hands and experienced the righteousness of desire. No longer a force at odds with the universe, it was right here, acknowledged between us. Her eyes glistened and she folded a leg back under herself on the upholstered seat.

'You're so easy to talk to,' she said. 'You're so relaxed you'd fall off a log.'

'Life's too short to take it seriously.' And again we went at each other, like spark to distillate, my breath on her ear, her fingers running down my back, a thin scent beyond perfume, her ankle splayed sideways with the shoe half off.

The lights stopped their stroboscopic dance, the beat died down. We stood, hand in hand.

'Time to go,' I said, 'Do you have to get home soon?'

'I don't have to get home any time,' she said.

'Then let's go,' I said, 'I know somewhere else to go.'

When I gazed on her slumbering face in the hotel room later that night, I thought of how much I had really needed this when I was seventeen or eighteen or nineteen, and how my smouldering desires had made me shame-faced and bitter. How the scoffers got the best-looking girlfriends, using chat-up lines I had always thought too despicable to use. And I thought, why had I made things so complicated?

It is a summer night, sports day for the local schools. Warm air rises from the concrete slabs. The radio talks of *Perestroika*. Inside the school sports hall, red drapes are hanging over the climbing frames, me laughing with friends, the air thin with excitement. Girls from The Holy Faith clustered along the opposite wall. Joking and jostling just like us, but the way they stretch a hand, their cheeks and lips, their piercing eyes; everything about them so alien and fabulous. A difference beyond description. So out of reach in mind and touch.

STRIPPED BARE

The places to visit that day are the warzone of tar and the shallow of leeches. One hour in the warzone and it reeks from your clothes for a week. It is a thrilling, strengthening smell. The lads bring a milk crate to help scale the block wall. Once inside they find cut-off pieces of sheet metal and drag them along the timbers, scraping up a good ooze. Nice to smear and stretch. Someone bangs the rods, but not so loud as to attract attention. When a match is brought close to smeared bits of paper the flame jumps the empty space and creeps to a glow of orange. A thick black streak races upwards from the flame. Too big a bundle of paper, and the flames would spurt burning drops, the whole thing turn to a hellish inferno. But what madman would want to do that? They would never do that, they always stamp the flame underfoot as soon as it begins to catch. Let it swell out for five seconds then a quick stamping of feet. But never let it out of control.

Yet the man in overalls roars at them and comes clattering down the metal steps. They retreat over the wall, spilling into the laneway, and leg it for the open end where traffic flies by. The man in overalls takes his time loosening the long bolts, dragging open the tall steel doors. They boom with a sound for the world. He stands and faces them, a quiet appraisal that unsettles the boys. They feel they should keep running. He is far off, his face indistinct. Then some implicit rule is violated as the man draws back his arm and launches a missile towards them – a weighty hexagonal wheel nut. They scatter like ragged pigeons.

The shallow of leeches is a stretch of the park river where it is easy to wade across. There are low concrete banks on both sides, and the concrete extends under the water too, but the middle part is covered with a spongy mass of weed. Cyril takes off his shoes and socks. The shock of cold on his feet catches him out. He grits his teeth like someone about to throw a punch. His pale feet glow from under the water. Little fish dart around him. It would be nice if they swarmed directly over his feet but they never do that.

There are other kids with a net on a stick that they swish through the water. Swish, they go, and peer at the weed they catch. He watches them dip and drag, and pick things out of the weed. He hangs around the grassy bank letting his feet dry, watching.

'Givvus a go,' he says to them.

'No,' one of the kids says.

'Go on, givvus a go,' he pesters them the length of the bank, until they reach where the grass verge narrows and changes to a strip of gravel. 'No,' they say each time, quietly, like adults stating the self-evident.

'Is that all you can say?' He turns from them with finality. They move on, still fishing, or pretending to fish, and he is on his own.

Feet can slip on the slimy bottom. The current could catch his legs, topple him, sweep him down to the rapids. Wiped away, swept away like a leaf. Floating on a crest, thrashing his arms and legs.

But he knows the water is not really dangerous. It reaches to his knee in the deepest parts. The current can seem fast and rough where it tumbles over rocks, but it's not dangerous. His legs are cold now and the thrill has gone.

He has never seen the leeches. Blood-sucking worms, that's what they say. He cannot doubt that they are real, and yet he finds the idea too fanciful. If there were girls up on the bank he would try the usual joke: *leeches*, he would scream and grip his foot in mock terror. The girls would run off screaming.

There's no time that day for the cavern of spare parts. It is getting dark and cold. Even the seagulls squabble and cry for food. There is no-one left in the park, and the scent of coal-smoke grits the air.

He can hear the voices stabbing at each other as he turns the corner to his home road. Short staccato bursts are exchanged. It might go on like that for a long time with no escalation, a sound as corrosive as a drilling machine in the warzone of tar. He crouches and listens until sense is lost and all he can hear is rhythm. His heart beats fast and tight.

It is a strange thrill to hide in the front garden. He is inside the gate and yet a stranger. If a neighbour sees him all he has to do is stand up straight and smile, at once an intruder no longer. The black slate roofs are slick with rain. He could walk away again, but there would be nobody playing football at the triangle, nobody in the lane.

The voices come through the walls of the house, grinding onward yet still under control. He is always able to recognise when the tension ramps up toward overload: it is a crescendo with steps marked by *for jaysus sake and just get the fuck out of my sight.*

He releases the hacking device. *Chop chop* it goes, its arms jab fast and smartly. *Chop chop*, and his father snorts and shakes his head. He is getting uncomfortable; the invisible powers are working on him. Time to leave, time to go. Persistent micro-blows urge him towards the door. The device used no physical force, but it would never let up. It is free of Cyril now; once released he cannot rein it in.

Bewildered, itched with impatience, the father flings some last words out. A pleasing sequence of sounds follow: rattle of keys, a drawer opening and closing, footsteps up the hallway. The front door opens. Cyril ducks behind the boards and watches his father's back. The lean figure in overalls fiddles at the van door to get it open. The engine however spurts into power on first turn.

This road has a hundred houses that are all variations on one pattern: two windows upstairs, one downstairs. His house however has a junkyard in the front garden. He emerges from behind a leaning sheet of plywood.

'It's me,' he says through the letterbox. 'Hey, it's only me.' The bell doesn't work and it would be too strange to knock on your own front door. She has gone inside somewhere, perhaps she has flung herself out on the bed, head pressed into a pillow. 'Hey,' he shouts, 'are you all right?' And then feels an odd, old tightness in his throat.

'Ma,' he says. 'Mammy, can you hear me? Mammy, I'm at the door.' The word makes him want to cry, even though he hears her coming up the hallway and there is nothing wrong, nothing wrong at all.

Sweet Caroline, Ma sings. *Sweet suffering Jaysus.* Sweet is one of her favourite words. When she used to take out the mixing bowl there would be as much as he could eat of spotted currant cake for a whole week. But now she boils and boils all day until the windows stream. There will be potatoes in their skins and pounded cabbage for dinner. Boiled bacon or boiled bones.

'Your father loves potatoes and cabbage, so that's what we'll get,' she says to him tearfully. 'This is a house of potato and cabbage from now on. It's good enough for us.'

Thus began the era of boiling everything. It had been going on for some time now, and he often thought back to the previous era, when his mother had made chicken kievs and roast potatoes, desserts of rice pudding and prunes. Now she was always tired, too tired to be cheerful. *Do you want me to dance?* she'd screech.

When Mrs Renn calls, the regime is suspended. The women put on eye-shadow together and a tin of biscuits is set on the table. Mrs Renn brings cake: tipsy cake or ginger cake, Oxford lunch or brack.

'Look at the shine off your shiny black hair,' she crows, and insists on combing it to one side till the white grains at the roots show. She cups his face in her hands and smiles warmly, but when she brings him to the mirror and looks at his reflection she makes a pretend gasp at the transformation.

Sometimes the happy mood will continue a while after Mrs Renn has gone. He will leave the last biscuit on the plate untouched. Sometimes it ends abruptly. 'Damn your skin Cyril. You're the same breed as your father.'

Mrs Renn doesn't know that Ma occasionally loses her mind. There are times when you have to shut off the words that Ma says because they don't make sense. She says he, Cyril, will betray her. She says he will turn to the bad and run wild.

That's not true. Ma doesn't know it, but he has banished evil from his soul. He has sworn allegiance to the side of good. He has never had rage in him – does she not see that? When has he hurled and smashed, when has he raised his fist against another? When has he said *fuck you*, and turned and walked away?

Ma is confused. She treats him like someone else, like a boy who has already turned rotten. She is a weepy vortex, who wants to drag him into tears of repentance. Sorrow for the world that will corrupt you. With Ma, life is often a valley of tears and she must struggle daily to keep going.

Though when she and Mrs Renn are together, they treat

him as a different kind of boy, as a boy who eats sticky buns and grins until his cheeks hurt. He is not really that boy either, one who smiles when his hair is tousled and who licks the sugar off his fingers.

Cyril his name is, though it's a silly, sissy name. There's nothing of his real self in his name. When people call him it's like they are calling someone else, and he steps forward instead to fill that place. So maybe it suits him after all.

'Cyril Conroy, have you no coat?' The boys chuckle until silenced by the teacher. He never has a coat, everybody knows that. But he is careful to give the right answers.

'I left it at home, it wasn't raining this morning,' he says. Why would he need a coat? *Cyril you're a hardy one*, they all agree.

Now he suffers the indignity of having to wear a grey wooly coat every day, just so the school won't think his parents are poor.

In the story the teacher makes them read, two children listen to their parents talking late at night. They crouch at the top bannister and listen. The voices percolate up from the kitchen below and they learn the Truth.

The children leave a trail of white breadcrumbs through the forest. The breadcrumbs glow in the moonlight. But in the city the street lights dazzle all night and the road home roars with traffic.

In the story there are two of them. That makes a difference.

One night he doesn't go home at all. He sneaks into the warzone of tar and makes a hideout. He collects oil in a shallow of metal and tears a wick from the pocket of his shirt. The flame rises with livid colours, then settles to a steady burn. The rain will not reach them under the tarred boards, he and his lamp. He curls around it, and the hot centre makes him aware of the cold. The flame does not warm him; he doesn't need it for warmth. He doesn't need it at all. He learns to keep still. But after some time he gets up and stretches his muscles, hobbles the way home. How long a time? There was a milkman out, one side of the sky was glowing. The night feeling had passed.

The mind controls matter. The mind creates reality. That's what the deep voice on the television says. *If belief is strong enough, matter will yield.* Bubbles of strange music follow, pictures of ancient tombs, quantum lasers firing. Reality is created in the moment of observation, that is the truth, and yet it is not acknowledged here in this room.

Bullshit, they say, without even paying attention. They would say that anyway, as predictable as a toilet flush. Ah bullshit, they say and switch channel.

Father is back again after working several weeks up the country.

'You got bored, is that it?' his mother says.

'Someone around here has to earn money.'

The voices wind and twine towards a climax. He can feel it coming. Doors will slam, his father march out the hallway. But this time his mother pushes and slaps at his father. He throws her to one side roaring, 'Stop your mad catfighting. You want me to hit you so you can call the guards, isn't that what you want?' She fights at him again, throwing her hands out in front of her. His father grasps her in a bearhug, presses her against the wall. She stops struggling. Her voice shakes with resolve.

'You pay me nothing. You give me no money. This is not your home.'

At last some words of sense. Words that mean something and are not just flung like pebbles against a wall. Why can he not stay away forever? The idea excites Cyril. That would be a conclusion to all the arguing. That would show that change is possible.

The father stands for a while watching her sobbing into the sofa cushions. He raises his eyes to heaven and curses.

Then it is now as it has been so many times before: keys jangle, door closes, engine roars into power. The dull whine of the car pulling away. He has stood here, exactly like this, listening to this sound before. It's a strange shameful pleasure: the car engine slows at the crossing just down the road, the sound thins out to nothing, then whines back into hearing one last time. This is comfort.

He thinks of what has been said and wants something to happen soon. His mother leaves for the shops and is gone a long time. When she comes back however she brings only bread and poundsaver jam. He makes a pot of tea without being told to. He sets the sugar and milk on the table.

'If he doesn't pay you anything, why do you let him back in?' he whispers.

'He owns the whole house.' She sniffles and dabs her eyes.

'Why don't you leave him? He can't throw you out. There's a law.'

The slap hits him unexpectedly. It isn't hard, but catches him mid-sentence and makes him blubber.

'Don't talk like that,' she says. 'Is that what you be saying out on the street?'

And later. 'Are you any better than him? All you do about the house is eat.'

And later again. 'What happens within these four walls stays within these four walls.'

It might be a scientific fact that mind can control matter, but the hacking device is a fantasy. He never truly believed in it. It was only some crazy idea from a Japanese cartoon. What really and truly works is Control of Time.

Think this: no matter what pain there is right now, in ten hours, or twelve, it will be gone. In a few days it will be just a memory. That's all there is to it. Time sweeps away the pain, so let time do its work. Even now, this moment, is already in the past and on the way to being forgotten.

When a teacher takes him to one side and starts asking stupid questions, there is a thought that can keep him calm: *this moment will pass*. And in the thought he is already outside the moment. It is already a memory. The teacher is powerless against this. Though his voice ratchets up in pitch, and his face turns red with rage.

On his night wanderings, Cyril keeps among the crowds along the small cobblestoned streets. The women's bright clothing warms the air and everyone is cheerful. Ha ha ha, throats open to the air, bare arms and legs, unsteady steps in high heels. People jostle in slow motion; he has plenty of time to dodge around the keeling bodies. Some call to him, *look at the young fella, c'mere young fella.* Three times he does a circuit of the streets and finds dozens of coins.

Onwards he walks, past leafy front gardens, high railings, the bright lobbies of international hotels, out to the wide roads where there are only trucks and taxis. On an overhead sign he reads a name he hears every day on the traffic bulletins. It is colder here and the sky is wider. Nobody is out walking. On one side there is coarse grass and sand, just like on a beach. On the other an immense yard with several scattered prefabs and containers. He observes the wind takes its rise down the road ahead; he can see it rustling up crisp bags and dead leaves. The whirl gathers force and begins to move. It hurtles towards him, one two THREE, hits him on the forehead, steady against it, eyes narrowed to slits.

Father is back again. They watch the flickering television but they do not understand what they see and hear.

Instead they repeat portions of time.

I'm tired, so very tired of it all.
You're one to be talking.
Off in your white van and I've no idea when you're back.
Become the slut again, is that what you want?
You let them all swindle you, yet if I take one single penny -
Like a parasite on my back.
Get out of my sight.

Have they no memory?
Have they no memory?

Things cannot go on like this. Things will go on like this. Repeat.

They try to cheat you – teachers, the television – by turning what was inside to the outside. They needle into you, squeezing out the tears. *I love you daddy*, say the children on the television programme. They hug like teddy bears in a shopping mall display.

Because the world is founded on love, the religion teacher was saying. Trying to drag them all into the vale of sorrow. Cyril blinks back a tear. He must be on guard against such wheedling strategies. Always this teacher was laying out his traps, to get you to be serious, to coax out some admission.

He despised this moment, but it is within time and time would pass.

'They brought you up from being a small child, didn't they Cyril?'

He sits resolute. This man wants something from him. This man wants to see his own life ratified. He wants to feed off assent.

'Do you know that they love you?'

He pictures his house on fire, the small boy of himself stumbling through the smoke, timbers cracking and falling in flames just inches behind him. One huge breath inside him, clambering fast and faster. The flames sting at his ankles, but they don't have time to burn him. He's quick, too quick for fire. Down in the front garden his mother is wailing, a man in uniform patting her on the shoulder.

It's a pleasant image, but no such catastrophe will ever happen.

'Do you love your parents?' the teacher asks. An infinitely patient voice.

'Yes,' Cyril says. The word he speaks is *Yes*, but it is spoken with the tone of *No*.

The teacher lowers his eyes. 'You may sit down,' he says. The boy feels a secret thrill course through him. This is a moment of pride. And pride is stronger than pity. Pride is stronger than hope.

In the story that is what really happens he listens at the top of the stairs. The voices grate against each other, die down and rise up again. At last he understands. What they mean is this: *He should never have been.* That is the Truth. The world will not acknowledge it, nor can he say it. The schoolteacher will not mention it, it will be in no prayer book, nor on any TV programme. He cannot be permitted to have this truth. For the world to continue on its way it cannot be supposed that he is even capable of thinking this.

Yes, he had said, with the tone of *No*. And the teacher had lowered his eyes and mumbled.

He knows how far his legs can carry him. If only the rain didn't always slash in horizontally. He sits inside a recessed porch in a building made of glass panes. It's probably a financial building. He knows about such things because the teacher at school had talked about this district of the city. He knows about exports and imports, suburbs and commuters.

Offices are packed into special blocks rising to eight or ten storeys. The workers drive in every day to sit at a desk.

And see! It is really true. Now at night the streets are deserted. The commuters have gone back to the suburbs by car and bus and tram. This is the real city, a deserted landscape of vacant buildings and empty streets. It's a comforting thought that things can be exactly and as simple as they are explained in a book. One element of the city sits inside on a leather chair. It is the security guard, who stares long at the boy, then ignores him.

Warm air streams from a ventilation grille. He finds a position where the air flows against him and keeps him cosy. In his dreams he is sure-footed, over a wall in one leap, clack clack down a lane, leaving the sound trailing behind him. His strength does not fade, no, it increases with each bounding step. The man in the blue overalls, he keeps following, but the streets are familiar, he knows each turn and dead-end.

Cyril wakes up, still eluding a pursuer, still tracing an escape down familiar laneways. He feels anxious, then realises there is nothing to fear in the waking world.

'You should go on home.' A man wearing a bulky coat is settling himself in the porch. His face is wrinkled, he keeps one hand folded over the other. 'You should be at home in your bed.' He speaks with an old man's voice, full of certainty. 'You have a home to go to, do you? Yer mammy is waiting for you.'

The boy shrugs, sets his face to neutral. Questions again, questions to trap you. He looks to one side so as not to give the idea he's about to answer any time soon. They always give up eventually.

Cyril watches the man set out layers of cardboard to form a bed. It hits him: this is not some teacher he's talking to. This is someone who lives outside of it all. He does not deserve the Control of Time treatment.

'Yeah, I have a home,' the boy answers. 'Most of the time there's no-one there though.' Actually he wanted to answer truthfully, but it comes out as a lie. Not much of a lie, but still. Now he notices the beery smell, and the red welts across the man's face. He is a true down-and-out, although surprisingly he speaks the same way as any old man. Cyril finds himself telling a long tale of a father who beats him with a belt, - a drinker, yes, cider and vodka. All the money is spent on booze, yes, so he goes to school hungry. He has to rob food sometimes, but only bread and milk.

The man nods and understands. Such a tale is familiar to him, he is not shocked at all.

'And I don't have a proper coat and I have to keep pretending I forgot it,' he says. This part is true, though it is also true he never needs a coat. 'The teacher at school asked me why I had no coat, and I lied and said I left it at home because there was rain. I mean because there was no rain.' The ingenuity of his lies confuses even himself.

'But I'm alright now,' he finishes implausibly.

Things are not so bad at home after all, he reflects. It's not so bad out on the street either. Nothing really bad can happen in the world.

A few days later he decides to throw himself at the mercy

of the world. To see what people are made of, as a probe, to give them a chance.

His mother throws open all the cupboard doors. 'For jaysus sake do you not get enough to eat? Look! There's every kind of food at home.' Cyril looks at the contents of the cupboards as though he might see something new, but there are only the usual rows of tins and boxes of cereal. He is conscious of having set in motion an important train of events. He feels big, beyond himself and beyond regret.

'Don't you know they'll take you in? They'll put you in an institution.'

'No they won't,' he says.

'They will! That woman from the department has the right to do that. She as much as told me so.' His mother puts her hands to her face and weeps. 'Oh Jesus. Why are you doing this to me? Begging on the streets when you have all the food you want in the house. Putting me to shame. Now that bitch can come in any time she wants and waltz around. Why were you sitting out on the street? What notion did you get?'

There is no explaining it, not to his mother nor to Miriam. His silence this time is not wilful; it's a lack of anything to say.

'What is it you want? You have food and a warm home, people looking after you constantly. I work my fingers to the bone for you. You have my heart broke.'

His mother sinks onto the sofa and curls up in a ball of tears. He thinks he should go to comfort her, that this is something he should want to do at that moment, and that maybe after all he has become a little bit brutal.

On the top shelf, for weeks afterwards, there is a carton of KIDZ superjuice in green and orange with bubble faces (we know why it's there).

She had been very kind, Miriam. She had watched him from across the road, then approached and placed a small coin on his tray. Later she came back again and hunkered down beside him. *Are you making much?* she asked. This embarrassed him. He stood up, pushed the money to one side. But she counted it up, as though the money was of great importance, and asked if it was a good night so far. Making fun of him maybe, because surely anyone could see he wasn't a beggar for real. So he admitted it was his first time. Half an hour is all he'd been there. She laughed, prettily, and he did too, seeing how ridiculous it was. He basked in a sense of being discovered, some secret sacrifice was at last revealed.

Well we can't leave you here, I'll give you a lift home, she said. Are you not taking the money with you?

He picked it up reluctantly, like collecting evidence against himself. If only she didn't keep noticing the money. Now it jangled in his pocket. He had expected that she would take it from him, as a sign that this part of his life was over. He got into her car with a warm feeling that something good was going to happen. Or at least something would happen at last.

Where do you live? she asked. The engine started with a nice burring sound. A warm hum enveloped them. He watched the vegetable shop pass, the novelty store with its glass front that went right into the ground, the stone wall lane, the bank porch, and all these familiar places. But now he was seeing them from inside a car, so he felt a long way off, and that he was seeing them for the last time. *Remember us, we are part of your past*, they seemed to say to him.

Give me a call tomorrow and tell me how you are, she said, writing out a number on a yellow rectangle.

Stupid stupid child. He understood now that this was someone whose business it was to look after children. It was her paid role. This was not the one he had been waiting for. No matter how nice she was (and she was paid to be) she was not the one to save him.

The rain rouses to a bluster. It spits in his face, pushes his hair to one side then the other. His cheeks are scrubbed raw by the wind, water drips from his nose. At last he stops, huddles in a bus shelter. He crouches in the most sheltered spot. If he holds his hands under his armpits the warmth is preserved within.

Three teenagers arrive. They shove and jostle each other: elbows bang against the perspex panels, slaps are exchanged, laughter all the while. They trip and fall in a confusion of limbs, then jump up again. They are of indestructible material.

Cyril gives a few cautious glances and keeps to himself. The rain will end soon.

LOOKA THE STEAM OFFA YOUR MAN!

The teenagers gather around him, drag him out under the street lamp. He is passed from hand to hand, rotated, admired. He sees it too, the wisps rising from him, his energy made manifest.

Jesus, you're mad hot.
Don't be queering the man.
Feel his arms, seriously.
You just walk around in the rain?
Don't mind him, he's only messin.
Fucking hell, you're an engine. What's your name?
'Cyril,' he says.

They offer him a bar of chocolate and the rest of a bag of chips. He accepts their tribute and goes on his way. Something of the power within him has been revealed.

'Jesus you scared the life out of me,' his mother says. 'What's up with you?' She's amazed to see him still in bed, because he always leaves on time for school. It's gone ten now and the traffic outside is quiet. His eyes and nose stream with moisture. He shivers uncontrollably. The motor within burns with excess energy.

'You've a fever,' she says, 'stay in your bed.' She is relieved to see him sick: it explains things. In a minute, just as she promised, she brings in a mug of tea and slices of toast.

He eats and sleeps. Wakes and eats. The house is empty. Next door he hears footsteps, floorboards creaking. There are people who do nothing but stay in a house all day. Cars slow and accelerate outside. These are all comforting sounds. He knows the sound that will disturb the quiet: that one particular car engine, the precise way the car door slams shut.

'Who ate all the bread? Every last slice is eaten!'

His mother barges into the room. She puts her hand to his forehead.

'That's no fever. You're stone cold.'

'It's a fever where I've a low temperature,' he says.

This is not something she has heard of, but it's not like Cyril to fake being sick. She has no intention of paying a doctor just to hear the advice: 'wrap up and keep warm'. Cyril is hardy, just a few hours rest and he'll be fine. The very next morning, in fact, he goes back to school. She doesn't have to encourage him, he gets up himself at breakfast time.

So his secret training continues. Five hours out in the cold, then six, then seven. He walks to distant places – once to the Phoenix Park, once to a place where the mountains look like they are rising from the back gardens of the very next row of houses. No-one would believe it possible, but there is no-one to tell.

'Put your jumper on you'll get the flu,' says Mrs Renn. 'There's a chill in the air, you'll catch your death,' says Mrs Guinn at the shop.

These are things that people say. But they do not apply to him. Like the words from television, like the religion teacher's fatuous ploys, they are words:

> for empty-headed people who know nothing
> for fakes and frauds
> for unreal people who live in a story
> for those who cannot bear the truth
> for those who force themselves to laugh
> for those who say what they have been told to say
> for those who will repeat portions of time forever

He is the bearer of a ruthless discipline. *I am the bearer of a ruthless discipline*, he thinks.

Another regular resting point is the train station. Warm air billows from the doorway grids (but Cyril doesn't need it). There are benches to sit on, no-one bothers him. He will find coins if he waits there long enough. They lie on the ground, perfectly visible, but people are too busy to notice.

The real down-and-outs talk to him. They have no home and no-one and yet they live on. See! The worst that can happen is nothing to fear.

The train pulls in with an extended shriek. People step down from the carriages, busy with their bags and smiles. Hundreds and hundreds. They file along the platform and through the ticket barriers. *Do you think I don't know the rules?* he thinks at them. *Do you think I don't know what it's all about?*

If things could be stripped bare, the sandwich boutiques fade to grey, shop fronts shatter, fan heaters stutter and grind to a halt, the tiles crack and the earth show through. Better to be all left walking across a field of cinders than this. Better to strip things to the bare reality, so each would see that he is truly alone and that the hidden growl will emerge from behind the polite words, and that the plastic people be torn through.

That at last the pretence may end.
That at last.

He walks away from the station with steady steps. The ground is frozen outside; ice sparkles hard from the pavement. The air is tight around him.

See! It is the (boy) striding out, his legs will take him as far as he wills, his forehead is steady, his course is set. He is out on the verge of the orbital highway, heading north. There, where no human has a right to be, a (boy) walks and survives. He can sleep on a bed of concrete, his nose can withstand the heaviest hail, his chest is a bulwark against the wind. He is going out to the cold, where there is no smell. That time may not repeat itself, that words may not be empty sounds, that something will at last have consequence.

And sometimes he burned within, and that was how he withstood the cold, and sometimes his temperature dropped to meet that of the icy wastes around, and that was also how he withstood the cold, and in this way he wandered far from the rooms where people live, and understood things he did not understand before. For those who will not yield to pretence must learn to endure an eternity of cold.

WORDS SPOKEN

Two years since he's emerged from zero by completing a course in web design, speaking in a clear even tone, and moving into the centre of town to an apartment that leaves him nothing saved at the end of each month. Less than nothing, for his income is supplemented by a claim for rent assistance. No shame in that, none at all; he'd be quite prepared to mention it if the subject came up, but so far it hasn't come up, not among the people he meets now, and there's no reason why it ever should.

He loves to look at the city lights from the fourth storey landing. A silent vista through double panes of glass. There is a feeling of contact, of being in the middle of life. The lines of red tail-lights move smoothly, each orange street lamp casts a circular glow on the pavement. The stronger halogen lights around business premises cast a glow on the air itself, creating a fuzz around each intense point. He blinks and rubs his eyes, wondering if the late nights have got to him, or if maybe the shampoo he uses has frosted the corneas. On the corridors and landings there are no windows that open, but when he opens those in in his room the air blows in damp and cold, only faintly charged with the fumes of an endless rush hour.

Amanda Bennett invited him. Sure you'll come, it's just people, not my friends. Half of them I'll hardly know, she'd said. You know the way you just invite a load of people because you know only half of them will turn up anyway?

But I'll definitely come, he said.

Right, you know the Bull Harbour building? It's block E, apartment 16 but the intercom doesn't work, so I just ask people to give me a call as soon as they get to the front door. You have my number, don't you?

Sure, I have your number somewhere, he said.

And you have a mobile?

Yes, I have a mobile, he confirmed in a level voice.

He'd met her in the foyer of Keystroke College where he'd been running an eye down the list of courses starting that month. Do you study here? he'd asked. She pouted, seemed about to say something sharp, then said carefully: Well, I've just finished up a course. Why? Are you thinking of doing one?

He took the cue. Maybe not, he said, I don't think it's that good. Still, it would be nice to have something else on the old CV.

What kind of work do you do?

Graphic design, he answered. He had completed a leaflet for a local karate club just two weeks before. The club rented some warehouse space in his uncle's scrapyard.

Really? she said with interest. Me too! But honestly you'd be better off without the course here. What kind of design work do you do?

Commercial flyers, clubs, that kind of thing.

There's a lot of freelance contracts going around but it's so hard to get anything steady don't you think?

When they parted she'd handed him her card as a matter of course, as though he might be another significant contact.

When Amanda comes down the stairs and opens the metal-framed door that evening she's in a different mood, more reckless and trusting, the same confidence, but now it's not based on her professional manner.

Hi, she says, sorry to make you ring. It's just the kids. They hang around outside and press all the buttons. The buzzer went off twice already today.

So your doorbell works again?

Yes, but the intercom doesn't, like I said earlier.

The precision of her memory irritates him. He wonders how she can be so involved with every detail that she remembers them all. He follows her up the carpeted stairs, snatching glimpses out the windows, or rather the continuous glass shell, at the tin-can profile of the gasometer and the dark hulk of the stadium. For though he lives in a high apartment himself, he never tires of the transformation from a height, the sudden revelation, like watching your home town become the setting for a Hollywood thriller.

Cathy, Conor, Alvin, Coreen, Louis, Chris. She performs the introductions with six waves of her left hand around the room. Each guest nods and mutters. This is Mervyn by the way, she adds at the end, I should complete my introductions.

No-one offers to shake hands. He figures it's just a mixed party, and wonders how he'll phrase it when they ask him what he works at. But everyone seems content to lounge across the chairs and sofas without conversing much.

Someone has gone to a lot of trouble with the food. Translucent rectangles of smoked salmon on soda bread, grilled cheese on baguette, shredded lettuce and rocket salad, cream cheese on crackers, small cylinders of sushi, bowls of tuna pasta salad, strips of red and green pepper, little sherry-glasses of prawn cocktail with each prawn bent over the rim of the glass, like a man leaning over a railing to puke.

You have a nice apartment, he says.

Don't you want to leave down your coat? she says. She points him through a door to a second room. He sees a desk and computer. There's a bed with papers and coats thrown across it. Cardboard boxes are wedged between the bed and the wall. Thick hard-backed books stacked on the floor. This is the spare room then; he sees another door opposite which must be her bedroom. A two-bedroomed apartment on a few freelance hours per week. Some things you just have to wonder at and and never ask.

Are you still a student? he asks.

No, why? Is it the books lying all over the place? They're just my old ones. I actually go back and read them sometimes.

Not something I'd ever do.

What did you study?

Web design, he answers.

She looks perplexed. But you didn't just do web design?

Indeed I did.

For four years?

What do you mean four years? he asks in a neutral voice, as though he hasn't figured out she assumes he's been to university. As do a lot of people he meets. It's just too unexpected: a presentable professional, or halfway to being a professional, who never went to university. Amanda waits a moment for him to elaborate, then passes into the living room.

Take one too, she says, I spent five hours slaving in the kitchen so you'd better appreciate it or you'll never get invited again. She hands him a plate and moves along the table piling on a little of each salad. He would hardly recognise her out of her career girl slacks. Mousy brown hair you can see the tangles in, mouth too wide and flat. But there's no-one going to tell her, she's too nice for that. She talks on and on in full confidence that talk makes everyone the same, like they are all in the same boat, everything is going to be all right so long as we can keep talking about it. You could introduce yourself with "I beg for money on Capel Street" and she'd say "Really, you must meet a lot of interesting people. But I wouldn't like to be doing it on a day like this."

He takes his plate over to the window, where some people are talking about the view. He points out Liberty

Hall and the gap where the river lies. It turns into a kind of puzzle, to guess what each significant cluster of lights could be. That stream of lights, he points, is the Stephen's Green centre. And that chimney there is way over in Smithfield.

In one of the dead ends, off the streets directly below, is the back entrance he knows too well. It's not true that he's emerged from zero, but the six years after leaving school were spent out of sight in the stockroom of a department store, taking deliveries from lorries. The boxes he stacked were huge, tall as a man, but light. He used a hand-operated hydraulic trolley. Pile on the boxes, raise it up with a few quick pumps of the lever. A forklift wasn't needed, so after all that time in a warehouse he didn't even have a forklift qualification. Not even that one small chance to gain something concrete from his time there. Six years spent in a cavernous space lit with bare bulbs, out back behind the heavy vinyl curtains that separated it from the shop floor. Any new girl who started on the shop floor assumed he must be a grade below them, a warehouse worker. One who didn't need any training, didn't have to shave or wear a tie, or neat clothes of any sort, and who was incapable of operating a cash register. They were surprised to see he got the same reduction on clothes as everyone else. At Christmas he was handed the same wad of vouchers.

Most of the staff were female – girls straight out of school, mothers with teenage children, mothers who didn't have any choice. It was the kind of job someone might take up for a few months then leave. People were rotated around the different departments, the bargain basement being the least favourite, even lower than the warehouse. But Mervyn was never rotated. He regretted that his CV didn't have the usual line on having experience in dealing with the public. In retrospect, he supposed, there was nobody forcing him to stay hidden out the back. All he'd had to do was ask and he would have been trained at the register. They'd have been happy for him to ask.

He can't rightly explain why he spent so long there. It seems almost to have been an experiment on himself. Perhaps he had wanted to see if he could be happy working at a simple job, just living, or if on the other hand something would rebel within him, force him out. But the real reason must be just indifference, he realises, falling into a habit. Everybody does it, it's just the way everybody gets by.

But Mervyn doesn't tell these people about the warehouse entrance below or the empty top floor of the store they could see into through the window. I know the city pretty well from a height, he tells them, you know not a lot of people can figure it out.

Nobody smokes inside the apartment, that's understood. A couple of tiled steps lead down to an aluminium door. Outside is a small terrace, on one side is a drop four storeys to the ground. A gravel oval, two shrubs shrivelled by the wind. The terrace is shared by three other apartments. A clothes rack is tethered to the door frame. Amanda's things flutter brazenly from it.

A guest sitting on the bottom step nods, moves to one side. Cigarette? the man asks, take one of mine. He taps the open end on the packet to firm the tobacco. You don't have to go outside, she allows it here when the door is open.

Not a bad party this.

Yes, Amanda's salads are really – well let's say they're designed to impress, no matter about the taste.

He looks behind himself, ironically checking to see if she is listening. He is in his late twenties, blond hair combed back. Almost film-star looks, but the accent is familiar. From Dublin anyway.

Where are you from?

Drimnagh.

Not a bad spot.

I haven't lived there for a while, Chris says. This must be Chris, he decides, there were a lot of names beginning 'K' introduced around the room.

Nice pad she has here, what? A balcony and the works.

It certainly is, the man replies.

Jays the city out there is a lot different to when I was running into town on the hop from school, going in *The Mint* to play pool.

Chris doesn't smile at the chummy language. He speaks like he has to pluck the words from the air.

Things look different. I got used to Canada when I was there.

You were in Canada? I thought you needed a visa for there.

I was there five years, maybe six. Working at various things.

You must've had a brilliant time there. Jays compared to the dump this place was then.

Yes it was great, said the stranger. It was different from Dublin. But it was also in a sense, the loneliest time in my life. A time when I had to come to terms with myself.

Mervyn can't see where this is going, there's nothing he can answer to this. His heart beats like he has entered a danger zone. Who is this person to say such things? He scrutinises the pale eyebrows and the fingers pointing the cigarette away so the smoke drifts past him. The grey eyes are turned to him, not sharply, but curious, testing. Like he has just told a riddle, and he is not sure if the listener appreciates riddles.

The listener jumps from the step, flicks his cigarette through the half-open door. Fuckin RAIN out there! he says, turns and takes the steps in one bound, rubbing his hands together in feigned anticipation of second helpings.

It's a week of new contacts, new work opportunities in the offing. An email arrives with a few casual sentences:

Hi, Amanda here.

Take a look at this message I got and see if you're interested. I don't have the time to handle it. You can reply yourself, or else I can take it on and just pass you the work – I know the people there and what they want.

\>> TCO here at Vigilant. Hi Amanda. Our office would like to produce a 20 - 30 page color spec for new clients. Full details at a later stage, but if you are interested in this project reply asap.

That was how it worked. No fretting about being clean shaven or how to knot your tie correctly, no sitting before a table with humble eyes, no churning up of school certificates, hobbies, achievements you are proud of. The farce of an interview – thinking about the humiliation brings blood to his face. Two or three in the months after leaving school had been enough for a lifetime. With this line of work his school results do not matter, nor does the certificate from his course, which wasn't even in graphic design. What mattered is who you worked for the month before, what names you can mention. And if it's a name that is recognised – and in a small country it often is – the job will fall to you.

His old friends, the ones from the department store days and even earlier, have a laugh at him when they meet. You're your own boss now, you can lie in the scratcher until two in the afternoon, they laugh, or rather sneer, for he never meets them intentionally now. They only run into each other by chance on the streets. There are the usual enquiries about friends in common: How's old Richie, how's Cully Mac? Enthusiastic questions, though in fact it is some five or six years since he has met these people, and he is not quite sure he would even recognise them if they passed on a busy street.

They inevitably ask what he's working at these days. He tries to explain, but it sounds too glib. He doesn't mean to, but he gives the impression that anyone still working on a nine to five job must be a fool. See you in Fagans sometime, they will say on parting, though nothing will come of it.

At the end of the week he rings Amanda and asks how the party went. Oh *that* party, she says after a moment to figure it. Sure, it was great. Yeah he agrees instantly, I really enjoyed it. Thanks for inviting me. He hesitates, he's about to ask casually about one of her guests when she says, I'll let you know when I'm having another one. That would be great, he says, and can't think of any way now to enquire about Chris that wouldn't sound downright weird.

For he had meant to pile a few salads on his plate and go back to the smoking exit, down the three steps. Get talking to Chris some more about Canada, about work there and gun licences, winter snow. Gradually circle back, approach the abruptly severed topic from a different angle.

But it was also in a sense, the loneliest time in my life. The sentence recurs to him at the oddest moments, intriguing him, irritating him. Who did he think he was, this blond-haired man no older than twenty-six, to speak like a teacher, a priest, a prophet? Were the ordinary bullshit words not good enough for him? Maybe it was a sophisticated joke and he'd missed the point. Like the gilt-framed image the guests had passed around at Amanda's that same evening. Bubbling over with laughter, the girls with hand to mouth, then hanging it back up on the wall with ironic reverence. It was a relief of the Sacred Heart. A ring of thorns around the iconic red heart, rays emanating from it. The soft beard and gentle features of the standardised Catholic Jesus. The intense blue eyes followed the viewer from left to right around the room. This was no high technology – just a simple optical illusion. He laughed too, but felt there was some extra hilarity that he'd missed.

Maybe Chris was a student of English, or Arts, and took him for another eternal student in touch with the latest ironies. Maybe it was a scene from some film everybody was supposed to have seen. That would explain the precision of the words spoken, and that little testing smile that seemed to taunt: *Do you recognise this? Who am I being now?*

But Chris couldn't possibly be a student. It didn't fit. He'd mentioned working for six years in Canada. It was understood that 'working' meant ordinary simple jobs, the kind that anyone might get when they need to pay the rent. There isn't a lot to mull over from just two minutes sitting on a step; everything suggested Chris was making a simple, sincere statement. But why did he have to speak like that, in a way that sealed off any ordinary reply?

His anger summons back the tiled steps, a man sitting on the bottom one, his grey eyes questioning the smoke curling from a cigarette, an empty pack at his side dented to form an ashtray. Just say what you mean to say don't make a speech of it, he wants to say in a harsh voice to the stranger who might possibly be called Chris. So you weren't too happy in Canada? Why was that? He speaks in a commonsense tone, forcing the stranger onto his level. He hears about difficulty in finding work, long hours in a dead-end job carrying boxes on a building site. Yeah, he sympathises, a few years of that and you're banging at the walls. You need to have contacts with the right people to get ahead. That's the way it is all over. Did you not try hanging around the Irish bars?

Then the second sentence: *A time when I had to come to terms with myself.*

Fucking queer, he rages to himself, springing up from the step again, pacing the room. For what else could the sentence mean? Who else but a gay man would speak like that? What other reason could there be? He's shot through the stomach with anger, not precisely at the possibility that Chris is gay, but the possibility that the words were a lure, testing the waters. He feels he has uncovered a fraud.

He sits down again at his desk. Pulls a draft guide for

mortgage providers in front of him, stares down at it, circles the images he wants moved. His eyes are sore, it's maybe the fifth time he's gotten up and come back with a coffee. Two half-empty cups are perched alongside the monitor, a third is on the floor at his feet. The conversation is waiting to be resumed, there, just to the left of him.

So Chris, he says, sitting down on the step again, slapping a knee. He's a man of the world now, not awkward, not nervous of ambiguities. There are matters to be resolved.

There was something about yourself that you had to change? Something about the way you were? Like, am I supposed to guess what it is?

Chris smiles, rubs his jaw a bit guiltily. His foot slips on the tiles and bangs against the door. No, I . . . I was involved in a lot of bad business. You know, I got in with this gang of con artists. Knocking at doors pretending to sell insurance, harvesting people's credit card numbers. Nobody would suspect me, Irish you know. It was pretty low stuff.

Jesus.

I had to sort myself out. Big time.

But you got away from it in the end?

Put away from it, he laughs drily. Yeah I didn't stay six years in Canada living the high life, that's for sure. A nice time seeing the world abroad.

I like it, said Amanda on the phone. When you say it took you all day it makes it hardly worthwhile in terms of money, but if you're still on for it, I can pass more on to you.

Sure, he says brightly.

There's a range of labels we have to adjust to Irish

regulations. A Canadian company.

Canada? There was a Canadian at your party a few weeks ago. A guy who used to live there I mean.

Yes. So there was.

What's he up to?

Up to? Well I suppose he's still putting in heating pumps. He's been in the block here so many times I just invited him along. But he's very interesting, not at all boring. You'd never guess he was a plumber.

Another variation: Yeah, "come to terms"? Maybe I don't want to come to terms. Maybe I want to obliterate instead. And the stranger sets his jaw and understands.

But would he really have said that?

It shouldn't be a big surprise to run into Chris one day on the ground-floor corridor. Yet Mervyn stops dead. There is something uncanny about the figure, down on his hunkers, clipping cables together.

Chris? he says uncertainly. Then he sees the tiles are indistinguishable from those at Amanda's apartment. Chris looks up, there's a moment of recognition untethered to place or time.

What's your name again?

Mervyn.

Right. Amanda's party. I just have to pack this stuff away. Do you live in this place?

They head towards the town centre, thinking of some cafe, but turn in at the doors of a fast-food outlet because they see a couple of free seats inside and it's getting on for lunchtime. He hears about Canada, about the frozen waterfalls, savage winters in Watson Lake, going for a walk through untracked forest and getting lost in the wilderness with the sound of a jam factory whistle cutting the silence every hour, always the same distance away.

Halfway through the coffee a couple of girls come in, throw a glance.

Doyles Stores girls, says Mervyn, that's the black and white zigzag. The warehouse entrance is up that laneway across the road. We used to come here for our lunch. Three at a time, forty-five minutes. Just enough time to get your food and get it down. I worked there in the stockroom packing boxes for six years.

Six years? Why did you stay there so long?

He looks over at the girls in uniform. They are fresh-faced, all laughing, probably still at school just two years before. He can't rightly explain why he spent so long there. It seems almost to have been an experiment on himself. He had wanted to see if he could be happy working at a simple job, just living, or if something would rebel within him, force him out. It was wrong to make of himself a small and shriveled thing, wrong to view himself from a height as one more figure walking along the pavement.

It seems to me now like my buried life. Like I wanted to see if I could bury myself under ten feet of earth and be silent and content, or if there was something within me that would make me wake up.

As he speaks it becomes clear that this is what happened, and that the dead self he had dragged along with him could finally be cut loose.

The girls throw a glance back as they pass out the door,

but it's not because they recognise him. All the girls from that time would have long since moved on.